T H E
C O M P A N Y

Thanks, Mandy!
your picture has hung from
the rafters at the Orlando Convention
Center. And I looked fabulous!!

TC+BG,

Chuck Graham

Heb 3:13

THE
COMPANY

A PARABLE FOR OUR TIME

CHUCK GRAHAM
AUTHOR OF *TAKE THE STAND*

WinePressPublishing
Great Books, Defined.

WinePress Publishing (PO Box 428, Enumclaw, WA 98022) functions only as book publisher. As such, the ultimate design, content, editorial accuracy, and views expressed or implied in this work are those of the author.

Unless otherwise noted, all Scriptures are taken from the *Holy Bible, New International Version®, NIV®*. Copyright © 1973, 1978, 1984 by Biblica, Inc.™ Used by permission of Zondervan. All rights reserved worldwide. www.zondervan.com

ISBN 13: 978-1-4141-2090-4
ISBN 10: 1-4141-2090-7
Library of Congress Catalog Card Number: 2011927678

To my wife, Beverly, and my mother, Martha, who have
always encouraged me to write and, from the
very first, believed in *The Company*

CONTENTS

Acknowledgments ix

1. Last Day 1
2. The Stranger 7
3. A Business 17
4. The Review 31
5. One Way 43
6. Heis 63
7. The Announcement 75
8. Assignments 87
9. A Visit 99
10. Interviews Begin 113
11. Seniors 125
12. Interviews End 145
13. The Report 157
14. Breakfast with Friends 167

15. Lord Mohae 177

16. A New Task 193

17. The Answer 213

Keys to *The Company* 225

Starting *The Company* 231

About the Author 235

Coming Soon—*The Rise of New Power*
1. The Breach 239

ACKNOWLEDGMENTS

WRITING IS VERY much an adventure, one that includes not only the author, but many others who willingly join in the experience. Few books are truly complete, even fewer possible, without the guidance, encouragement, and often the imagination of those who sincerely believe in the project. That has especially been true in the writing of *The Company*.

First and foremost, I would like to thank Susan Paradise, for the countless hours she read and reread the many drafts, her excellent suggestions and comments along the way, and especially for her excitement and belief in the message of *The Company*.

Thanks to all who reviewed the manuscripts, provided incredible insight, and eagerly kept me humble in the process with the occasional, "I don't think you've quite got it." Especially to Beverly Graham, Hal Harris, Martha Swanson, Matt Graham, Frank Stanley, Pam Lunsford, and my fellow author buddies, Janet Perez Eckles and Michael K. Brown.

And last, but certainly not least, to all who have faithfully prayed for this book and that God would guide my hand so others would know Him better. I appreciate you more than words can express.

Thank you all, for helping me turn an interesting tale into a pretty good story. I have been profoundly blessed to have you along for the adventure.

Take care & be God's,
Chuck

CHAPTER 1

LAST DAY

THE BLAST HIT without warning.

The rock exploded into the planet with unbelievable force. Massive, invisible shock waves raced across the land, and with them came immediate destruction. The sound alone instantly killed millions, and millions more were vaporized where they stood, sat, worked, or played. They were the fortunate ones. Others burned alive in the searing heat or were crushed by falling rubble or drowned in the sudden rush of the tides. The impact spared no one.

Violent winds leveled the landscape for hundreds of miles. Trees, houses, structures...all were flattened into the dirt as though a wandering giant had stepped on them. The land heaved. Enormous seismic power sped through the earth's crust, creating terrifying global quakes as tectonic plates moved violently...side to side, up and down. Volcanoes were summoned to life with gigantic eruptions. Each explosion sent concussion waves rippling through towering plumes of tumbling debris. Bright red fountains of lava burst into the sky. Glaciers became fleeing rivers. Mountains fell. Dams breached. Fires raged with nothing to stop them. Tsunamis shattered coastlines, stripped trees, and washed away life, leaving nothing in their wake.

Thick clouds billowed into the atmosphere. Suffocating shrouds of smoke, toxic gas, and ash as small as dust rose with the wind and covered the darkening earth, driving away the sunlight. Soon there was no dawn, no dusk. Only constant night. And for what seemed an eternity, the air remained heavy with the stench of death.

No one had believed that life of any kind could survive a direct hit by such a large meteor. Scientists with their studies and theories had been so confident in all the carefully crafted "what if" scenarios, so certain of their conclusions. "End of the world as we know it. Total annihilation. No one left." But they were wrong. There was a village…tucked away in a deep, long valley, hidden in the shadows. Brigos Glen.

Maybe the surrounding mountains had shielded it from the horrible blast. Maybe the high winds had spared it from much of the fallout. Maybe the solid earth underneath had allowed the harsher shock waves to pass through. Or maybe they were just lucky. Homes were heavily damaged. Buildings had toppled into the streets. Water mains were broken and power lines severed. But in a world filled with the dead and dying, the Brigons had lived.

Life would adapt. It had to. Nothing would ever be the same. Not as it had been. Not before Last Day.

Time passed. Quickly, slowly…the Brigons could not honestly say. The darkness weighed heavily on them. Time could have been standing still for all they knew, and yet, each moment seemed a lifetime. No one could tell any longer when Last Day had occurred. Few cared. Watches, clocks, other instruments for measuring time—almost all required batteries or electric current—eventually became useless or, in the oppressive darkness, were simply ignored.

What was a day anymore? Or a week or month? Years even, for that matter? They blended together in the darkness, especially in those early times. In such desperation and confusion, dates had no meaning; calendars even less. Finding shelter, searching for food—staying alive—held far more importance.

Brigos Glen had been governed by a Council of Elders, mostly retired men who stopped by the Village Center once a month to socialize. They discussed a few world affairs they deemed relevant and made even fewer administrative decisions. This had become their routine. With Last Day, that, too, changed. Nothing was routine any longer. Now their families, friends, and neighbors wanted answers...answers to questions the Elders had never considered.

Among their first order of business was the organization of search parties to scope out the lay of the land, assess the condition of the village, and determine what resources might still be available. Each group was given a flashlight to guide them and a flare in case of emergency. They set out to scour the village and within hours found reason for hope.

The Brigons had long prided themselves on being an independent, self-sustaining community, one that needed no help from anyone. Through carefully managed farms and ranches, they produced their own food. Wild game was abundant for hunting. And deep, reliable wells provided more than enough water. A treatment facility stood near the northern boundary of the village. Across the street was a distribution terminal where farm products from the valley were stored for local sales as well as shipped to faraway towns and cities.

It took little effort to determine the extent of the damage to the village's water system. The effect of the broken mains could be seen everywhere...water poured into the streets, fountains sprayed from dislodged fire hydrants, and ponds formed where once there were paved parking lots. One group continued to the treatment facility. Though the great storage tank had emptied, they found the well system in good shape. They activated the backup generators and the system sprang to life. They immediately turned them off to conserve power and sent a report to the Elders.

Another group headed to the distribution terminal and found the large warehouses intact with little damage. Best of all, since scheduled shipments had not been made before the impact, they were filled with fresh fruit and vegetables. They also checked a number of smaller warehouses nearby. These contained stores of food that had been grown with artificial light sources...ongoing experiments a private lab had been conducting to bring an end to world hunger, or so it claimed. No one ever saw those shipments going anywhere except to distant military posts.

Two other groups made their way outside the village to a state-of-the-art solar plant. Designed and built by the Brigons, the plant had generated all the power they believed they would ever need, with plenty left over to recharge their electric vehicles...the only kind allowed in Brigos Glen. Once at the plant, they succeeded in locating a number of batteries and several portable generators, along with fuel that had been reserved for emergencies. Everything was carefully gathered and after long, grueling hours, they managed to carry it all back to Village Center.

With these few resources, the Elders were able to provide limited light and electricity, especially for the well pumps to bring much needed water to the surface. Then they assigned guards to the warehouses as they developed a plan for distributing the food among the Brigons. Meanwhile, more search parties formed and dispersed throughout the village. Others joined in—assisting the injured, gathering firewood, and looking for the lost, all accomplished with considerable efficiency.

Their successes greatly encouraged them, and soon four rescue teams were selected to leave the valley in search of other survivors. The Elders sent each team in a different direction to cross the surrounding mountains—one to the jagged range of the north, another to the rocky crests of the west, and a third to the rolling heights of the south. The last team traveled the most difficult journey, to the east and the land of the Great Peaks... Chokmah and Sunesis.

Once the teams had vanished into the darkness, little remained for the Brigons to do except cling to the hope that they would pull themselves up from their pit of destruction. Before long, however, that hope faded. The generators worked well at first but used a great amount of fuel, and soon no more gasoline, diesel, or kerosene could be found. With no sustainable source of power, the batteries grew weaker and died. The machines in the village became silent and useless. Technology gave way to primitive survival, and the darkness crept ever closer.

In time, Brigos Glen looked less like a village than a gathering of small camps, each with its own fire blazing in the long, cold night. As refrigerators, coolers, and freezers sat dormant, food wilted, withered, and rotted. The Brigons were forced to hunt for wild game, but hunting meant leaving the safety of their fires and venturing into the darkness.

Eventually, the rescue teams made their way back. In the north, west, and south, they had crossed the mountains and searched for many miles on the other side. And in each case, no sign of human life had been found. They returned, despondent and weary. But the last team...the one that had made its way to the east...to Chokmah and Sunesis...was never seen again.

The Brigons were utterly alone. Nothing the Elders attempted could penetrate the darkness that enveloped them. The people struggled. Food became scarce. What they managed to find, capture, and kill was only enough to keep them alive. A few of the deepest wells still had water, but it took great labor to draw that precious water out. Frustration spread from one person to the next. And in the heart of every Brigon grew the terrifying fear that the night would never end.

Many died in the early times—men, women, children. The will to survive became but a memory, ever waning in a deepening depression—a constant companion that robbed them of their remaining hope.

Until the stranger arrived.

CHAPTER 2

THE STRANGER

THE DEEPEST FEAR DOES NOT COME FROM FACING THE KNOWN, BUT IN BEING SURPRISED BY THE UNKNOWN. — Prophet of the Glen

THE BRIGONS LEARNED to be cautious, guarded, and alert; and for the longest time they were afraid. They did not dare stray from the camps or their ever-burning fires. Wild animals had always roamed the surrounding mountains, so most survivors already owned a rifle, pistol, or other weapons. But it was more than what lurked in the wild that concerned them. The very presence of the darkness drew their fear, as though it were the most dangerous of creatures.

The Elders issued strict orders to never venture outside alone and always travel in groups of five or more. The rules worked well for the most part. The only Brigons truly at risk were those charged with gathering more fuel for the fires and trapping animals for food. Even then, enough people carrying torches assured an adequate degree of safety.

But apart from an occasional and easily explained accident, nothing ever happened. Nothing ever changed. Nothing was unexpected. They moved through the same routines, over and over. In time their fear subsided. They carried their weapons only out of habit. No one seemed afraid anymore, though not because they had found new courage. They no longer cared. The darkness had dulled their senses and desires, their hopes and dreams... which is why the Voice that called out in the darkness brought such terror.

"Would you like some help?"

That was all, but that was enough. Instantly, panic filled those nearest the Voice, and it spread quickly. Screams and shouts of alarm rose as many ran for the nearest buildings, knocking others down in their flight to get inside. Some jumped behind anything that might hide them, grabbing their weapons and brandishing them about so their would-be attacker could see they were armed. In the excitement someone wildly fired into the darkness, barely missing a feeble old man trying to restore calm and order. In a remarkably short time, all of Brigos Glen was on alert, staring into the darkness that surrounded them.

"Would you like some help?"

Now the Voice sprang at them from a different location. Weapons swung toward the Voice, but the old man signaled them to hold their fire. This time there was no shot. Having regained some semblance of control, he steadied himself, stepped cautiously toward the darkness, and spoke to the invisible Voice.

"I am Thomas, Chief Elder of Brigos Glen. Who...who are you? Where are you from?"

No answer came. Thomas peered into the darkness, straining for any sign of movement that might give away the Voice's location. But there was none, only silence. He nervously looked about.

"A friend," the Voice finally answered. "From beyond Chokmah and Sunesis. I was sent to see if you would like some help."

Men behind the Chief Elder stirred, and whispered questions poured out. "Sent? Are there others? How did he find us? Why hasn't he come before? How was he able to cross those mountains? Is it better on the far side? Could he take us there?"

"Quiet," Thomas ordered. "I'll do the talking." He turned back to the Voice. "There are things we must know before we can consider accepting help, especially from someone who will not show himself," he said. Then he carefully repeated each of the questions. "So, what say you?" This time he did not have to wait for a reply.

"I've been sent," the Voice explained. "Yes, there are others, and if you would like us to help you, we will be glad to. We saw your fires. Finding you was not a problem, but the path here is difficult. Very steep. I came because I was sent, but more than that I cannot say. It is different where we are. One day we may take you there, but not now. It would be far too dangerous for you."

Those who could hear the Voice struggled with his words. Not since Last Day had they seen the slightest evidence that anyone else on the planet had survived the blast. And the Chief Elder had far too often seen the ruin caused by broken dreams and dying hope. No hope had become better than false hope. He sighed deeply and looked into the void.

"What can you *possibly* do for us?" He waited, but the silence had returned. "Are you there?" he called out.

"Yes."

"Then answer," Thomas commanded. "What is it you think you could do for us? Do you have food or water to share? Do you have supplies and materials to help us restore our houses and buildings?"

"Better," came the reply. "We have power and can bring you light."

The Brigons proved to be amazing creatures. For so long they had barely existed. They expected hardships and disappointment. Then a stranger came with the promise of light. Word spread and—though help had not yet arrived nor been accepted—laughter could be heard once more.

Suddenly, the Brigons felt a burning desire to truly live again. They did not understand where the desire came from, but it was there, all the same. And for the moment, that was what they needed. On the day the Voice called out in the darkness, everything changed.

The Elders wanted to trust this stranger from beyond the mountains. They needed to. But caution and fear forced them to move slowly. It did not seem to bother him, however. He waited patiently and answered what questions he could. Perhaps he was not eager to return to his home. No one would have blamed him. There were many dangers in that journey and the people of Brigos Glen were well aware of them. They remembered the men who had never returned.

After much discussion, the Elders asked the stranger to explain more of what he was proposing. To their surprise, the man stepped out of the darkness. He walked to the nearest fire, sat on the ground, and warmed himself. Though taller than the Brigons, the man's appearance indicated nothing unusual or remarkable. The lines of age crept near his eyes, but he did not appear particularly old. He looked strong, sturdy, and confident. He had a ready smile with a light of its own…a warm, comforting light that softened their fears and concerns. Despite their own instinct to maintain caution, the Elders felt drawn to this man they did not know. As their best sharpshooter kept a steady aim, they made their way to the fire and joined him on the ground. The Chief Elder sat closest, facing him.

"You said…you could bring us light?" Thomas asked. "You have generators? What do they run on? Where did you find fuel? We ran out a long time ago, but…" The questions spilled out more quickly than the Chief Elder had intended, and he suddenly realized the man did not have time to answer even one. "I'm sorry. I'm trying to keep this in perspective, but if what you say is true…" His words hung in the air.

"It's true," the man gently replied.

"But how can that be? We have tried so many things and nothing has worked, at least not for long. What is this power source?" Thomas begged for an answer.

The man looked at the Chief Elder, then at all the others who had now gathered around them. "I don't know what the power source is," he finally conceded. "I don't understand such things." A few Elders frowned while others seemed impatient with the apparently unsatisfactory reply. "But, it is there."

"Have you seen it?" an Elder asked.

"No. Well, not really. Sometimes I can see the glow that comes from it. But it's incredibly bright, and very dangerous. If you get near it, you will die."

"Then how can you use it if you can't get near it?" asked another. "How can anyone use it?"

Doubts rose about the man's offer. Some of the Elders openly challenged such talk as mere nonsense while others mumbled their agreement. As questions were thrown at the stranger and batted about among themselves, they became angry at the man whom only moments earlier they had grown to like. In the midst of the commotion, the stranger calmly raised his hand.

"Stop," he said sternly. Immediately there was silence, and the Elders stared at the man seated before them. "You have asked me questions I cannot answer. But giving you answers was not why I was sent." His dark eyes looked intently at each of the Elders. "Listen very carefully to what I am about to say."

The man paused, making sure he had the full attention of the Elders and all who had pushed and shoved to get near that fire. It seemed the entire village was crowding in.

A young boy somehow managed to force his way through the dense forest of legs and arms. With his last effort he burst from the crowd, stumbled forward, and fell facedown in the dirt near the stranger's feet. The crowd gasped as most of the Elders jumped in surprise, then glared at the intruder. A woman hissed for her Brian to "get back here," though it was impossible to know for certain where exactly "here" might be. Frightened, the child glanced up at the man, who gently smiled down at him. Suddenly, the boy felt different…warm inside. He smiled back. Then noticing the angry stares around him, he jumped up, mumbled, "Sorry, mister," and hurried back to the crowd.

The man watched as the boy disappeared once again into the forest. Then, he returned his attention to the Elders.

"There's only one question that matters. Would you like some help?" He paused as the Elders glanced at each other. "Would you like some help?" he repeated. "We will lay the first lines, get you started with training, and provide help when you run into problems."

"Will a power plant be built here?" asked Thomas.

"No." The man seemed pleased that at least someone was moving closer to accepting the offer. "The power will come from the far side of Chokmah and Sunesis. It can't be here. Like I said, the source is far too dangerous for your people to be exposed to it. But a branch will eventually be located here."

"Will your people run it?"

"No. It will be very important for you to become involved in this. Each one of you. The citizens here. Everyone. As I said, we will help from time to time, but this isn't our job." The man looked at the bewildered faces surrounding him.

"How much will we have to pay for this?" someone asked. "Yes, how much will it cost?" asked another. The Brigons waited anxiously for the reply.

The stranger smiled. "It's free." Hushed sounds of surprise and relief mixed among the crowd. Then he added, "But it will cost you everything. You must understand. You are either with us…or against us."

No one dared move or make a sound, as though an overwhelming, mystical force had turned them to stone. The crowd. The Elders. Every eye focused on this one man as he eyed all those around him. Then he got to his feet, brushed the dirt from his pants, and nodded slightly as if to say, "We are done." The man stepped toward the old Chief Elder, who was still sitting on the ground, and helped him to his feet.

"Now," the stranger said, extending a strong, firm hand, "would you like some help?"

The stranger met with the Elders only that one time, though he stayed to direct the early work that returned power to the village. After the Council accepted his offer, many others like him soon arrived. No one could ever figure out how he had signaled them, yet they came nonetheless—from beyond the Great Peaks, over the high crests, and down the treacherous slopes.

Every now and again a Brigon shouted, "Yonder comes one," "Yonder comes another," and "Yonder come more." Soon all in the valley came to know them as Yonders. They did not talk much, being more content to do the work at hand, and never did any mention their home or what it was like there. But that did not stop the Brigons from asking. Since these strangers offered no name for their home—the land beyond the mountains—the Brigons named it themselves. Farside.

For a long time the Yonders from Farside worked alone. Heavy cables were laid across the eastern range, threading their way through the narrow pass between Chokmah and Sunesis, then down the rocky, steep slopes. From there, the Brigons were allowed to work alongside the Yonders, and together they brought the lines into the valley and finally to the boundary of Brigos Glen. But the old electrical lines in the village, unused and neglected, were in serious decay. When word reached the stranger, he ordered his men to carefully restore them, making certain the old lines would handle the surge of new power. He tirelessly oversaw their work, observing even the smallest details and inspecting each and every repair.

Then, with the last line fully repaired and ready for operation, he left. No goodbye. No fond farewell. Never to return. And all anyone really knew about him was his name. Karis.

Before his abrupt departure, Karis sent to the Elders an extensive manual entitled *The Brigos Plan*. The document contained blueprints, diagrams, descriptions, and directions for the distribution of power within the village. The Plan had been designed especially with Brigos Glen in mind, taking into account everything from its terrain and available resources to the abilities and skills of the Brigons. And, as stated on the very first page, the Plan had been developed *for* the Brigons, not *with* them. There had been no discussions, no attempt at cooperation of any kind. This bothered many of the Elders and more than a few took issue with their exclusion. They reminded the Council of Karis's words: "It will cost you everything." But their cries of indignation went ignored as the majority wasted no time in studying the manual.

For the most part, everything would be very simple for the Brigons. In the beginning, each of the three major operations—transmission, distribution, and support—were to be administered remotely from Farside. Transmission within the system would be the responsibility of Brighten Power Authority. It would direct power from the primary source in Farside through the high intensity cables and down to the repaired lines in Brigos Glen. There, the distribution of the power fell to Olasom Contracting.

While Brighten Power Authority would operate exclusively from Farside, the Plan called for distribution services to locate in Brigos Glen. Olasom would further develop, maintain, and expand the system, laying new lines to reach more people. Initially it would perform all the work with no outside assistance, which angered several Elders, but in time a group of Brigons would be specially trained to assume significant responsibilities. Working as a local branch of Olasom, they would carry out its directions to restore light throughout the valley. This promised involvement satisfied most of the riled Elders, who did not hesitate to point out that any Brigon was certainly as capable as any Yonder.

Once the transfer of responsibilities began, the Brigons would receive additional technical support and guidance through QolCom, a communications firm based in Farside. Using an elaborate and complicated network, none of which was sufficiently explained to the Elders' satisfaction, QolCom would serve as the primary link between the system's foreign management and the local branch in Brigos Glen. Information concerning system operations, power transmission, distribution procedures, on-site training, and further education would be transmitted from Farside. The Brigons would also be able to interact with QolCom, primarily to communicate any needs, identify issues, and request assistance and conflict resolution.

All seemed straightforward. The village would again have power and light. And yet, an uneasiness filled the Council. Whoever prepared the Plan had a very detailed and, for the Elders, unsettling knowledge of Brigos Glen and its people. But it was the operations' administration that most concerned the Elders. While input and requests would be permitted, all final decisions would issue solely from beyond the mountains. Though this system would operate for the benefit of those in Brigos Glen, no Brigon would be allowed to assume any position of control. Not now. Not ever.

Much work remained for the Yonders. Power grids had to be configured, a training center built, offices constructed, and countless testings and trials completed. But in time, each of the Yonders returned to Farside. For months upon months they had worked long and hard, closely following the Plan. Then one day the Brigons awoke to find everything completed. Power flowed from beyond the mountains. The darkness retreated from the village as light came to the valley. And the Yonders...were gone.

CHAPTER 3

A BUSINESS

SEVENTY YEARS HAD passed since the Voice called out in the darkness. Seventy years to the day. And the Brigons knew. They counted the years again, and the weeks and the months. With the return of power, a new day had come to Brigos Glen, one simulated by the many light towers constructed throughout the village. They dimmed for dusk and brightened for dawn. Nothing could manufacture a clear blue sky or puffy white clouds, but few of the original survivors still lived and even they found it difficult to remember the time before Last Day. Now, after all those years, the Brigons could only dream of what might lay beyond the deep, black clouds that covered the land like an impenetrable ceiling. And as always, past the light towers, the darkness remained.

But no one thought of the darkness on this day…this very special day. Laughter and music filled the air. Colorful pennants and bunting hung from every building. Festive parties carried on throughout the village while streets filled with noisy revelers. This was a time for remembering, a time for rejoicing, a time for shouting defiance to the lingering darkness that surrounded Brigos Glen. For this was Marturia…the celebration of the day the stranger came.

Few businesses remained open…restaurants, caterers, a shop or two. All the others closed while their owners and employees celebrated. All, except the local offices of Brighten Power Authority. Though the Plan called for only one branch, three now covered the village—First Brigos Branch, Glen Community Branch, and New Power Branch. In those early days everything had operated well with only one, but in time, disagreements arose concerning the best way to distribute the power, how and where to provide new lines, and even as to the specific directions and instructions of the manual itself. Eventually there was such division within the original branch that many of the managers left and set up two additional offices. After much debate, an agreement was reached to divide the village into service districts, one for each of the three branches. Then names were adopted so the Brigons would be clear as to which branch was which. That was deemed important since each claimed to have the correct interpretation of the Plan.

First Brigos Branch held to a very conservative interpretation. It determined early on that while a branch should assist in the distribution, its primary purpose was to protect the power. If there were no instructions to provide power for uses not specifically described in the manual, then no such power would be provided, regardless of needs that might exist. Much effort was used in teaching the methods of laying lines as had first been applied by Olasom Contracting. But since First Brigos did not tolerate change or new ideas, it serviced only the older, established areas of the village where there was no development or growth. So its teaching had no clear purpose, though that did nothing to hinder the mandatory classes.

Glen Community Branch, on the other hand, applied a broader interpretation of the Plan. It looked to serve all the different needs of the village, whether or not those needs were a wise use of the power. Brigons wanting more buildings, more shops, more houses, and more services were more than welcome at Glen Community where power was provided with no strings attached. But unlike First Brigos, little time was given to teaching, none to the old methods for repairing and maintaining the lines. In fact, caring for the new lines was largely ignored as Glen Community looked always to the next development.

The last branch differed greatly from the other two and, except for rare occasions, would not associate with them at all. It even refused to have "Branch" appear in its signage, referring to itself only as New Power. Of the three, New Power had the most open and, according to the others, most radical interpretation of the Plan, which it considered merely a guide with suggestions. Its leaders claimed to have discovered the truth of the Plan, that the power existed for all to enjoy any way they wished: no controls for any application, no restriction on the amount used, no requirement for obtaining the power, and no consequent responsibilities.

New Power, unlike the other branches, did not view Farside as the only acceptable source. It strongly encouraged its staff to explore and develop ways in which it might generate its own power and thereby attain complete independence from Farside, as well as its sister branches. In fact, New Power claimed on several occasions to have succeeded, though it was never able to sufficiently demonstrate a new source it could adequately control. And while continuing to distribute the power that came from Farside, it largely ignored the Plan and any information from Olasom, as well as any further instructions that might issue through QolCom.

Glen Community established its headquarters in Three Rivers, a growing neighborhood in the western territory of Brigos Glen. Only one river flowed in the valley. It wasn't especially significant and was a distance away. However, the neighborhood's name made the residents feel good, which seemed far more important.

Three Rivers thrived in the new—new stores, new businesses, new housing, new parks. It provided the perfect location for Glen Community, which at long last had settled into its new offices—a renovated shopping mall that once held great promise as a premier site for designer retail and fine dining. Unfortunately, it had failed due to a lack of planning, which would have revealed the inability of the area's residents to afford such services, regardless of how much they may have wanted them.

One new venture after another closed for lack of sales. The mall became an empty shell, desolate and abandoned, until Glen Community took over, renaming it Vanguard Center. The move greatly cheered those in Three Rivers, while also diverting the longstanding question of how the branch could have approved such an ill-fated project.

Normally the hallways were filled with people hurrying from meeting to meeting, scurrying from one important conference to another. But not today. It was Marturia, after all, and even the always busy Glen Community wanted to celebrate. Only a skeleton crew remained on duty in case a dire emergency arose, which never occurred.

Usually filled with brightly colored electric cars, now brightly colored tents and balloons cluttered the parking lot. Singers, musicians, artists, jugglers, magicians, clowns, even a mime or two, and hundreds of men, women, and children milled about from one exhibit and performance to the next.

The light towers worked beautifully, shining down on a cheery vision of happiness and joy…at least it seemed that way from behind a lonely window far down the side of the Center. A young man stared out from a sterile, half lit corridor.

He was dressed in crisply ironed khakis and a navy blue dress shirt, as required of all employees. Stitched across the shirt pocket in gold letters was *Glen Community—Your Community*. The side of his face pressed against the window. A lock of brown hair fell carelessly across his brow. He sighed, never hearing the footsteps coming from behind.

"Hey, there," came a friendly call. "What are you looking at?"

The man by the window recognized the voice immediately. He turned around and smiled.

"Mr. Ellington," he replied, "don't tell me they have you working today, too?"

The much older man gave a slight laugh. "Now, Sam, I couldn't leave you here all alone, could I? It just wouldn't do." He continued, without waiting for a reply. "Besides, I've seen the other sixty-nine of these things, and they're all pretty much the same. Certainly won't hurt to miss one." He laughed again.

Sam politely nodded, trying to conceal his disappointment.

"Hey," Ellington said, his bushy eyebrows raised as though a great thought had occurred to him. "I've got a few minutes to spare. Why don't you join me for a quick cup of coffee? My treat."

"I don't know. I've still got the Lexington report to do, and there are piles of new applications to review, and…"

Ellington held up his hand. "A quick cup. That's all. I promise not to keep you," he said with a quick smile.

Sam usually preferred hot tea, but he did enjoy spending time with Ellington, who was the only true friend he had at Glen Community. Sam could unload his burdens, divulge secret fears, and speak his mind. He never worried that Ellington might judge him, or worse, rat him out. Such trust was rare at the branch.

For most, one's own problems far outweighed any concern for those of another. Conversations were reduced to mere business-speak. "What's happening with project so and so? Where are those work requisitions? How's the latest development coming? Why can't we move faster? Who's in charge of the power grid this week?"

and on and on. Even their language was veiled with one acronym or another, as though they wanted their true plans kept secret.

But Ellington was different. There was his age, for one thing. Well into his seventies and with his short cropped hair, Ellington easily stood out among the branch's youthful workforce, who held much more interest in his retirement than he did. Ellington had taken good care of himself over the years and remained fit...unlike most at Glen Community, who lived the majority of their waking lives behind a desk. He refused to use an electric car—the normal means of transportation in the village—and each day could be seen briskly walking to work...always swinging his long arms, always smiling regardless of how he might feel that day, and always, always, greeting everyone he met.

Ellington did not merely appear to care about others. He genuinely did care. And *that*, Sam found most different of all. The old man sincerely cared. If he sensed someone was upset and wanted to talk, he listened. If they asked for advice, he thought carefully and gave it. If they needed someone to be there with never a word between them, he was. Ellington's wife had died ten years earlier and he never had children. As he was fond of saying to his young friend, "Sam, I have the time. Why not give it?"

Sam liked Ellington from the very first time they met. Five years earlier Sam had managed a rare transfer from New Power. It was rare not because those at New Power cared...which they did not in the least...but because those at Glen Community generally did not feel comfortable with anyone or anything that might have come into contact with the New Power way of thinking. It took a great amount of salesmanship to convince them he had been mis-assigned and should never have been placed there.

But he had a deeper reason for wanting to get away from New Power—the "acceptance" it required. Every thought, every idea, every notion, every belief had to be accepted, regardless of any differences or conflicts that might exist among all those accepted thoughts, ideas, notions, and beliefs. As he later confided to Ellington, "If you're willing to accept anything, you'll soon believe in nothing."

The transfer came through on Sam's tenth anniversary with the Company, which was what most Brigons called the overall power system. Everyone in the system technically worked for a particular branch, though—personal feelings and differences aside—all three were connected within the greater structure. Each branch had its own individual relations with Brighten Power Authority, Olasom Contracting, and QolCom. They in turn had their own connections and relations with each other, even to the extent that often directions and instructions to the branches might be delivered by one, but issued by another. It was confusing and no one truly understood it all, though many claimed they did. Perhaps the Yonders knew the mystery of how everything worked together. However, since no one had seen a Yonder in such a very long time, it would have been no use to anyone even if they did. So rather than attempt anything remotely resembling a clear explanation, the Brigons casually referred to the whole lot of it as "the Company."

Sam followed Ellington down a long corridor. They passed a large room filled with cubicles, work stations, and a few other unlucky souls forced to work during the celebration. At the end of the corridor, a door opened into a small room set aside for employees, furnished with a rickety wooden table and a few plastic chairs. Sam opted for one of the more sturdy chairs while Ellington walked to the counter where a pot of coffee had been aging most of the day. He poured two cups, heated them in the microwave, and then took a seat at the table. Sam drank his coffee black, but Ellington took his with a bit of cream. As the old man stirred his coffee, he leaned back in his chair and studied his downcast friend.

"So…what's on your mind? Problem with the projects? Report due?"

"Everything's fine," Sam lied. He took a long drink of coffee as Ellington eyed him suspiciously.

"I've seen that look before, Sammy. I know how difficult it can be here. It's tomorrow, isn't it?" Sam glanced away. "Ah, thought so," Ellington acknowledged with a nod. "Don't worry. It will be fine. You've always done well in your reviews."

"I don't know about this time." Sam sighed.

"Eh, what's so different from all the others?"

"For one thing," Sam absentmindedly counted on his fingers, "there was last year's lecture on production. Everything was about developing newer, bigger, and even more projects. If you recall, they took a rather dim view of the time I spent reviewing the completed ones and doing those stability assistance reports."

"Why, yes," Ellington laughed. "If they had taken those reports seriously, my boy, this shopping mall might never have failed and we would still be working out of those drab offices in Commerce Center." He could not suppress another laugh, but Sam found no humor in the situation.

"I'm not sure they actually thought so far ahead. That would've required a plan," Sam said sarcastically. "I don't get it. I really don't. It's like all we're supposed to be interested in is the next great project, not whether any of them succeed or make a difference."

Ellington nodded. They had discussed this before, yet what those higher up the corporate ladder might do had never so intensely affected Sam.

"Anything else?"

"Not unless you consider *attitude adjustment* anything," Sam replied.

A few months before, the supervisor had called Sam into his office—a large cubicle with no door—about a problem raised by many of the assistant managers. For some time they had become greatly concerned about Sam's attitude toward fellow employees, one they felt needed...*adjustment.* Taken aback, Sam quickly explained that if he had offended or upset anyone in the slightest way, it certainly had not been intentional and he would immediately apologize. All he ever wanted was to help and encourage...

Precisely at that moment the supervisor interrupted in a stoic manner, "It is not *your* business to help or encourage *anyone* here. Nor is it the business of Glen Community. We are here to distribute power to new developments," the supervisor droned. "We do not have the luxury of listening to every poor, pathetic story of some poor, pathetic life. It isn't that we don't care to take such time, it's that we don't have such time to care." The supervisor had ended the one-sided discussion abruptly, clearly impressed with his choice of words.

There had been many conversations between Ellington and Sam about that meeting. But as much as they talked, discussed, and analyzed, neither had come to an acceptable solution. The attitude that so vexed the assistant managers was not a new one. Several had complained of this before...about Ellington. But they had gotten nowhere with him. He never changed one iota of the way he carried on...or his caring attitude. Eventually, they were resigned to wait him out. As one conceded, "He's bound to retire soon."

But then they noticed the same "aberrant behavior" in their young engineer. It angered them to consider even the possibility of Sam learning at the hands of the old master—which indeed he was. Like Ellington, Sam genuinely cared for others and it brought him great joy to be of help, even in the slightest ways. However, unlike Ellington, Sam had a considerably longer future, a wife, and two small children. He needed this job, as he frequently reminded his older friend.

Ellington rocked a bit in his chair.

"So, what do you plan to do? I didn't notice you refusing to help Stevens a few weeks ago when he needed to talk about his divorce, or Mrs. Patel when she asked for advice about that son of hers, or even the girl who was concerned about her upcoming surgery. What's her name?"

"Angie Cho," Sam replied, staring at his coffee.

"I could name quite a few others, you know."

"Yes, thank you for not doing that."

"And what does Ali think about all this?"

"She had some advice." Sam thought about his wife and smiled.

"For you?"

"For *them*. But I don't use that kind of language." Sam laughed as did Ellington, who had met Ali many times and knew she could be strong-willed and a bit feisty. "Yeah, she's pretty upset about it all, but she said she'd support me in whatever I choose to do. It's just…" He paused, glanced at his friend, then stared again into his coffee. "I don't know what I choose to do."

"Hmm." Ellington leaned closer to his protégé. "Would you like some help?"

The celebration wore on well into the evening. The crowd moved like a mighty river—flowing from one party, pouring out onto the street, sloshing about the walkway, briefly joining a pool of people here, leaving another there, finally spilling through an open door and into another party—only to repeat it all in due course. With great effort, Sam struggled through the festive Brigons in the Glen Community parking lot. Being careful not to get swept away in the happy flood, he made his way to a side alley that ran off the main thoroughfare.

He hurried down the alley to an empty street and continued on for several blocks. He reached a private drive reserved for deliveries to the shops nearby. There would be no deliveries this day, but it did provide a safe out-of-the-way location. Like a loyal pet, Sam's car sat there waiting for him. He got in, closed the door, and slumped into his seat. It was quiet inside. Sam was finally alone. And the sounds of Marturia grew faint.

The Mitchells' apartment was modest. A family room with a galley kitchen to one side, a bedroom for Sam and Ali, and another bedroom for the children. Only the one bathroom. And something a bit larger than a storage closet that Sam had converted into a cramped, but serviceable, office. They found the apartment large enough, though barely.

Sam had been lucky to get it after his transfer. As always, the area boasted extensive new residential construction, intended primarily for those with considerably more income than someone mired in the midst of middle management. Ironically, the housing units being built far outnumbered those who could afford them. But due to the desires of the Brigons—and their willingness to go into tremendous debt—construction continued.

Sam and Ali lived in an old complex that dated back to before Last Day. After light returned to Brigos Glen, it had been restored and kept in decent repair, but most considered the apartments ancient and run-down. A place to move *from* rather than move *to*. Not the place of choice to raise a family. Except for Sam and Ali. Their neighbors were older, many already retired, and they were friendly. They took time for each other, talked and walked together. Had each other over for dinner and tea. When the young couple moved in, this humble community embraced them as though they were long-lost friends. And friends they became. Sam and Ali truly loved starting their family there, living there… enjoying life there.

Just before midnight, Sam finally made his way home. A dimly lit floor lamp in the corner provided the only light. Next to it sat a well-used overstuffed chair, and buried in the cushions was a young woman with a child in each arm. All fast asleep.

Sam smiled as he imagined the pleading that must have gone on so Mark and Molly could stay up to see their dad. Ali seldom gave in to such things, but being together as a family was intensely important to them, and these days Sam often left for work early and came home late. Family time had become rare.

Sam gently touched Ali's arm, rousing her from a deep sleep, and motioned for her to stay there. Then he carefully picked up the two toddlers, rested one on each shoulder, and carried them off to bed. Their room was small, like everything else in the apartment, but Ali had painted it bright and fun for the kids. A deep blue ceiling displayed white, puffy clouds. Snow-capped mountains adorned the wall behind the one bed. Trees and streams graced either side, and on the far wall…a beaming, red sun rose between two large peaks. Ali had gotten the idea from a picture that had decorated her bedroom wall when she was a child. Her mother had hung it there so Ali would know what the world had been like before the darkness and to give her hope of what it could be again.

Sam softly laid them on their bed and pulled the covers up under their chins. "Sweet dreams," he whispered, tucking them in. As he was about to leave the room, he paused to look at them once more. *So peaceful. Never enough time*, he thought, then carefully eased the door closed behind him. He wearily returned to the family room and plopped onto the worn couch across from his yawning wife.

She tossed aside her long auburn hair and rubbed the sleep from soft brown eyes. "How'd it go today?"

"The same." He did not want to mention his review in the morning. *At least one of us should get some sleep*, he thought. "Not much going on with it being Marturia."

"I don't see why they make *you* work it at all," Ali said with renewed energy.

"Now, Ali, we've been over this."

"But it's not fair, Sam. You know it's not! You have to work during Marturia every year. Other people get to stay at home with *their* families."

"I'm low man."

"In *all* of Glen Community?" she replied sternly. It was not so much a question, as questioning.

"In my division. Besides, we need the extra money."

Ali could not argue with that. Sam made enough, but good jobs were hard to come by, and he certainly could not afford to lose this one. As she sat silently, Sam took advantage of the moment and changed the subject.

"Talked with Ellington a bit today. He asked about you."

Ali smiled. She had grown fond of the old gentleman.

"And how is Mr. E today? In good health I hope."

"Oh yes. Nothing to worry about there. Don't think I've ever seen him even with a cold. He's got more energy than all the rest of us, I'm sure."

"And what did the two of you talk about?"

"You know," Sam laughed a little, "I'm really not sure."

Ali frowned a bit. "You don't know what you talked about? You were there, weren't you?" she teased him.

"Yeah, I think so," Sam answered playfully. He scratched the back of his head and looked down at the floor as though it were a monitor replaying the scene from earlier in the day. "It's just that… he's a funny old guy. Sometimes he talks and sometimes he sits there and listens, and sometimes he says things that don't make a lot of sense, but he never really explains them either."

"And which did he do today?" This was beginning to sound like a great mystery. Ali leaned toward Sam, elbows on her knees and chin resting on folded hands. She gazed into Sam's steel gray eyes.

"All the above, " Sam said with a grin. "He's a good guy." Sam yawned and, without thinking, added, "Wanted to help with the review in the morning." His eyes immediately closed tight in a grimace.

"*What* review?"

CHAPTER 4

THE REVIEW

SAM HATED WAITING. The review was to begin at "07:00, precisely!" as he had been told several times over the last few days. Three hours earlier he had dragged himself out of bed, showered, shaved, dressed, and rushed out the door. He arrived so early the parking lot was still empty. The light towers had not yet summoned dawn. A few lamps lit the walkway to the main entrance and fewer shone from the building itself. Sam had hurried inside, rushed to his cubicle, picked up his project reports and development assessments, and taken a seat outside his supervisor's cubicle.

An hour later, no one had arrived. Sam nervously checked his watch. 07:15. He glanced at one end of the work room, then to the other. Nothing. He was absolutely alone. With no real purpose but to pass the time, he opened a folder and scanned one of the reports. Then he flipped through another, and another. He checked the time again. 07:28. Sam was about to rummage through the assessments in the next folder when, at last, he heard footsteps approaching.

Be calm, be calm, he thought. *This is going to be all right.*

The footsteps grew louder.

After all, you work hard. Haven't asked for a raise or promotion. Can be depended on. Why would they risk losing...

His thoughts abruptly ended as did the footsteps. Sam looked up in time to see an impassive face glance in his general direction, then disappear into the cubicle. The face belonged to Roger Carrington, Sam's supervisor. He was a very large man, a foot taller than Sam and at least two hundred pounds heavier. Each day Carrington would wile away the hours sitting inside his cubicle—ordering plans, reviewing plans, approving plans—always alone except for the annual reviews. He made no secret that he found these terribly bothersome ordeals, which he dreaded, loathed, and would have avoided at any cost were it not a part of his job description. Usually he made short work of them, giving each of his charges a summary "Meets Expectations" rating that required little thought or effort on his part.

"If you're not causing me trouble," he would tell them, "you're meeting my expectations."

But as he had made clear to Sam on more than one occasion, two of his engineers seemed particularly gifted in creating a stir among those above him. He never understood why anyone cared, but because they did, he was forced to. And he hated being forced to do anything out of his routine.

A chair groaned as it took on the massive weight. A drawer scraped open, then slammed shut. A stack of papers dropped onto a desk. Then nothing but an unsettling silence. Sam anxiously waited for the impending unknown. His palms grew sweaty, and he unconsciously rubbed them on his pants. Finally, a heavy sigh floated out of the cubicle, and Sam considered peeking inside.

"Mitchell!"

Sam jumped, startled at suddenly hearing his name. The folders slipped out of his hand and scattered about the floor.

"Get in here!" the supervisor barked. "I don't have all day."

Sam gathered up his files and hurried into the cubicle.

Lining the four walls stood tall bookcases, each filled to over-flowing with manuals, folders, folded plats, progress evaluations, and dozens of unopened assessment reports. A large metal desk, with Carrington seated behind it, occupied most of the available space. Everything appeared normal in the cramped little office... except for the two empty chairs facing the desk.

Normally Carrington dispensed with such comforts, always requiring his unfortunate visitors to stand. "Standing encourages you to keep the meetings short," he would explain. It never occurred to him that it was not they, but he, who was in charge.

His large meaty hands held a single sheet of paper. He stared at it, possibly reading, though there was no way to be certain from his rather blank expression.

"Sit," he ordered, without making the slightest move. Sam started toward the nearest chair. "Not that one. The other one."

His supervisor pointed to a chair farther from the view of passing employees. Carrington had often complained he should have an actual door. Now Sam also wished the supervisor had one. Sam slid into the designated space.

Why two chairs? There's never been two before. This can't be good.

He waited for an explanation, but the supervisor sat there, silently staring at the sheet of paper. Finally, Sam could take the suspense no longer.

"Um...will anyone be joining us?"

Carrington glanced at Sam, his face impassive. "There will be." Then he returned to studying the paper.

Not good, not good.

Sam's anxiety swelled in his chest until he felt his heart pounding. He wrung his hands and kept glancing out the cubicle for a sign of anyone else. A few more workers had arrived, but they were either already safely within or headed to their own little cubicles. No one appeared to have any interest in coming near the supervisor's. Sam looked at his watch. 07:30.

Only 07:30? Did time stop all of a sudden?

Sam had reason for concern…the employee manual. In spite of his worrying about any of the past reviews, he had always found solace in Regulation 347(a)(1)(ii) which specified that one supervisor had authority only to discipline an employee. Termination, on the other hand, required the agreement of two.

Sam looked at the second chair. *What will we do? Where will I go? How will I tell Ali?*

"Am I late?" rang out a cheery voice as the next man entered the cramped, little office.

Sam jerked around, shocked.

"My boy, glad to see you're here, too."

"El…Ellington?" Sam stuttered.

"Ellington," the old man laughed. "Yes, yes, as far as I'm aware at any rate. Can't be too sure at my age," he teased. "Why, the other day…"

"Would you sit…please?" the supervisor asked, as if he were begging not to be regaled with any delightful or witty story that might take up his precious time.

"Certainly," came the dutiful reply.

With a broad smile, Ellington sat in the chair beside Sam and nodded to his young friend. As Carrington continued to study the paper, Sam leaned toward Ellington and whispered.

"Any idea what's going on?"

"Not remotely."

Then suddenly Sam remembered Ellington's words from the day before: "Would you like some help?" He straightened up in alarm and whispered much more emphatically, "What did you do?"

"Nothing," replied the supervisor. Sam's eyes darted back. "Ellington has done nothing, Mitchell."

"I'm sorry, sir. It's just…," Sam stammered. "It's just that I knew it was time for my review and…"

"That will have to wait, I'm afraid," the supervisor interrupted, unconcerned.

For the first time since Sam had entered his cluttered cubicle, the supervisor appeared relaxed. He even appeared to have a slight grin, though since neither Sam nor Ellington had ever witnessed such an event, they could not be sure. Sam nervously glanced at Ellington as Carrington placed the sheet of paper onto the desk and leaned back in his ever-straining chair.

"We will reserve any further review for another day. I have another matter I must briefly mention to you…*each* of you… which is why you're both here. May as well kill two birds with one stone." He motioned to the sheet of paper. "This is a CDO," he said nonchalantly.

Carrington had a well-earned reputation for speaking in acronyms, especially to those who had no idea what he was talking about. They gave him a sense of superiority, even if only for the moment. He looked with false pity at their quizzical faces.

"CDO? Company…Direct…Order?" he said with deliberate enunciation, as though better diction would assist their understanding. "I receive these from time to time." Seeing his audience was not impressed, he continued. "Says here the two of you are to attend a BPA conference."

"Brighten Power Authority?" asked Sam.

"Yes," Carrington curtly replied, annoyed at missing the opportunity to explain this as well.

"I don't understand," Sam said. "Why us? What's it about?"

"I'm not at liberty to answer that," droned the supervisor.

In spite of his answer, Sam realized Carrington had no clue what the meeting could be about. In fact, through all the years since Last Day, no one had ever heard of such a thing. Brighten Power Authority had never held a conference…*ever*.

"Where will it be?" asked Ellington.

"I can't say."

"You can't say?" asked Sam. "But how are we to get there if we don't know where we're going?"

Ellington nodded in agreement. As they waited for an answer, Carrington took up the piece of paper and read.

"The Company will provide transportation both to and from Heis Center in the mountains of the eastern range. Attendees will be picked up at and returned to their homes, and each should bring enough clothing for five days. Rooms and meals will be provided. However, no outside communication will be allowed during the conference. The Company will conduct all sessions and meetings, and any necessary materials will be supplied."

Sam was so shocked he could not speak. This directive was more than unexpected. The eastern range stretched far beyond the boundaries of Brigos Glen, in a dangerous area known as the Outlands. Few had ventured there, and none since the Yonders had left.

Ellington acted as though such things occurred all the time. He took over.

"Will you be going with us?"

Carrington shook his head. "No, sadly, there's too much work here to be done. The Company wants me to stay and make sure everything continues smoothly." Sam suspected the CDO had not said anything of the sort, but the supervisor obviously felt much better with this assumption.

"Too bad. Does the CDO say when this conference will begin?"

"Uh, yes, here it is. Today."

Sam jumped to attention and even Ellington looked surprised.

"Today?" Sam asked, astonished. "You mean *today* today?"

"I know of no other," droned the supervisor who appeared thoroughly bored with the entire affair.

"And they'll pick us up?"

"Yes."

"At our homes?"

"Yes," came the long sigh.

"But when?" Sam asked.

"Yes, when would that be?" added Ellington.

Carrington mechanically scanned the sheet of paper, located the proper information, and retrieved the requested data. Sam guessed the image of two empty cubicles must have formed in his mind, for the supervisor grinned…a little more than slightly.

"One hour."

Sam had never packed so quickly in his life. Of course, he had also never been anywhere in his life. Over the last twenty years, Brigos Glen had grown, expanding more and more into the valley. Adding light towers and redistributing the power had made that possible. Travel, such as it was, consisted of visits to one another's homes or to the small resort Glen Community had helped develop. But travel beyond the valley was strictly prohibited.

Few towers had been installed outside the boundaries of Brigos Glen, none in the Outlands where the only source of light had to be carried. The darkness ruled there, or so it had always been believed. And yet, that is exactly where Sam and Ellington were headed—a fact not lost on Ali. She watched her husband frantically throwing clothes into an old, battered suitcase that lay open on their bed.

"I don't like this," she said, just above a whisper.

Sam concentrated on the task at hand, avoiding the look of concern he knew was being cast his way. "It will be fine."

"How do you know?"

Sam paused. "They wouldn't send us into any danger, Ali," he said, as reassuringly as he could, then began packing again.

Ali stepped up from behind, put her arms around him, and hugged him close. He could feel her heartbeat. Sam turned in her arms and looked deeply into her eyes.

"It's going to be okay. There's nothing to worry about. Ellington will be there, too."

Ali frowned. "And having a man in his seventies helps how, exactly?"

"Well," Sam said, "I figure that if anything chases us…"

"Yes?"

"…all I have to do is outrun him."

Ali laughed. "And can you?"

"Not certain, actually," Sam replied, trying to sound serious. "He *is* in pretty good shape. But I'm sure he could beat you." Ali shoved him away and he fell back onto the bed, laughing.

"I'm serious, Sam," she said, then turned and stormed out of the room.

"Ali," Sam called after her. "I was kidding. Come on, Ali."

He sat up and waited, but she did not return. Ali had been upset since she first learned of this trip into the Outlands. She railed against the thought of it, listing each of the unknowns and dangers. But Sam never doubted he would go. He had to, really. He needed the job, of course, but there was something else compelling him… something he could not put his finger on. And now that he had time to consider everything, he had a peace about it…and he had not had a peace about anything for a very long time. It felt good. But Ali did not share that feeling.

Sam ran his hand through his hair, then looked about the room. *What a day*, he thought. He got up and returned to the few things left to pack. A suit, just in case. An extra belt. His razor, a toothbrush. And last, a small framed picture of Ali and the kids. He carefully tucked it safely inside the clothes. Then, with the snap of the locks, he was done. He carried the suitcase into the living room and set it beside the door.

A beckoning aroma filled the kitchen as Ali prepared breakfast for Mark and Molly, who sat, squirming, in the two tall chairs that stood at the counter. Space did not allow for a proper kitchen table, so this had to suffice. But the children did not care. It was great fun to be so high and so close to Mommy while she cooked. As soon as they noticed Sam, they squealed with delight. Never did they see him during a workday unless he was very ill, which seldom occurred.

"Hey, my little munchkins," he said and hurried over to give them a hug and a peck on the cheek. "Are you going to be good for Mommy while I'm gone?" They both nodded with great enthusiasm. "And mind her like you're supposed to?" Again they eagerly nodded. "And pick up your toys?" This time they giggled. Sam looked over at Ali. "Two out of three's not bad."

Ali said nothing. She gave a quick smile, then returned to her cooking. Sam looked at her, hoping for an additional reaction… maybe even a sign of support…but nothing came. He hated that she felt this way, but there really was no choice. He had to go, and deep down, he wanted to. He tousled his kids' hair, making them squeal again, then walked up close behind Ali and put his hand on her shoulder.

"I love you," he whispered.

"I know," she said softly.

With her face still turned toward the cooking food, she reached up and held his hand. Suddenly, there was a knock at the door. Her grip tightened.

A tall and slender man, neatly dressed in a plain, dark suit, stood outside. Sam could tell the man was older than he, but beyond that, it was difficult to say. He had a full head of gray hair, but his face bore a youthful quality and, oddly enough, was very tan. The only tans in Brigos Glen came from a bottle, except for the wealthy who could afford the expensive treatments at the salons…treatments far too expensive for a hired driver.

"The name's Davidson," he said, extending his hand. "And you would be Sam Mitchell?"

"Yes," Sam replied. He shook the man's hand and received a surprisingly firm grip in return. "Pardon our apartment. It's a mess with the kids and all."

"Oh, certainly. No problem at all. I believe everything is quite nice."

"Thank you, sir," Ali called out from the kitchen. Her tone made it clear she was not happy with Sam apologizing for the appearance of their apartment, which may have seemed more as an apology for her.

"You're quite welcome, ma'am."

Sam was about to show him his suitcase when suddenly Mark and Molly came flying out of the kitchen. He had not noticed them scrambling out of their chairs. They always ran to greet their neighbors whenever one dropped by for a visit, and to them, this man was simply another visitor to welcome.

"Wait!" Ali cried out, but the children kept running.

Then Sam yelled, "Stop!" and the two immediately came to an abrupt halt. "What are you doing?" he scolded them. "That's no way to act to a stran…I mean, to treat our guest." Tears welled up in their eyes.

"No, no, that's quite all right," Davidson replied. "I love children, Mr. Mitchell." And with that, he knelt down and held out his arms to them. A warm smile spread across his tan face.

With no reasonable explanation, Sam felt…no, knew…it really was all right. The man's voice held a certain quality—a kindness, a gentleness, maybe even something more. And Sam knew.

He looked at his frightened kids and nodded. They instantly squealed again and ran into the man's open arms, knocking him backward to the floor, laughing all the way. He gave them each a hug, then Sam and Ali came to his rescue, lifting Mark and Molly into their own arms and hugs.

"They pack a wallop!" Davidson said, still laughing.

"Oh, I'm so sorry," Ali replied, though she was trying not to laugh herself.

"Here, let me help you up," Sam offered. He reached down, grasped Davidson's hand, and with one easy motion lifted him to his feet. "You know," he said, brushing dust off the man's suit, "most people wouldn't have been so gracious with little children."

"What do you mean?" Davidson asked, straightening his coat.

"Most people I know wouldn't have given them the time of day, I'm afraid."

"Mr. Mitchell..." He paused. "Sadly, I'm not into *most* people."

Sam nodded, though not entirely certain what he was agreeing with. Once again neat and tidy, Davidson straightened up and resumed a more business-like manner.

"I believe it's time."

"Oh...oh yes," Sam stuttered. He handed his little one to Ali and gave them all a warm embrace. "I'll be back soon," he promised, then whispered to Ali, "It will be okay, really."

She smiled. "I know," and this time it was clear she meant it. She looked to the waiting driver. "Be sure you take good care of him, sir."

"Oh, I will, indeed," he replied, and it was clear he meant it, too.

"And thank you again for tolerating the children. They're so used to having company come round. They can be a bit much."

"Oh, not at all, ma'am," Davidson said, with another broad smile. "Today it is every bit my pleasure to be the company." And with that, he grabbed Sam's suitcase, gave a departing nod, and headed outside.

Sam turned to the kids, now standing on either side of Ali. "Take care of Mommy, you hear?" They nodded as vigorously as always, but this time there were no smiles. He bent down and kissed each on the forehead. Then he stood and looked at his loving wife. The smile was still there, but it had become much more of a struggle. Sam gave Ali one last hug and kissed her gently before finally heading outside.

Ali and the kids followed as far as the door and watched as he walked away. Sam glanced back only once and saw Ali pat her chest over her heart, their personal sign for "I love you." He turned away and followed Davidson, not daring to look back to their tearful eyes...for fear they would see the tears in his own.

Sam hurried down the enclosed stairs and through a door that led outside. The light towers had manufactured a very bright day, and there was the usual chill in the air, though he hardly noticed. Such things were not important at the moment. He crossed the lawn the short distance to a waiting minibus. It looked like it could carry about twenty-four people, but for now, at least, it was empty. As Davidson loaded the luggage into an outside storage bin, Sam boarded the minibus and settled in a seat three rows back on the left side of the vehicle. He thought sitting a distance from the driver might lessen the opportunity for idle talk, which he suddenly felt he was not up to.

"You ready then?" Davidson called out, stepping inside. Sam silently nodded. "Good then. We're off."

Sam looked back at the apartment complex. As the minibus pulled away, he sank into his seat and suddenly wished he had never left.

CHAPTER 5

ONE WAY

THE MINIBUS WOULD never be mistaken for anything elegant. Still, Sam found it comfortable. Passengers had individual seats; two per row, separated by a narrow aisle with an identical set on the other side. Five rows covered the length of the vehicle, with a bench in the rear that stretched its width. Arm rests, handrails, the typical fare in a commuter. The upholstery, while far from new, showed no rips or tears. But the dominant feature was its awkward emptiness. Davidson had no other passengers and ever since they pulled out of the complex, neither of them had said a word.

Davidson deftly steered among, around, and through the traffic. Brigos Glen had not become a large city by anyone's comparison, but the Brigons did love their electric cars, which provided a sense of freedom in this altered world. They took advantage of any opportunity for a nice, leisurely drive, especially on non-working days such as this.

The day after the official celebration of Marturia was another holiday for all but essential services. This was due primarily to the elaborate parties of the previous night, which carried well into the wee hours of the morning. Presumably to avoid the inevitable avalanche of employee "sick day" calls, the Elders had issued an edict extending Marturia one more day. "For the welfare of the citizenry," the order proclaimed, though most Brigons believed it was more for the Elders' own recoveries from those parties.

Sam did not care about that. He never got any portion of Marturia off, and not just since he arrived at Glen Community. The same had been true at New Power, where they never observed the holiday. Some felt the ideals of Marturia should be celebrated throughout the year. "Every day," they claimed, "should be special, not just one." That sounded nice enough, but as Sam discovered, when every day is special, none are. At first, New Power made a valiant attempt to focus on each day, but soon only the day, itself, was being honored, not what had happened so long ago. After all, they reasoned, one can hear the old tales only so often before they become worn, tired, and no longer especially interesting. In due time, no one at New Power celebrated at all, though they did manage to dispense judgment on those who did.

There were those who had refused to follow this *particular* chosen day, originally set aside by First Brigos and later avidly supported by Glen Community. The Day of the Voice, as this group at New Power preferred to call it, was long before the light towers were erected, which necessarily meant long before the Elders had instituted the new calendaring system that simulated days. The Day of the Voice occurred in the dark times when no one could be sure even what month it might be, much less the actual day. "It would be wrong and disrespectful to Karis and his fellow Yonders," they argued, "to risk celebrating the wrong day."

First Brigos felt certain it had decided correctly, though never offered any proof for its claim, and Glen Community had always shown more interest in the parties. Neither believed it important enough to ask their customers how they might feel. Instead, they chose to ignore the issue altogether, labeling the matter as utter nonsense and creating an even further divide with their sister branch…not that New Power cared.

Sam had been there. He had seen it all. And he had escaped. He shook his head as he remembered. Then the words of a poem came to mind.

> *How lost such pointless souls become*
> *That ne'er do seek to find their way*
> *Back to the source they've long strayed from*
> *Back to the meaning of Today*
> *What lies in lies some fill their mind*
> *What pride in pride some dare to take*
> *What greed in greed some use to bind*
> *What life in life some choose to make*
> *How lost such pointless souls become*
> *That ne'er do seek to find their way*
> *Back to the source they've long strayed from*
> *Back to the meaning of Today*

He smiled, puzzled. *Where did that come from?* he wondered. *I haven't thought of that since…*

The minibus suddenly jerked to a stop, sending Sam flying into the back of the seat in front of him. Fortunately, there was not enough room for him to fall to the floor. He pulled himself into his own seat again.

"Sorry," Davidson called out.

"No problem," Sam replied, a little flustered. "My fault. Should have been paying attention." He looked outside the tinted window, while he regained his composure and dignity. "So, where are we?"

The composure may not have been there, but the question was sincere enough. He had not been paying attention and honestly had no idea where they could be.

"We're *here*," Davidson said, and headed for the door. "Going to fetch Mr. Ellington."

"So this is where he lives," Sam said to no one in particular.

He had never been to Ellington's home, though he and his family had been invited repeatedly. There was so much to do—at the office, at home, anywhere and everywhere—that little time was left for anything else.

Ellington often asked them over for afternoon tea. "Nothing grand," he would assure them. "Just an hour or so for a visit."

But they always had a reason or an excuse. In five years, they had never found even a few minutes to go see their old friend. And Sam suddenly felt ashamed, realizing how hard Ellington had tried.

The minibus was parked along a narrow lane not far from the main road, leaving only enough room for annoyed drivers of small electric cars to squeeze by one at a time. They did, and tossed a few words in Sam's general direction for good measure. The vehicle's tires pressed against a stone curb bordering a broken sidewalk that traveled along the front of a stone cottage. Two steps led up to a large wooden door. On either side planters displayed a variety of flowers in assorted colors, all somewhat faded due to the artificial light.

By the time Sam took notice of the green wooden door, it was opening. Davidson had already gone inside and now exited with an old suitcase in hand. The always cheery Ellington followed close behind. He stopped long enough to lock the door before quickly hurrying to the minibus and climbing on board. At the sight of Sam, Ellington's face lit up.

"Sam, my boy. Wonderful to see you again. Ready for the adventure? Mind if I sit here with you?"

"Yes."

Ellington was about to take the seat next to Sam, but stopped in mid-sitting.

"No." Sam corrected himself. "Of course, you can sit here." And Ellington gladly did. "What I meant was that I'm ready for our adventure. At least, I think I am. I'm still not sure what to make of it all."

Ellington stroked his chin and feigned a wise posture. "As my ol' father used to say, 'Bad Boy...' He called me Bad Boy. He never liked my real name. It was my mother's father's name and they never got along. But he would tease me and call me Bad Boy, as I was always doing something I ought not to be doing. There was this one time..." Ellington paused and laughed at a memory, then suddenly remembered why he was talking to begin with. "My father, yes...he'd say, 'Bad Boy, when you don't know what to make of a situation, sit tight and watch it make itself.' Ah!" Ellington laughed. "What do you make of that?"

Sam laughed along with him and shrugged. "I've no idea. What's it mean?"

"Ah, well, that's where it all falls down," Ellington said with a grin. "I've never known either. I was hoping you could tell me."

As they laughed again, Davidson stepped back into the minibus and resumed his position behind the wheel, never seeming to take the slightest notice of his passengers. Ellington wiped a tear from his eye, then saw their driver. He leaned toward Sam.

"Have the two of you talked much?"

"No, not really. A little when he picked me up, but nothing since."

Ellington called out to the front. "Mr. Davidson."

"Just Davidson, sir," the driver answered, starting the motor.

"Davidson sir," came the playful reply, "will we be taking on others? This seems rather large for only the three of us."

"Yes, sir. We have four more stops to make, then we'll head on to Heis. It's a long trip, but we should be there for dinner."

"Fine, fine. You have directions to Heis then, I take it?" Ellington continued, searching for something to carry on the conversation with the not-so-talkative fellow.

"No need, sir."

"No need?" Ellington asked doubtfully. "Isn't it beyond the towers, in the Outlands?"

"It is. Hidden in the eastern range, between the Great Peaks."

Sam had only been half listening, but what he had heard made him feel uneasy. He was not sure why. He straightened up and stared at the back of their driver's head. Their playful banter had taken on a more serious quality.

"How can he find this place?" he whispered to Ellington. "The Outlands are restricted. No Brigon is allowed there." Ellington appeared puzzled as well, and shook his head slightly.

Then a thought occurred to Sam. It quickly took shape, presenting a possibility he had never considered—one that greatly bothered him. Sam glanced at Ellington, then nervously looked back to the driver who was moving the minibus into traffic.

"Uh, Davidson," Sam said, though it sounded more like he was clearing his throat.

"Yes, sir?"

"You seem to know a lot about us, but we don't know anything about you. Since it's likely to be a long day, we should at least get to know each other a little. Mind telling us a bit?"

"Not at all," came the easy reply. "What would you like to know?"

"Oh, I don't know…are you married?"

"No sir, only to my job."

"Yeah, I hear that," Sam said, trying to sound as chummy as possible. "Um, been with the Company long?"

"Forever!"

"Yeah, I feel that way, too, sometimes." Sam hesitated, then summoning resolve he did not remember having, asked what he really wanted to know. "Where do you call home?" He and Ellington held their breath for what seemed an eternity, though it was but a moment.

"Farside."

Not much was said after that. Davidson drove along as Sam and Ellington sat still and silent, staring at the mysterious driver. Sam thought about his promise to Ali that everything would be all right and was angry for not having already considered this bit of news.

Of course, he's from Farside. How could anyone else have known how to get there? No one ever goes into the Outlands. What an idiot! I wonder if anyone at Glen Community knows about this?

But he immediately dismissed that thought. Anyone back at the branch would be far too busy preparing for a new development to be concerned about what danger might befall Ellington and him.

Arriving at their next stop, Davidson, as before, pulled to the curb, annoyed more drivers, and hurried off to "fetch another passenger." They were parked directly in front of a small, weathered sign that read Hopewell. It belonged to an equally weathered group of buildings that at one time had been a quaint neighborhood, but over the years had become a retirement community for those without the means to do better.

Hopewell stood in what was popularly known as the Forgotten Zone. None of the branches claimed it as part of their service area. First Brigon saw nothing to be gained by including its residents, except a drain on its own time and resources. Certainly no opportunity for new development appeared to exist, so just as certainly, Glen Community had no interest. And New Power found Hopewell to have no ambition for new ideas. "They would never fit in. It's for their own good," they all claimed.

Sam watched Davidson enter an old brick building, then he leaned toward Ellington.

"What are we going to do?" he whispered, as though Davidson might somehow hear.

"About what?" Ellington replied, surprised. "Are you thinking about bolting? Then what would you say back at the branch? Won't look good on your next review, I would think."

"No, I wasn't thinking of that," though that was exactly what he was thinking. "But we need a plan."

"A plan?" Ellington echoed, this time even more surprised. "My dear boy, get a hold of yourself. I'm sure everything will be fine. We may not know where we're going or why, or for that matter, what we'll find when we get there, or who...but I'm sure we're perfectly safe."

There was not a bit of that which Sam found even remotely reassuring.

"How can you be certain?" he asked, frustrated with Ellington's logic and apparent calm. "If Ali were here..."

"She's not," Ellington said gently, though firmly. "She's not, Sam. You are. And for whatever reason...you and I, and apparently a few others, have been chosen for this. I truly believe we're perfectly safe."

Sam was about to demand once more how he could be sure when Ellington interrupted him again.

"And I'm so certain because...well...I've got a peace about this. We're meant to go. We're meant to do this." He looked at the door Davidson had entered. "Besides, I don't recall ever hearing of any problems with those who came here from Farside. You wouldn't remember, of course. You weren't even born, then." He laughed. "There were quite a few. They came a long way back then, on foot, to help us. No, I believe we'll be fine." He turned back to his young friend. "I want to do this, Sam, and I'd be very pleased to share this adventure with you."

Sam felt like a coward. Nothing at all in Davidson's manner appeared alarming or threatening. He seemed kind enough, exceptionally polite, and very helpful. Even the kids had loved him. All of Sam's fears were based solely on where Davidson said he had come from.

Just then the door to the building opened and out stepped a small, elderly woman with perfectly groomed white hair. Davidson, carrying another suitcase, followed. Sam and Ellington watched as they approached the minibus.

"So," Sam concluded, "he's a Yonder."

"No." Ellington barely spoke, but the word was clear.

Still focused on the driver, Sam sighed. "You're not helping."

Once they were again underway, Ellington introduced himself and Sam to their new companion, Madame Miriam Couteau. She listened with great interest as he told her about themselves…where they lived and worked, even mentioning Ali and the kids, as well as insisting that Sam show her a picture of the happy little family. He also related their brief story of how they came to be a part of this strange trip. But he did not mention Sam's concerns about Davidson.

A warmth and kindness radiated from the lady, immediately drawing Sam to her. She was unabashedly honest. She told them with no reservation that she was ninety-two years of age. "And not a day younger!" she said proudly. Although she had lived her entire life in the village, in her younger days she had traveled behind the mountains, seen new sights, and had new experiences. "But there was nothing ever as good or as welcome as coming home," she sighed.

Mme. Couteau had never married—"Never found anyone crazy enough to have me." She laughed. She had spent most of her life working for the Company. When Sam pressed her for which branch, she laughed again, "All of them. Each of them. They're all the same to me, Sam." She told them stories of those early times when everyone was trying to figure out how to handle the power that came into the village, and the egos that got in the way.

"It was a shame, really," she said sadly. "Early on everyone cared more for each other. At least it seemed that way. We were just so thankful to have some help and be alive. Everyone was sharing everything. Those were happy times. You remember," she prodded Ellington, who nodded thoughtfully. "Yes, happy times. But, then people being people…"

Her words faded as she remembered. The minibus became very quiet, and Sam sensed she and Ellington wanted to be alone with their memories. He sat back in his seat and looked out the window with no particular interest, watching the scenery pass by.

The remaining three stops were made during the next two hours, the first in South End, a rather dismal area and the closely guarded district of New Power. The people there did not care much for the old ways nor, for that matter, the new ones. In fact, they did not seem to care about much at all, other than themselves.

Sam shuddered as they passed the cold, gray buildings of the bleak community. This had been his home for ten years before the transfer and the memories were still fresh. A woman, in her mid-forties and sharply dressed in a business suit, boarded the minibus and silently took her seat. Then Davidson, to Sam's considerable relief, drove the vehicle out of New Power's territory.

The next destination was Lakeview, the latest, upscale development in the Glen Community district. There was no actual view of a lake, just as there was no actual lake, but the name sounded quaint and that alone attracted new residents to the colorful area. Lakeview followed a pure "out with the old, in with the new" approach. Protocols, procedures, and plans of yesterday were tossed aside for new ones of today, with little thought for how well they might work tomorrow. Within the branch, this was popularly known as the Mettenger Method, and its architect had become their newest passenger.

The final stop was in Old Brigos, the historic center of the village. Here the philosophy was quite different and very clear—at all costs and with no exceptions, maintain the old ways. Great care was taken to restore buildings, roads, and even the street lamps to how they appeared before Last Day. Nothing new could be added. No improvements could be made. Builders and artisans were not even allowed to use new methods to carry out the restoration and repairs. Everything had to be as it had always been, only now governed by countless detailed rules and regulations. And no one enforced them as strictly as Guy Williams of First Brigos, the last passenger for the journey to Heis.

At each location, Davidson followed the same routine he had used with the others—parking the minibus, hurrying inside an adjacent building, helping the latest person on board, then driving off again—leaving it to his passengers to introduce themselves, if they felt so inclined. And Ellington always felt so inclined, though his enthusiasm was returned only once. These last few passengers were the Senior Managers, the chief executive officers of the three branches. To varying degrees, they left no doubt as to their irritation at the sudden command to attend a conference they knew nothing about, especially Williams.

"What? You've got to be kidding!" he bellowed from the front door of his very large house. Though forty yards away, everyone in the minibus easily heard the short, heavy-set man. "Where's the limo? I'll not be going in *that*!"

"Mr. Williams, sir," Davidson calmly replied, carrying two suitcases and a third smaller one, easily the most luggage any of the passengers had brought. "*That* is the transport which has been provided."

Williams stopped dead in his tracks. Widely known as a proud man, he was accustomed to getting his own way about pretty much everything. He often referred to himself as the leader of the Senior

Managers. Though such a position was never part of the Plan, he made clear it would not do for anyone to think otherwise.

"I said," Williams announced, his anger rising, "I'll not be going in that. I did not come to this point in life to be hauled about in a common commuter. You will have to call something else. I will accept nothing less than an executive limousine."

"Sir," Davidson said, "this is your transport. There will be none other."

"Look here," Williams shouted. "I'll not be spoken to in that tone."

Sam looked at Ellington. *What tone?* Davidson was calmness itself.

Williams went on. "I don't know who you work for, but I guarantee it won't be for much longer. I'll have my own driver take me, then. Just give him the directions. And when we arrive, I'll have a word with your superiors about your conduct, I can assure you."

Davidson, heavy luggage in hand, had been steadily heading toward the minibus. With Williams's last salvo he stopped, placed the suitcases on the ground, and turned resolutely toward the defiant Senior Manager. He eyed Williams from his shiny bald head, down the tailored suit, to the supple leather shoes, and back again.

"I will say this only once, Mr. Williams." Davidson remained civil but had a distinct firmness in his voice…a definite *tone*, as Sam would later recall. "You have been invited to Heis. You can choose not to come. You may stay here while your colleagues and my other passengers continue on. But…" he said the word most emphatically, "if you attempt to get there by your own means, you will be lost and you will die. You must understand that I'm telling you the truth."

Red faced, Williams stammered, searching for an indignant retort. He glanced at the lowly minibus where the other Senior Managers stared back. Then he turned to Davidson.

"So, you are the *only* way I have?" He spoke with defiance in his voice.

Davidson was not fazed in the least. "I am."

Williams glared at him, then stomped off toward the others. "Bring my bags," he barked.

With the journey finally underway, Williams took his station in the rear of the minibus, distancing himself from the others as much as possible. He sat on the right side and deliberately tossed his coat and briefcase about so as to take up the entire bench.

Laura Stürn from New Power was in the next row, but far to the left, next to the window. Straight, black hair sharply framed her smooth, pale face. She was undoubtedly attractive, but there was a coldness about her. Though polite enough when she boarded, she was not much of a talker, preferring instead to sit quietly without a trace of emotion regarding anything transpiring around her.

Sam and Ellington sat two rows in front of her with Mme. Couteau of Hopewell in front of them. On the very first row, to the right of the aisle, was Otto Mettenger, Senior Manager of Glen Community. Wearing a tan sports coat and an open collar shirt similar to Sam's, he was clearly more relaxed than his colleagues. He was also much older. He seemed friendly and did not hesitate to speak with Sam, Ellington, and Mme. Couteau. Sam had previously met him at several official branch functions, but Mettenger did not appear to recognize him.

Just as well, Sam thought. *No need to discuss attitude adjustments then.*

Mettenger did recognize Ellington. He rushed over to give Ellington a hug, and Ellington gladly hugged him back.

"How are you doing, you old coot?" Mettenger exclaimed. "What's it been…six, seven years now? How's retirement going?"

Ellington laughed. "Oh, I'm not retired…not yet anyway. Still plugging away down in Project Design."

"You're kidding! I would have sworn you had retired long ago. You could have, you know. You've certainly earned it."

"Maybe one day. Besides, what would I do with myself? This way I stay out of trouble."

"Ha!" Mettenger let out a loud laugh. "As if you could. Well, I'm glad to see you on this trip. Very glad." Then he leaned closer. "I'd heard all the Senior Managers were invited, but who wants to hang out with them? Am I right?" He nudged Ellington, who smiled in return. "Well, I've got work to do, but we'll get together later," Mettenger said, returning to his seat. "Yes, very glad, very glad."

As Mettenger immersed himself in a stack of paper, Sam leaned toward Ellington and whispered, "Old pals, I take it."

His friend nodded. "We grew up together. We were best of friends for a long time…a long time."

The words trailed off. Ellington offered nothing further, and Sam sensed sadness there. He decided to leave the matter alone for the time being.

With all the passengers on board, Davidson guided the minibus out of Old Brigos and onto Perimeter Parkway, a four lane road that circled the entire village. Built three years earlier, it served as the fastest means of traveling from one district to another. The traffic was again heavy with Brigons taking advantage of their last day off, but it moved along smoothly—not that it mattered to Williams, who could be heard complaining about everything from the discomfort of his seat to the inadequate legroom.

As they neared the easternmost section of the Parkway, Davidson turned onto a single-lane road just wide enough for the minibus. By the looks of it, the road had not been maintained for a long time. The pavement was frequently broken, missing altogether in areas, and filled with potholes, forcing them to creep along. Occasionally the lane widened, creating a space—a lay-by Ellington called it—just large enough to allow oncoming vehicles to pass. But that was not a concern as everything before them appeared desolate.

They drove on, far beyond the boundaries of Brigos Glen. Few towers had been erected in this part of the valley and with each passing minute, the light diminished. For several miles little changed. The road remained rough and worn. Conversation was kept to a minimum. And the light from the village continued to fade.

Eventually the minibus slowed. Sam leaned forward and looked through the front windshield. In the distance stood a lonely guard-house flanked by a high fence with concertina wire rolled across the top. The fence reached as far to the left and to the right as he could see. Standing nearby, one light tower dimly lit the area, giving the feel of dusk though it would still be bright back in the village. Sam guessed this was not part of the solar simulation service that covered Brigos Glen, but was there specifically to provide security.

The light was not diffused like that of other towers. Instead, it focused on the guardhouse, spreading out no more than fifty yards from the tower.

Sam looked past the fence. There the light grew dimmer still. The trees, rocks, and road faded into the darkness.

"The Outlands?" he murmured to Ellington, who nodded.

As they drew closer, the minibus slowed even more. Two men in uniform stood in front of the fence, each carrying automatic weapons and 9 mm handguns strapped to their sides. One of the guards, a sergeant by the stripes on his sleeves, raised a gloved hand, signaling them to stop. Davidson pulled up to the guardhouse and, to Sam's surprise, turned off the motor.

"We will be changing transport here," he said, turning around to face everyone. "The remainder of our journey will be rougher, not as nice as what we've been on." Williams groaned, but Davidson continued. "And it will get rather steep in places. So we'll need something with more power and a firmer grip. It will be here shortly and we'll join it on the other side of the barrier. I suggest you get out and stretch a bit. It will be your last opportunity before we arrive at Heis." And with that, he opened the door, climbed out, and went to talk with the sergeant.

Sam, Ellington, and Mme. Couteau made their way off the minibus, followed by Mettenger and Stürn.

Williams stubbornly remained. Even outside they could hear him complaining of the "horrid service" and how "someone will certainly hear about this."

The others ignored him and wandered about, though not far from the guardhouse. No one spoke. They grew more anxious, especially with the darkness so close. Each avoided looking toward it and gazed instead at the glow of their distant village.

They had been outside for less than ten minutes when Sam saw a vehicle approaching. But it was not coming out of the darkness. This one was coming from the village…and it was roaring toward them.

Sam stared at it, then got Ellington's attention. "Look at that. What do you suppose it is?"

"At my age, dear boy, I don't *suppose* anymore. Requires too much effort, is too often wrong, and causes too much grief. These days I much prefer to wait and observe," he explained, observing the oncoming vehicle.

Soon the others joined them…except Davidson, who continued his discussion with the guard. Even Williams had seen the speeding vehicle and had finally exited the minibus to get a better look. As the others wondered out loud who it might be or what it could mean, Williams stared at the target and grinned.

"Thought they might," he muttered.

It took little time for the vehicle to cover the last stretch to the guardhouse. A black limousine with miniature flags attached to the front fenders screeched to a halt behind the minibus, kicking up a cloud of dust. Doors flew open and six men in business suits scrambled out. Upon seeing Williams, they headed straight to him, ignoring the others.

"What's the meaning of this?" one demanded. "And where do you think you're going?" asked another. "Why were we not informed?" cried a third, as they all rushed to Williams, who had a broad and not-too-friendly smile.

"Gentlemen, gentlemen," he replied, "for what do I have the pleasure of addressing the Elder Council?"

"You know exactly why we're here!" exclaimed a fourth. "No one goes beyond the barrier without permission of the Council."

"No one," echoed a fifth.

"Well, my dear sirs," Williams replied, not attempting to hide his disdain for the group, "first of all, this is *Company* business. Are any of you a part of the Company?" he asked, then added, "No, I did not think so. Second, this is by special invitation. Were any of you invited?" This time he paused for a response, but there was no reply from the six angry men. "And last, this isn't *my* party."

"What do you mean, Guy?" asked the first Elder. "Are you trying to tell us you don't know what's going on? You're the head Senior Manager, or so you've said on many occasions."

Williams bristled. His nostrils flared like a bull preparing to charge. The Elder nervously stepped back.

"I don't care for your insinuation, Stanley," he said through clenched teeth. "If you want to know anything further, ask my driver." Williams turned on his heel and walked back to the minibus.

The Elders were appalled by such behavior—at least that is what several of them said—and they would have hurried after him, but Davidson suddenly stepped between them and their prey.

"May I assist you?" he asked in his usual calm manner.

An Elder, the one Williams had called Stanley, stepped up.

"What's your name, driver?"

"Davidson, sir."

"Where are you going and what is the purpose of this...this... whatever it is?" he stammered.

"Mr. Williams and these other passengers have been summoned by Brighten Power Authority to Heis Center for meetings scheduled over the next several days. They will discuss the affairs of the Company within Brigos Glen."

"Brigos Glen?"

"Yes, sir."

"Well, if it concerns Brigos Glen, then that's our jurisdiction. We will accompany you to this Heis location."

"No, sir."

"No?! *You dare tell me no?*" the Elder yelled.

"Yes, sir," Davidson said, without missing a beat. "This is for these six and no more. They have direct relations with the Company, and the Company has made it clear that only those with such relations may attend."

"What? That's preposterous," the Elder exclaimed, and he was joined by his fellow Elders. "I'll have you know that *we* govern Brigos Glen. *We* have taken care of the people there. *We* sanction all that goes on. If it were not for *us*, there would be no one there for Brighten to have relations with!" he shouted. "Brighten has worked with us for years. I demand," he said harshly, "that we accompany you."

"No, sir." This time Davidson was much firmer and focused on the Elder.

"This is ridiculous!" the Elder said, frustrated. He looked at his fellow Elders, then glared back at Davidson. "Who's in charge here?"

"I am," came the resolute reply.

The Elder was about to ask how a mere driver could possibly be in charge, but Davidson's stare held him in check. Instead, he asked, "And why, may I ask, can we not join in this matter?"

Without batting an eye, Davidson answered. "Because I don't know you."

Davidson turned his back to the stunned Elder and walked away. As he passed among his six passengers, he gave the instruction, "Follow me," and headed toward the guards. Even Williams hurried after him, though he could not repress casting a smile at the Elders as he did. Sam looked back at the minibus.

"Your baggage will follow," Davidson said, as though he knew the question Sam was about to ask. "Come now, everyone. Our transport has arrived." Just then a stout, square-bodied vehicle appeared out of the darkness and stopped on the other side of the fence.

"Are we going to climb over?" Sam whispered to Ellington.

The guards had resumed their positions, but as the seven travelers approached, they moved to either side, revealing a small gate. Davidson reached the gate first and opened it. "Come along," he said, and quickly stepped through to the other side. Sam, Ellington, and the others followed, hurrying between the guards who had left only enough room for them to pass single file.

Mettenger stumbled into one of the guards, who stood rock solid and never moved. He apologized, but the guard remained silent, as did the other. Their focus was solely on the Elders… preventing anyone other than Davidson and his passengers from passing through.

Once everyone cleared the fence, the gate closed securely behind them. They stepped up to the vehicle, with Sam the first to board. He quickly looked about the spartan interior.

If Williams didn't like the minibus, his attitude's not likely to improve.

Then he reached back and helped each of the others climb in.

Williams entered last. As the door closed, he yelled out, "Bye, bye Stanley. I'll try to write."

Davidson had a few more words with the guards, then hurried back to the transport. Inside were two bench seats that faced each other, such that three could see where they were headed while the others could see where they had been. The Senior Managers chose the forward facing seats before anyone else had time to consider; so Sam, Ellington, and Mme. Couteau sat with their backs to Davidson.

As they drove away, Sam looked to the other side of the fence. The Elders were quite animated. One boldly stepped toward the gate…until the guards raised their weapons. He rejoined the others, who were piling into the limousine. Sam watched them speed away, as the guardhouse became smaller and smaller.

Then a sudden coldness swept up his back and enveloped him. Instantly, he was consumed by the darkness.

CHAPTER 6

HEIS

D AVIDSON HAD NOT been joking about the road to Heis. If anything, he had not done it justice. Without the light towers, everything was pitch black, the darkness broken only by the headlights of the transport.

The road climbed steadily into the foothills, then rose to a steep ascent farther into the mountains. Deep holes and ditches stretching across the road required deft maneuvering and slow going. Pavement gave way to dirt covered by loose rock that caused them to slide. Twice, Sam was certain the next curve would send them careening off the road and into what he could only imagine. But Davidson drove very well. Each time he maintained control, shifting gears and correcting direction.

No conversation stirred among the passengers this time. They looked at their hands, the floor, and the inside of the transport, occasionally taking a brief glance at a fellow passenger. Nothing could be seen through the windows, though a few looked, mostly out of habit. The darkness closed in as if a heavy curtain had been drawn around them.

Sam sat immediately behind Davidson on the left side of the transport, with Mme. Couteau between Ellington and himself to keep her from being jostled against the doors. There were no armrests like those in the minibus, so she held onto their hands to help keep her steady. Across from Ellington sat Stürn, with Mettenger to her left and then Williams.

Once, after being flung into the side of the transport, Williams appeared on the verge of firing off another round of complaints and protests in Davidson's direction, but held his tongue. Nothing could be gained in the middle of nowhere.

Left turns. Right turns. Briefly down, then up. Gravel spewing from spinning tires. Sam's ears popped as the transport climbed. This part of their journey was taking much longer than he had hoped, especially with the destination unknown. When the road leveled, Sam looked at his watch. He had recently received it from Glen Community for his fifteen years of service with the Company. It was cheap and unattractive, but at least it worked. He touched the face plate and it sprang to life.

"What's the time?" Ellington asked, noticing the light from Sam's wrist.

"20:15."

"That late already?"

"Oh, for the love of Brighten," Williams grumbled. "We're never going to get there at this rate."

"And what rate is that, Guy?" asked Stürn, coldly.

Her question caught him off guard, as the Senior Manager of New Power had said very little the entire trip. She made no attempt to look at Williams, whose glaring eyes shone even in the darkened interior of the transport.

"Can you *see* how fast we're traveling?" Her tone was more that of an adult talking to an annoying child than a peer. "Why don't you calm down, sit back, and enjoy the ride?" she sneered.

"Why don't *you*..."

"What is that?" Mettenger interrupted.

Williams stopped his assault and looked out the front, as did everyone else. Davidson was guiding the transport up a slight incline, the crest being no more than a hundred yards away. The darkness hugged the road on either side, but farther ahead—beyond the crest—shone a soft, blue glow.

They could see nothing of Heis Center. Sheltered in an otherwise darkened gap, it was well hidden…though Sam could not make out exactly what was doing the hiding. From what appeared to be a jagged edge across the top, he assumed it must be a fence, though it was difficult to be sure in the blue light emanating from the Center. He dismissed the idea as they drove farther and farther down into the gap. Given their previous position along the crest, the angle of sight, and the fact that absolutely nothing of the Center could be seen, such a fence would have been ridiculously high.

As the transport continued its descent, the blue light slowly faded until they were once again surrounded by the dense darkness. Occasionally, Sam saw a bit of the light here, then over there, maybe even high in the sky, but it disappeared immediately. Soon, the only light came from the headlights of the transport, and the only thing visible was the road before them.

Davidson guided them along several switchbacks, continuing their descent until at last the road leveled out. They lumbered on for about a mile, then turned left. The road suddenly changed from rough terrain to something much smoother, and even with the windows closed, the unmistakable sounds of creaking wood and rushing water echoed underneath. A little farther and the transport was again on solid ground, much better than before. Gravel still crunched beneath the tires, but this portion of the road had been graded.

Davidson turned sharply to the right, and the sound of the water faded. The darkness drew even closer around them, as though trying to enter the transport itself. They continued a short distance, then stopped. No one said a word as they waited for Davidson's next move.

A thin, vertical blue line appeared thirty feet in front of the transport. The six passengers stared in amazement as it grew wider and brighter. Sam squinted, trying to block the glare so he could get a better look. "It's a gate," he whispered.

Davidson eased forward. The gate opened just wide enough, and they passed through to the other side. Immediately a brilliant blue light surrounded them, so bright they had to shield their eyes a moment to give them time to adjust. With his hands cupped over his eyes like the bill of a cap, Sam scanned their new surroundings.

The gravel road turned briefly to the right before making a wide circle, rejoining itself at the top of the loop, not far from the gate that was now closing behind them. At the bottom of the loop, stood a stone and wood canopy. Nothing else.

"Driver!" Williams growled. "Where is this you've taken us?"

"Heis," came the curt reply.

"This can't be Heis. Where's the conference center? Where's the hotel? There's nothing here at all."

"Do not assume, Mr. Williams," Davidson said. "Assumptions can destroy you."

"What did you say to me?" But there was only silence from the front as Davidson moved the transport under the canopy. "I'm talking to you," Williams said harshly, but Davidson merely switched off the motor and got out.

Before Williams could say another word, two men appeared to the left of the transport. They wore a uniform, though in the blue light it was impossible to determine even the color. Their broad smiles, however, could have been seen a distance away. One man opened the door nearest Sam.

"Let me help you there," he said cheerfully, extending his hand to Sam. "We've been expecting you all day. I hope the ride was not too unpleasant."

Sam took his hand, receiving a surprisingly strong grip in return, and awkwardly made his way out of the transport. He had been sitting a long time and had not realized how stiff he had become. He walked around and stretched as the two men helped the others.

"Watch your step, sir," the second called to Williams. He held out his hand but the Senior Manager jerked his shoulder back and pushed his way past the startled man.

"I can manage on my own," Williams muttered and strode off.

Giving no attention to his new surroundings, Williams immediately stepped into a shallow hole and lost his footing. He lunged forward, falling face forward toward the gravel. But the man he had spurned leapt with cat-like reflexes and caught him in midair. Williams scrambled to his feet, uttered something unintelligible, and hurried away. The man, unmoved by the incident, returned to his duties.

"Easy does it," he cautioned, as Mme. Couteau carefully exited. Unlike Williams, she gratefully accepted the assistance and safely reached the outside.

The two men efficiently helped the remaining passengers off the transport, with Ellington being the last. Everyone remained close by as they regained the use of their legs. Once they were ready, the two men led them to a stone walkway and from there, to what appeared to be a circular, tiled patio. An iron railing surrounded it except where the walkway entered, and toward the back stood Davidson waiting for them.

"Thank you, Kenneth," Davidson said to the first of the men, then turned to the passengers. "Everyone, this is Kenneth and the gentleman over there is Madhu." Davidson motioned to the second man, who had followed them onto the patio. "They will be glad to assist you while you are here, and you should feel free to call on them. Now, it has been a rather long day and I am certain you are quite hungry. So I suggest you proceed to the dining hall where your dinner awaits."

The passengers glanced bewilderedly at each other, then Ellington spoke up.

"Uh, Davidson…" he began.

"Yes, sir," replied the driver.

"I don't mean to be a bother, but there doesn't seem to be anything here. Where are we to be going?"

Davidson smiled. "With me."

Upon Davidson's signal, Kenneth extended a portion of the railing, enclosing the patio. Near Madhu stood an iron post with a metal box on top. Madhu lifted a cover on the side of the box, revealing two buttons. He pushed one and immediately the entire patio sank…except that it was not the ground they were sinking into. As they moved downward, smooth steel walls grew upward around them. They were descending a metallic tube. But for an occasional comment of astonishment from Mettenger and Mme. Couteau, the ride was remarkably silent.

"It's an elevator," Ellington laughed, at last. "That's what it is, an elevator."

"Wonder where it stops?" asked Sam.

They watched as the tube grew taller and taller. Lighting was sporadically placed about the smooth walls, though there was nothing of interest to see since the ever-growing walls were solid all around. After a descent of five hundred feet, they eased to a stop. Davidson gave a slight nod, and the two men immediately went to one part of the wall. They took their positions about ten feet apart. Suddenly panels smoothly slid to either side.

"Ladies and gentlemen," Davidson said softly, "welcome to Heis Center."

Sam could now see their hosts more clearly. Kenneth and Madhu wore deep red vests with small brass buttons, white long-sleeved shirts, and dark gray pants. They were both tall, but there the similarity ended. Kenneth had a ruddy complexion that matched a head full of unruly red hair. Madhu, on the other hand, was dark skinned. His blue black hair glinted with the reflection of overhead lights.

Kenneth led them into a large open room. Twenty round tables were scattered about, each with six chairs.

"Heis Center has been built into the side of a ridge," Kenneth explained. "There are three main areas, each extending off the central lobby, which you have seen. We are now in the dining wing. This is the main hall and below us is another hall about half this size, a private dining room, and the kitchens. The next area—you will happily see soon—is the housing wing. As you exit here, it is located across the central lobby to the far right. Guests have the main floor, our staff has the one below. On each level, we have enough rooms for fifty…or one hundred if we need to double up. And no, Mr. Williams," Kenneth said in anticipation of the question, "you need not be concerned. Each of you will have your own room."

Williams appeared satisfied and gave a slight nod.

"The last area is the conference wing…located to the left of the central lobby. You will see that tomorrow. It contains an auditorium and several meeting rooms of various shapes and sizes."

"Sir," Sam blurted out to their guide.

"Kenneth," he corrected him.

"Yeah, uh, Kenneth…I hear what you've said about how many this facility can hold, the rooms, an auditorium and all…that's a lot of people." He paused trying to choose his words carefully. "Where do they come from?"

Kenneth looked puzzled. "What do you mean, sir?"

"Well, and correct me if I'm wrong, but no one else has ever been here from Brigos Glen. Is this place used a lot by people in Farside?"

"Farside?"

"Oh, I'm sorry," Sam apologized. "That's what *we* call it, I guess. I meant where you come from."

Kenneth smiled. "Ah, I see. Well, we have a different name for our home, but to answer your question, many of us live here most of the year, but Heis has seen many from around the world, though I'm sad to say it has been a long time." The words faded as Kenneth looked far away to a distant past. Bringing himself back to the present, he added, "But now *you're* here, and we are very glad."

He took them to a table near a black, glass wall.

"You may sit anywhere you wish. I prefer this table myself, but since it is so late, it will not make much difference, though I strongly recommend it for the morning. Now, I have other duties to attend to. Madhu will alert the kitchen that you are ready and your meal will be served shortly. Later he will escort you to your rooms. If you should need anything, all you need do is ask."

With that, he made a short bow and walked out of the dining hall. Madhu did likewise and left for what Sam assumed was the kitchen. The room was now entirely empty except for the six weary travelers. Mme. Couteau walked to the table, and Mettenger helped her with her seat.

Sam and Ellington also took their places. As Mettenger was about to join them, Williams gruffly cleared his throat. Sam suddenly realized that Williams and Stürn had wandered away from the rest.

"Mettenger," Williams said, frowning at the Senior Manager of Glen Community. "Come here. We have things to discuss."

Without waiting for a reply, Williams turned his back to Sam's table and took a seat near the center of the dining hall. Stürn sat with him, leaving an empty chair between them. Mettenger appeared very irritated, and for a moment Sam thought he might stay as an act of defiance. But after a brief pause, Mettenger made his apologies to Mme. Couteau, then to Sam and Ellington, and left to join the others.

"What could they possibly have to discuss?" Sam asked, watching Mettenger take his seat with the other Senior Managers. "They don't know any more than we do about why we're here... do they?" He looked at Ellington, who shook his head.

"I don't believe so," Mme. Couteau said, "especially with the way Guy's acted the entire trip. He's been horrible, certainly toward Davidson, poor dear. I've known Guy for many years now and he can have quite a disagreeable manner when he chooses."

Ellington nodded. "Yes, but I believe there's more to it."

"Like what? He's a jerk?" Sam laughed softly.

"Well, he may be a jerk, but I believe he's afraid."

Sam leaned toward Ellington, as though they were sharing deep secrets. "Afraid? Afraid of what?"

"Not sure. Maybe not knowing what's going on or why he's here. Maybe realizing he's not in control after all."

"He doesn't look like the *afraid* type," Sam observed.

Mme. Couteau patted Sam's arm. "Anyone can be afraid, Sam. It's what you do in your fear that matters. When you first heard you were to come here, weren't you afraid? I certainly was. I've been around a long time and have never heard of this place."

Sam looked a little sheepish. "Well, I guess I like to think of it more as *concern*," he said with a smile.

"Fear. Concern. It still matters what actions you choose to take." Then she looked up and exclaimed, "Ah! Dinner, I believe."

Madhu approached their table, followed by three others carrying trays with plates loaded with food. The servers carefully placed a setting before each, provided them something to drink, and then did the same for the Senior Managers at the other table.

Sam did not feel hungry until he took that first bite. The taste was incredible, far better than anything he could remember. They all fell silent as they focused on their fine meal.

For more than an hour they dined. As plates were cleaned and glasses emptied, a server appeared immediately to replenish them.

Different and even tastier food…more drink, like a fruit punch… all provided in abundance until they were completely satisfied. Ellington finally pushed his plate away and leaned back in his chair. A server appeared at his side, but he waved him off.

"No more," he laughed. "It was wonderful, but I can't eat another bite. Thank you." The server bowed and left.

Finally, the servers cleared the tables, made a last offer of tea and coffee, then retired for the evening. With fatigue reminding him of the day's long journey, Sam gratefully took the opportunity to sit and rest, making little effort toward any meaningful conversation… just a polite word here, a brief comment there. He closed his eyes, completely relaxed and at peace.

"Excuse me."

Sam was startled by the voice. He turned, and Madhu stood behind him.

"Sorry. I didn't hear you come up."

"No apologies necessary, sir," came the polite reply. He glanced at all three. "I wanted to let you know that your rooms are waiting whenever you are ready. Can I get you anything else?" he asked.

After convincing him they could not possibly swallow another bite or take even another sip, Mme. Couteau, Ellington, and Sam stood and stepped away from their table. Sam gaped at the Senior Managers still seated.

"Don't tell me they're still eating."

"No sir," replied Madhu. "They would like to continue their conversation for a while longer." Madhu summoned the servers to remove the plates and glasses. "Would you like to have this table again in the morning?"

"I think we should," Mme. Couteau spoke up. "The other fellow…what was his name?"

"Kenneth," Madhu replied courteously.

"Yes, Kenneth seems to think this table is special. So I say, why not?" Sam and Ellington nodded.

"You will not be disappointed," Madhu said, smiling.

After a few brief instructions to the servers, Madhu escorted Mme. Couteau, Ellington, and Sam back to the central lobby. As they were about to leave the dining hall, Sam glanced at Williams, who was in a serious discussion with Stürn and Mettenger. They were too far away for him to hear, but Stürn and Mettenger were paying close attention.

"I wonder what he's on about?" he asked Ellington.

"There's no telling, my boy. Sometimes people talk to feel important. Sometimes they talk just to hear themselves talk."

"Which do you think it is?"

"With him," Ellington said, nodding slightly toward Williams, "bit of both, most likely. But I wouldn't be concerned about them."

"Why's that?"

"It's clear, isn't it? They're not in charge here."

Entering the lobby, Madhu led them across to the housing wing. They entered a hallway with doors evenly spaced every twenty feet along the right side. Only a few were scattered on the left and, as Madhu explained, were for staff services, cleaning, maintenance, and certain administrative functions. All guest rooms were located on the right.

Madhu went to the first door, which opened automatically. On the wall a small metal sign with a black insert read M. Couteau.

"Mme. Couteau," he said, turning to the elderly lady, "this will be your room. We have already brought your luggage and everything you need should be here. However, if you should require anything further, please let us know. There is an intercom located on the wall near your bed and another on the table across the room. We will use those to wake you in the morning for breakfast."

Mme. Couteau graciously thanked Madhu and said her good-nights to Sam and Ellington. Once the door closed behind her, they continued down the hall and Sam noted the signs by each door as they passed—L. Stürn, G. Williams, O. Mettenger.

They stopped at B. Ellington.

"Looks like this one's for me," Ellington said, in his usual cheerful manner. "I believe I will enjoy a good night's sleep." He patted Sam on the back, then stepped into the room. "See you at breakfast."

Sam waved, then watched the door silently close. Sleepier by the second, the thought of finally getting to bed was a welcome one.

"Sir," Madhu said, interrupting his thoughts, "right this way."

Sam wearily followed him down the hallway and automatically stopped at the next door. But he did not see his name on the wall. Madhu had walked several doors farther down before noticing Sam was no longer with him. He turned back and saw Sam, a bit bewildered, staring at the door.

"I'm sorry, sir. Your room is this way."

Sam frowned slightly. "I don't understand. Why am I not with the others?"

"It was Davidson's instruction, Mr. Mitchell. We have prepared a room for you down here."

Sam sighed and continued on, this time paying closer attention to his guide. After passing another ten rooms, the hallway angled to the right, revealing several more, still along the right side of the hall. Madhu walked briskly to the third door and patiently waited for Sam. As he approached, the door silently opened. On the wall hung his own sign, S. Mitchell. Sam nodded toward the sign, and turned into the room.

"Goodnight, Madhu."

"Goodnight, sir."

As Sam stepped farther into the room, dim light came from a small table lamp. Next to the table sprawled a large bed. The sheets were already pulled down, an invitation he had no intention of refusing. *At last*, Sam thought. He fell forward onto the bed and deep into dreams.

CHAPTER 7

THE ANNOUNCEMENT

SOOTHING MUSIC FLOATED gently through the room. Fresh, cool air flowed silently from the vents. And it was dark. All of which beckoned Sam to remain snug in his cozy bed, curled up and dreaming of home, Ali, and the kids. So relaxed and comfortable, he failed to hear the alarm, which had been growing steadily louder.

"Awake, Mr. Mitchell. It is time." The voice was that of a woman, or had been before a recording made it part of the time alarm system at Heis. "Awake, Mr. Mitchell. It is time." The softness had a comforting quality, like a mother rousing a sleepy child. "Awake, Mr. Mitchell. It is time." Even as the volume increased, that quality remained, never demanding or urgent. "Awake, Mr. Mitchell. It is time."

"Awake," Sam mumbled along with the recording. "I'm awake."

"Would you like a few more minutes of rest?" the recording automatically asked.

Sam rolled onto his back. "No, thank you," he yawned. "I'm okay. I'm going to get up now." Immediately, two lamps activated with a light that steadily brightened. Sam rubbed the stubble on his face. He tried looking around the room, but his vision was too blurred from sleep. "Um, what time is it?"

"The time is 06:30. Breakfast will be served until 08:00. Meetings will begin at 09:15 in Conference Room Twelve."

As the recording described the morning's dining fare, Sam adjusted to the growing light and took the opportunity to more closely survey his room. He had been far too tired on his arrival, when the only thing of interest had been the bed.

But now he discovered that his room was not merely a room, but part of a suite. It had been dark when Madhu showed Sam to his quarters the night before. Once inside, he had crossed a narrow, interior hallway and entered a bedroom, the only area the table lamp had allowed him to see. The bedroom easily held two full-size beds, a dresser, and a gentleman's wardrobe. A separate door led to the bath, which also connected to the hall.

"Will there be anything else?" the recording asked.

"Uh, no...no, thank you."

Sam decided to do a bit of exploring. With great reluctance, he withdrew from the warm, comfortable bed and stepped into the adjacent hallway. Straight ahead was the suite's entrance and to his right, the other door that led into the bath. The hall continued to the left, and he decided to see what might be there. With each step, spots of recessed lighting activated, one after the other, leading him on until he reached a large open area. He cautiously entered. A ceiling fixture immediately illuminated a room twice the size of that where he had slept.

A small round table stood directly in front of him and in the far right corner of the room sat a chair, angled back toward the center. A large writing desk took up much of the wall to the left of the chair. Three shallow drawers spanned its width, protective glass covered the top, and a swivel chair tucked in neatly underneath. In the far left corner of the room, another chair mirrored that in the right.

Sam stepped in a little farther. The left wall of the hallway extended into the room, creating an alcove behind it. Inside, a couch spread along the wall shared with the bedroom, with a coffee table and two chairs facing the couch. Across from Sam, deep green drapes extended the full length of the room.

"Nice," Sam remarked, admiring the suite. "Wonder why there's so much space for one person. Even if they have two in here, it's still a bit of overkill. But I don't think I'm going to complain."

He walked across the room to the curtain and moved it aside far enough to see what it might be hiding. The wall was solid glass and outside…that same blue light. The air was filled with it as far as he could see to the left and to the right; its source was somewhere far below. Beyond that light, he could see nothing except the ink-black darkness surrounding Heis. He let the curtain fall back into place.

After a hot shower, Sam dressed and set out for the dining hall. He thought he might catch up with someone else on the way, but the corridor was completely empty. In the central lobby, Kenneth and Madhu stood off to one side. He was about to wish them good morning but they were engaged in conversation. Not wanting to disturb them, he continued on. As he drew near the dining hall, the welcoming aromas beckoned him inside.

"Sam, my boy," called a familiar voice. There at the same table they had shared for dinner, Ellington and Mme. Couteau waved him over. "We've been waiting for you…and we're starving." Ellington laughed.

Sam gladly joined them.

"Good morning, all," he said. Sam took the seat next to Mme. Couteau. He had his back to the black, glass wall, which allowed a better view of everything in the dining hall. "I hope you haven't waited long."

"No, no," Mme. Couteau replied. "We've had a nice chat. Did you sleep well?"

"Must have. I don't remember much of it. And the bed was very comfortable."

"Oh yes, mine, as well," Ellington chimed in. "I honestly don't believe I've had such a good night's sleep in quite some time."

"And what about that room, isn't it amazing?" Sam asked, with a broad smile.

"Quite functional," replied Mme. Couteau.

"Yes, it will certainly do," agreed Ellington. "The room's a bit cramped, and I'm not sure what the window's all about since you can't very well see anything, but the chair's good enough and I do like the bed. Then again, I don't believe this is supposed to be a holiday. We probably won't be spending much time in our rooms."

While Ellington and Mme. Couteau's rooms may have been similar to each other, they certainly had nothing in common with Sam's. He was about to launch into a detailed description of his suite, but then decided nothing positive would be served. If anything, such news might upset them. At least for the time being, Sam chose to keep it a secret. *It's probably a mistake and I'll be moved to a new room today anyway.*

Sam looked around the empty dining hall. "Where are the others?"

"Most likely overslept," Ellington answered.

"Waiting for their grand entrance is more like it," corrected Mme. Couteau.

"Not Otto," came a weak protest.

Ellington looked sad and uncomfortable. Mme. Couteau reached over and placed her hand on his arm.

"He's changed over the years," she said, sympathetically. "You know that."

Ellington did not reply, but gave an almost imperceptible nod. Sam could not help feeling sorry for him. Ellington was always so cheery that it felt strange to see him this way. Sam tried to think of something to say that might make his friend feel a little better, but before he had the chance, the servers appeared and it was time to eat.

As with their last meal, this also proved delicious and equally welcome. Mme. Couteau, Ellington, and Sam made polite conversation during breakfast, with no further mention of Mettenger. Everything seemed at peace once more and whatever remorse Ellington had experienced appeared forgotten. They were having such a good time, it never occurred to them to look at the glass wall...until Mme. Couteau happened to glance that way.

"Oh my," she said, in hushed surprise.

Ellington stared blankly past him, so Sam turned to see what had caught their attention. Instantly his fork clattered onto the plate. The black glass wall was no longer a wall, but a huge window. Beyond, a beautiful world materialized in the artificial dawn. On the other side of the glass, perhaps twenty feet down, grew deep green shrubs with large purple blooms, others with bright orange, still more with multiple white blossoms. An assortment of flowers were scattered about...violet, blue, red, yellow. Green plants dotted the dark soil.

A stream flowed from the left, another from the right. Each moved in, around, and over rocks, occasionally making little pools before moving along. Eventually they swirled into each other above a mound of smooth stones, then disappeared together over a stone ledge. From there the landscape dropped significantly and, farther down, the now singular stream could be seen continuing its journey through even more shrubs, flowers, and plants. Standing their ground, like guards protecting it all, were wooden giants with enormous arms spread high and broad.

"Trees," Sam whispered.

Just a few were near the Center, but they grew closer together farther away until the forest was so dense that Sam could not see past them. He could make out the tops of the trees straining high into the growing light. They appeared to be one continuous expanse. It was neither smooth nor all of one level, but rose and fell depending on the reach of the many limbs that formed it, creating a rougher, more jagged edge to the outline of the canopy.

This is the fence.

Awestruck, the three sat in stunned silence as they took in the beauty of the view. The colors were so much more vibrant than anything manufactured in Brigos Glen—the richness of the brown soil, the clarity of the water in the stream—everything was so much more, even the deep sense of life in the scene spread out before them. How long they gazed out the window, they did not know nor care. They were completely captivated.

"Rhododendron," whispered a man behind them.

The hushed voice brought them back inside the Center, where they saw Mettenger standing there, lost in the same vision, a slight smile on his face.

"The purple ones. They're called rhododendron," he said, to no one in particular. "And those orange ones there are flame azaleas. They were common in the mountains, but it was hard to get them to grow in the village. And that one there…" He paused, then pointed to the large bush with pale pink blooms. "Mountain laurel."

"You remember well, Otto," said Mme. Couteau.

Mettenger smiled weakly. "Well, my father had a nursery and grew them…all of them…even those azaleas. I remember them from when I was a boy."

Ellington brightened. "Otto, what's that large green plant near the water's edge?"

Mettenger squinted, then zeroed in on the plant. "Ah, you know that one. It's red trillium. We used to call it toad shade. I haven't seen that since before Last Day. Remember when the ferns and toad shade would cover the forest in late spring and we would…"

"Mettenger!" called an irritating voice, forcing its way into the gentle memory. Williams and Stürn were taking their seats at the table they had used the night before. "Come along," Williams ordered, not bothering to look in his direction.

Mettenger continued looking at the vision beyond the glass wall, but the pleasure had drained from his face. He sighed deeply.

"Why don't you dine here, Otto?" Mme. Couteau asked. "We have a better view."

Mettenger's lips tightened as he glanced at the other table where a server arrived.

"Perhaps later. Definitely later."

He turned to join his fellow Senior Managers, but stopped suddenly as Williams exploded.

"What do you mean we're too late!"

Sam, Ellington, and Mme. Couteau walked down a new corridor, carefully eyeing each door they passed in search of the conference room. They had left the dining hall when Williams's rant grew ever louder about not being served after the designated breakfast hours. That scene had made it difficult to enjoy the one beyond the glass wall. Before they left, Ellington convinced Mettenger to take the last cinnamon roll for himself as he hurried off to help Stürn calm Williams. It was now after 09:00 and their meeting would begin soon.

"I don't understand the numbering here," Sam said in frustration. "The last three have been seven, twenty-one, three…nothing in between…and no twelve."

"I don't know what to make of it either," Ellington said. "You'd think there would be some rhyme or reason to this, but I certainly don't see it. What's this one?" he asked, as they approached another door.

"One forty-four."

"Lovely," Ellington sighed.

"This is ridiculous!" Sam looked down the corridor. Doors were scattered on either side. "So what do we do?"

"We will keep searching until we find it," Mme. Couteau replied, as though there was never any question about what course they should take. And with that, she strode past Sam and Ellington, who then followed dutifully behind.

The corridor curved continually to the right. More doors. More strange numbers that made no sense. More frustration, especially for Sam who kept checking his watch. 09:10. With time getting late, he thought of turning back, then saw stairs ahead. On the left wall a sign announced To Twelve.

"Finally!" Sam exclaimed.

The stairs were broad, carpeted, and descended at an even, gentle rate. Mme. Couteau appeared to be in good physical condition, but was very cautious about the stairs. So Ellington remained behind to assist her while Sam went ahead to see how much farther they had to go. The stairs led him down another thirty feet, turned sharply to the right, and then a few feet more to a single door. Above it was a brass plate. Twelve.

Sam hurried back to the others who, being encouraged by his report, picked up their pace. As they finally reached the conference room, Sam held the door open for Mme. Couteau and Ellington, then followed them in. His watch indicated 09:15. Kenneth and Madhu were already there waiting, but no one else.

At least we're not last, Sam thought.

They stood along the left side of the room, near the front and directly across from a door identical to the one through which they had entered. To the right was tiered seating like that in a theater, with four slightly curved rows of ten seats each. Adequately spaced, the rows allowed ample room for any moving about that might be necessary and faced a small stage with red curtains along the back and on either side. On the stage stood a simple wooden lectern… nothing else. As Madhu and Ellington assisted an exhausted Mme. Couteau to a seat in the front row, Kenneth walked over to Sam.

"Good morning, sir. Has everything been satisfactory?"

Sam had been watching Madhu and Ellington help Mme. Couteau, and was surprised by Kenneth's voice.

"Oh, uh, yeah, sure…everything's been fine." Then he reconsidered. "Well, not quite."

"Oh, I'm sorry, sir. What has been the problem? Please let me know and we will take care of it immediately."

There was no doubt about Kenneth's sincerity as his smile immediately vanished, replaced by genuine concern. Sam suddenly felt guilty about mentioning anything at all.

"It was just getting here…finding the room, actually."

"Sir?" Kenneth said, confused.

"The numbers on the rooms…they weren't in order or didn't appear to be."

"Oh, yes." Kenneth smiled as one who had finally figured out a puzzle. "Each number was chosen for a specific room. They are not designations of order, but the names of the rooms themselves." He gestured to the room in which they were standing. "Welcome to Twelve."

"Okay," Sam said, "but it makes it difficult to find."

"Certainly," Kenneth agreed. "Did you ask for help?"

"Well, no. I thought we could find it on our own, I guess. Besides, I didn't see anyone to ask."

Kenneth motioned to the ceiling as if he were painting it with his hand. "Throughout Heis, sir, there are sensors. If at any time you require assistance, all you have to do is ask and we will be there."

"Oh, okay. Thanks," Sam said, looking a bit confused.

"I'm sure Davidson mentioned it upon your arrival."

Sam nodded. "Yes, he did. I didn't realize he meant...well, doesn't matter. We're here."

"Yes, you are, sir." Kenneth beamed. "And if you will have a seat, I believe it is time we begin."

As he finished, the door across the room suddenly swung open. Stürn and Mettenger rushed in.

"Ah, welcome," Kenneth called out. "And is Mr. Williams with you?"

"No," Mettenger panted. "He said he wasn't coming until he'd been fed."

"Then he will be very disappointed, I'm afraid. Lunch will not be for some time yet."

"Serves him right," Stürn broke in. "He can certainly be a fool."

The harshness of her tone slashed through the pleasantries, leaving Kenneth at a loss for words, but not Mettenger.

"As can we all, Laura," he said, with considerably more compassion.

Stürn ignored him and selected a seat on the first row near the middle, several down from Mme. Couteau.

"W-well," Kenneth stammered, "shall we start then?"

Ellington took a seat to Mme. Couteau's left, while Sam chose one on the row behind them. Mettenger appeared as though he was about to join him there, but after a moment, chose instead a seat two down from Stürn. Kenneth looked on as everyone settled in, then took his place in front of the empty stage.

"Thank you for coming. We are very glad you have joined us here at Heis Center. It has been a long time since we have had visitors, and on behalf of all of us here, you are most welcome." He smiled broadly and nodded to the five people before him.

"I am also glad you were able to find Twelve. As I mentioned to Mr. Mitchell, if you should need any help finding your way, please do not hesitate to ask. But as I am sure you have discovered, if you seek earnestly, you will find what you need.

"Now, briefly, I would like to review the order for today, as well as that for the remainder of your stay here. This morning, Madhu will provide you with a history of time since Last Day. For some of you this will be a review of what you experienced firsthand, but this information will prove important for each of you in the following days, especially for the assignments."

"Excuse me," Stürn interrupted. "Did you say…*assignments?*"

"Yes, ma'am."

"What kind of assignments?"

"That will be further described in our afternoon session. However, it concerns your meeting with Lord Mohae. Now, I would like…"

"Mohae?" This time it was Mettenger who interrupted. "Did I understand you correctly? Lord Mohae…*the* Lord Mohae?"

The name meant nothing to Sam, but great significance was clearly attached to it. Stürn and Mettenger had come to life at the mere mention of the name. He glanced at Mme. Couteau, who looked to be in shock. Ellington was literally sitting on the edge of his seat.

"Yes, sir," Kenneth replied. "Lord Mohae will be meeting with you in three days' time during the final general session."

Stürn and Mettenger launched into a frantic and private conversation. Sam could not hear what they were saying, but it was obvious they were very concerned. Ellington looked at Mme. Couteau and grinned.

"He's alive," Mme. Couteau said softly, pleasantly surprised.

Kenneth overheard her and nodded.

"Yes, Madame. Quite."

It was clear everyone understood the importance of this announcement, everyone except Sam. He waited for an explanation, then finally leaned down to Ellington and whispered into his ear.

"Who's Mohae?"

Ellington turned around and looked at his young friend. Sam could not make out whether he, too, was in a state of shock, but like Mme. Couteau, he certainly appeared pleased with the unexpected news. Ellington cupped his hand around his mouth so only Sam could hear.

"He wrote the Plan. He's the leader of the Yonders."

CHAPTER 8

ASSIGNMENTS

SAM, ELLINGTON, AND Mme. Couteau sat at their usual table. The scene outside was once again beautiful and breathtaking. They were just as captivated. Everything was as it had been during breakfast, except there was someone new at the table. This time Otto Mettenger had gladly accepted their invitation for lunch. Stürn had also been invited, but she declined, expressing the need to "talk some sense into Williams." As she strode off, Mettenger gazed out the window, barely touching his meal.

"It's truly amazing," he remarked. "They've got to be using a different system here."

"Different system?" asked Mme. Couteau.

"Different lighting. Different placement, at the very least."

"Why do you say that?" Ellington mumbled, his mouth stuffed.

"Well, look at it," he replied, gesturing with his fork. "It isn't that everything is so clear. We have that, but not the depth of the colors here. It's just, I don't know…it's like it's real."

"Like it used to be," agreed Mme. Couteau.

"What do you think causes that?" asked Sam.

Until now he had remained quiet, finding it awkward sitting there with those who either had known each other a very long time or shared some historical bond. He did not feel as though he fit in with this crowd, so he had chosen to hide in his silence...which was why he was surprised to hear himself speak.

Mettenger never looked in his direction, though not out of arrogance or any sense of deference to the system of position. He stared at the wonder beyond the glass. Finally, he turned to Sam and grinned.

"If I knew that, Mr. Mitchell, we could transform Brigos Glen." He looked again outside. "Maybe it's the fixtures they use. Maybe they've figured out a way to better duplicate the sun's rays and get more energy to the plants. I honestly don't know. But they've figured something out. There's only one thing I am certain of and that's the placement. Our lighting comes from the towers. We've managed to construct a few tall ones that provide better light distribution, but it's still nothing like this. Wherever their lighting originates, it's considerably higher. They can't duplicate the sky, of course."

He waited for some agreement, then apparently remembered that Sam had never seen the sky.

"Well, I mean...they *can't*...but they've given a good impression of one." Looking at the artificial sky, he absent-mindedly took a bite of his salad. "Sure would like to know how they do it."

Sam followed his gaze to the bright, manufactured sky and understood what Mettenger meant by the light distribution. In Brigos Glen, even in the middle of the day, one could easily make out the location of the banks of lights that covered the village. But this sky had a uniform brightness with no such groupings. For that matter, he could not see a single tower.

"Well, while I find all this quite illuminating," Ellington chuckled, pushing his plate away, "I'm more interested in these assignments Kenneth mentioned. I wonder what they could be. Any ideas?" He looked about the table.

"Not a clue," Sam replied. "He said we would know more this afternoon. I'm just glad we finished the history lesson this morning. No offense to Madhu, but that was like being back in school. Pretty dull and boring stuff, huh?"

"Not if you were there, my boy."

Sam had only been thinking of his own discomfort over the last three hours, completely forgetting he was sitting with those who had experienced this "dull and boring stuff." He shifted uneasily in his seat, hoping he had not offended anyone.

"I mean for someone my age…because I'm so much younger… oh, not that any of you are ancient or anything." He laughed nervously. "Because you're not, it's just that…uh…that I…"

"It's getting worse," Ellington whispered with a smile, then said louder so everyone could hear, "I agree with Sam about it being over. Enough of the old. Let's hear something new."

His reference to "something new" perked up Mettenger.

"Exactly! Like this lighting. And maybe they've got even more advances they can share with us. Think of the new developments we could have. Why, one day all of Brigos Glen could become something new and we'd never have to bother with those old ways again."

"Well, that's not what I meant," Ellington broke in. "New *with* the old is what I like. And right now I'm ready to hear something new. Maybe that's what the assignments are about. Time to move forward, now that Madhu fully covered everything since Last Day."

Mme. Couteau finished her meal and gently laid down her fork. She looked up from her plate to Ellington and Mettenger. "No he did not," she said solemnly, but nothing more.

This puzzled Sam. Everything that morning had been straight out of the textbooks he had been forced to read as a young boy. Nothing unusual or out of the ordinary. And he certainly could not remember any more to the old stories and lessons he had heard so often growing up. He considered asking what she meant, but a strange feeling came over him and he thought better of it. Something was wrong, or had been. He glanced at Ellington and Mettenger. Both sat motionless, sadly returning Mme. Couteau's stare.

Madhu approached the table.

"Madame, sirs…it is time."

His announcement did not startle anyone, not even Sam, though he was totally absorbed in what had just occurred. He was also incredibly confused. He glanced at Ellington and Mettenger, who appeared relieved by the interruption.

They know something.

No one spoke on the way to Twelve. Back in the room, everyone took the same seats they had occupied in the morning session. Stürn had already arrived and next to her sat Williams. Mettenger nodded in his direction, but no one else paid Williams any attention, which did not bother him at all as he paid them no attention either, including Mettenger.

Kenneth and Madhu stood in the front, facing the six, and on the stage near them was a small box. Sam was certain it had not been there during the morning session. The box was open and several manila envelopes peeked over the top edge.

"Ladies and gentlemen," Kenneth began, "I trust you had an excellent lunch and are now ready for what should be a brief afternoon session. You will need the remainder of the day to work on your assignments. This morning went very well, and I am sure you are all anxious to get started on the reason you are here."

Then, tag-team fashion, Madhu took over.

"Seventy years have passed since *The Brigos Plan* was first developed and provided to the citizens of Brigos Glen. The system was then established and the Plan was implemented throughout your village. During this time there has, of course, been consistent monitoring of the system and resulting power distribution, but it is now time for a more thorough reporting of the system's overall management, development, and expansion."

As he spoke these last few words, Madhu glanced at each Senior Manager, emphasizing a particular word with that particular person—*management* to Williams, *development* to Mettenger, *expansion* to Stürn. The Senior Managers smiled in succession as they received his special recognition. Sam found it curious that Madhu never smiled in return.

"Each of you was specially selected to participate in this reporting process, which will provide historical documentation concerning the future advancement of the system."

As Madhu paused, Kenneth went to the box on the stage and withdrew three sealed envelopes. He gave one to each of the Senior Managers, as Madhu resumed.

"These are *your* assignments. They are to be opened *after* this meeting and in the privacy of your own room. Each is unique and has been prepared only for you. You may discuss them among yourselves if you wish, but the submissions will be made on an individual basis, and each of you will be solely responsible for his or her assignment, regardless of the input or assistance of others. Do you have any questions?"

Mettenger partially raised his hand.

"Can we request assistance from you or Kenneth?"

"No, sir, but I am sure you will not find that necessary. The information to be provided will be based upon your own personal observations, impressions, actions, and ideas as to past, present, and future issues. There is nothing either Kenneth or I could do to assist you in those areas." As Mettenger nodded, Madhu looked at the other two. "Any other questions?" Williams and Stürn did not budge. "If there are none, Kenneth will discuss the remaining assignments."

Kenneth again stepped up to the box, took out two sealed envelopes, and handed one to Mme. Couteau and one to Ellington. Sam suddenly felt completely alone. *Everyone has something to do but me. I'm not supposed to be here.*

"I give you these with the same descriptions and under the same instructions as Madhu has shared concerning the first three assignments. They are solely for you. Each of you has a long history with Brigos Glen and the Plan, extending back to the very beginning, and you have significantly different perspectives from Mr. Williams, Ms. Stürn, and Mr. Mettenger, which will be of great value in the reporting. Please consider carefully the information you are asked to provide and be thorough. Do you have any questions?"

As Ellington and Mme. Couteau replied they did not, Sam looked for a way to silently slip out of the room and save himself embarrassment. But that was impossible. He sat motionless, as though that would allow him to go unnoticed—a hope that was short-lived.

"Now," Kenneth said, turning to Sam, "that leaves us with Mr. Mitchell."

"Yeah, about that," Sam said nervously, "I'm not sure you understand. I'm just another employee of the Company."

Williams smirked and nodded. Stürn remained impassive, while Mettenger and the others seemed sympathetic.

"I don't have the positions or history the others do. There really isn't anything I can add to what they will be doing. I wouldn't even know where to begin."

"So, what is it you are saying, Mr. Mitchell?" Kenneth asked.

"Well," he replied, thinking of the spacious suite he had been given, "maybe there's been a mistake."

"A mistake, sir?"

"A mistake," Sam echoed, with a slight nod. "Maybe Davidson picked up the wrong guy…is what I'm saying." Sam felt awkward. Everyone had a clear role in this project, except him.

"No, sir," Kenneth replied politely. "There has been no mistake. You were chosen for your role and no one else here can adequately fill it."

The smirk immediately vanished from Williams's face. He joined Stürn's impassive gaze, while the others smiled. Sam looked on, confused. Kenneth took the last envelope from the box and handed it to Sam.

"Unlike the assignments for the others, Mr. Mitchell, I must briefly discuss yours so everyone else will understand the role they, too, have in it." Immediately, the other five became very attentive. "Further explanation and instructions are provided there, but your role is that of the recorder. After everyone has had ample opportunity to consider their assignments and gather their thoughts, you will meet with each person individually, review their submissions, pull together the most relevant information, and then prepare a comprehensive and final report."

"If I understand correctly," Williams interrupted, "the Senior Managers will provide…"

"And Mme. Couteau and Mr. Ellington," Kenneth added.

"Yes, of course," Williams said, irritated at being interrupted himself. "*We* will provide this fellow…"

"Mr. Mitchell."

"Mr. Mitchell," Williams echoed, "…with our information and he will essentially serve as the clerk for this. Am I correct?" Williams said *clerk* as though it were a lowly servant's role. Positions and knowing one's place were clearly important to him.

"Essentially. Yes, sir. He will receive whatever information you provide, but we also expect him to assist each of you in presenting that information…asking questions, making suggestions, and that sort of thing…but the submission to Mr. Mitchell will be entirely your own."

"Ah, I see, thank you for clarifying that," Williams replied, mechanically.

"However, sir," Kenneth continued, "you should also be aware…you should *all* be aware…" He glanced at each person in the room before settling on Sam. "…that the final report will be his and his alone."

As Kenneth had indicated, the remainder of the session was brief. Madhu reviewed a few items regarding the interviews Sam would be conducting. Upon his announcement the location would be Sam's room, Williams snorted. With no hesitation, Madhu moved on.

"The schedule will consist of two-hour sessions. The first is slated for 07:00 tomorrow morning with Mr. Ellington, followed by Mr. Williams at 09:30, a one-hour lunch, and then Mr. Mettenger and Ms. Stürn in similar fashion. Mme. Couteau's interview will be after dinner at 19:00.

"There will be no further meetings today. We want you to have ample opportunity to review your material and prepare the information you will be providing Mr. Mitchell. On the day following the interviews, a morning session has been scheduled for the Senior Managers and a separate one for Mme. Couteau and Mr. Ellington. But please be assured that generally that will be a day for you to relax…except for Mr. Mitchell, of course. The final report—*his* report—will be due that very evening."

After fielding a few questions, Kenneth encouraged everyone to spend their time wisely. With a slight nod toward Williams, he reminded them when dinner would be served and then adjourned the session.

Mme. Couteau, Mettenger, Ellington, and Sam walked together down the corridor toward the central lobby.

"Well, Williams and Stürn wasted no time getting out of there," Ellington laughed. "Didn't look like they were very pleased."

"I'd say not," Mme. Couteau agreed. "Guy, especially, when he heard Sam would be preparing the final report."

"It's an issue of control," Mettenger added matter-of-factly.

"Stubbornness!" Ellington added.

Mettenger laughed. "Well, maybe that as well. But don't forget, he is a Senior Manager and of the oldest branch."

"Ah now, Otto," Ellington said, exasperated. "No one's better than anyone else, and especially not that pompous blowhard. What's that got to do with it?"

"I'm not trying to defend him or the way he acts," Mettenger said, "but you can't completely disregard the fact that he's a Senior Manager."

"It's all about positions, then?" Ellington asked, sounding agitated.

"Not positions, but *responsibilities*," Mettenger explained, rather emphatically. "I don't care what you think of Williams personally, I'm not crazy about the guy either, but being a Senior Manager has enormous responsibility attached to it and I should know. I *am* one."

"All right, all right," Ellington said more calmly. "I wasn't saying anything about you."

"It's *not* about me!" Mettenger exclaimed. He paused, then sighed. "You don't understand. What we do…it's all to the extreme. Decisions about power distribution, who gets what and how much, what can be shared, maintaining a seventy-year-old system, laying new lines, monitoring the light towers, commissioning new ones, approving requests for new developments…"

Sounds like it is about him, Sam thought.

"…it can be overwhelming."

Mettenger stopped walking and stared down the corridor. The others walked a few more steps, then turned back to him.

"It's about lives," he murmured.

Mettenger looked directly at Ellington, but something in his tone made Sam feel those words were intended for someone else. Ellington walked over and patted Mettenger on the back.

"I'm sorry."

Mettenger smiled weakly. "That's okay. A lot of pressure comes with this. Everything falls on our shoulders, so I guess we get used to being in control."

"Well, I promise to be more considerate…to that blowhard."

At that Mettenger laughed, followed by the others.

"Now, let's go, my friend," Ellington said cheerfully. "We've got work to do."

They continued the short distance to the lobby, and Ellington invited everyone to join him for afternoon tea in the dining hall. Mettenger and Mme. Couteau gladly agreed, but Sam begged off, wanting to get back to his room and read over the material Kenneth had given him.

"I think each of you probably has a good idea of what you will be doing, but I'm still not certain how I'm supposed to go about this. Hopefully, there are better directions in here," he said, clutching the envelope.

"You sure, now?" Ellington implored. "We won't be long. We've got work to do today, as well." He added, with a twinkle in his eye, "They may even have some scones in there, chocolate chip muffins, date nut bread…"

"No, that's okay." Sam laughed. "I'm not hungry."

"Well, I *wasn't*," Mettenger said, now eyeing the dining hall.

"I'll catch up with you at dinner," Sam promised.

"At *our* table," Mme. Couteau insisted.

"Yes." Sam smiled, enjoying his inclusion as one of the owners of that choice area. "At our table."

After brief goodbyes, Ellington, Mme. Couteau, and Mettenger headed toward the dining hall and Sam crossed the lobby to the housing wing. He retraced his steps down the corridor, intent on going straight to his room. But as he walked past the other rooms, he slowed and glanced at the five doors.

"Guess that's why I got the suite," he said to himself. "All those interviews. Well, there will be plenty of room and it will be comfortable...at least for them. And I've got the desk. That will help, too. I wonder if they'll give me a computer. I don't even have a notepad. Why didn't I bring a notepad?" He was startled at his lack of foresight. "I am *so* not prepared for this."

Continuing along the corridor, he finally reached his room, activated the door, and stepped inside. The bedroom was dark, just as he had left it, but light shone from the far end of the suite.

"That's odd. I don't remember leaving any lamps on."

Walking cautiously down the hallway, he stepped into the large room. Silhouetted in front of the glass wall, a man stood like a statue. With his back to Sam and hands clasped behind him, he gazed outside. The drapes had been drawn back and light from the outside flooded the room, making it difficult for Sam to see. He stared at the man but could not make out who he might be.

For some time, neither moved nor made a sound. They stood there—the man staring outside, and Sam staring at the man. And much to his surprise, Sam felt no fear at all, just intense curiosity.

Why doesn't he say something? He must have heard me.

"Excuse me," Sam said softly, as though he were interrupting an invited guest. "Can I help you?"

A heavy sigh echoed off the glass. The man calmly reached up and closed the drapes. Sam's eyes widened in the dimmer light. The man turned around.

"Davidson?"

CHAPTER 9

A VISIT

SAM PACED OUTSIDE the dining hall. *I've got to tell Ellington.* He peeked around the door. Ellington was already seated, but Mme. Couteau and Mettenger were there as well. He saw Ellington check the time.

"Sam did say he would join us for dinner?"

"That's what I understood," replied Mme. Couteau. "I'm sure he'll be along."

"It's not like him to be late and it's now 18:45. I wonder how much longer they'll serve dinner."

Their conversation was as clear to Sam as if they were standing next to him.

Mettenger was looking over papers he had scattered on the table in front of him and without so much as glancing up, muttered, "19:30. He's got plenty of time. I wouldn't worry about Sam. He's a very resourceful young man. He'll be here soon."

"You sound as though you know him," commented Mme. Couteau.

"Oh, I know him," laughed Mettenger. He stacked the papers into a neat pile and looked at his companions seated at the dining table. "Yes, I know Sam Mitchell. Many at Glen Community know him. And probably New Power for that matter."

Safely out of their hearing, Sam sighed.

"Why, has he been a problem?" Mme. Couteau asked, surprised.

"No, not at all. Well, not really." He grinned at Ellington. "Have you ever seen the reports he prepares?"

Ellington nodded.

"Well I can assure you, so have I. Long, extensive ones, filled with an analysis of this and discussion of that. And on everything imaginable. He must submit a different one every other day. Why, I'd bet we have at least three times as many reports from Sam as we've had total projects since he's been with us. He's quite thorough, that one, perhaps a bit too much to suit our project coordinators, but, all in all, he does a good job."

Sam grinned.

"That must be why he was chosen as the recorder," Mme. Couteau reasoned.

"Absolutely. I knew that as soon as Kenneth mentioned it. And I can assure you, if they were looking for someone with an eye for detail who is willing to speak his mind, they got him."

"So you don't believe Williams will be a problem for him?" asked Ellington. "I've been concerned about that."

Me, too, Sam agreed.

"Guy's a problem for everyone. But no, from what I've seen of our Mr. Mitchell, when it comes down to it, he'll be able to hold his own."

Sam stepped back from the door. It was good to finally hear some encouragement. He straightened up, took a deep breath, and walked into the dining hall.

"Here he is," Mme. Couteau announced.

"Sorry, everyone," he said on reaching the table. "I got tied up." He took a seat next to Ellington and upon noticing the puzzled looks, added, "Turns out there was more to what was in my envelope than I thought there'd be."

"Like what?" Ellington asked.

"Oh, you know…instructions, directions on how to prepare it, how to set it up…that sort of thing. Have you already eaten?" he asked, changing the subject.

"No, we were waiting on you, dear," Mme. Couteau replied.

"Oh, I'm sorry. You should have gone ahead."

"It's been no problem at all," she assured him. "We've had a delightful time catching up, discussing the events of the day… attempting to get Otto to reveal what was in his envelope."

She glanced at Mettenger, who raised his eyebrows in return.

"I've already explained that. My instructions make it clear that while I can speak with Williams and Stürn, I am not to discuss anything with either of you until after all the interviews are completed."

"Yes, yes, so you say," she replied playfully. "Besides, ours said much the same in regard to you, so you will not have the benefit of our wisdom in preparing your material."

Mettenger laughed, and then looked over one of the sheets from his stack of paper.

"Wow, you had all that in your envelope?" Sam asked.

"No," Mettenger replied, studying the papers. "These are my notes and ideas. *This*—" he paused "—is for your benefit."

Sam nodded. *That's a lot of notes and ideas. I hope for your sake it won't have been a waste of time.*

"Well," Sam said, turning to the others, "what do we have to do to get some food around here? I'm starved."

"Your order, sir?"

The voice startled him so much that he jumped in his seat, hitting the table and tipping over Ellington's glass, which immediately dumped ice water into his lap. Ellington let out a yell, scaring Mme. Couteau, who in her alarm struck Mettenger's stack of papers. The sheets flew in different directions as though they, too, had been frightened and were trying to escape.

The only one at the table relatively undisturbed by the calamity was Mettenger. He sat there, casually watching the sheets of paper float to the floor like very large confetti. With a blank expression, he looked at Sam.

"So glad you could make it," he sighed.

Much to everyone's satisfaction, the dinner proceeded without further incident. Mettenger and the server had been able to gather up his papers, which he then sorted, restacked, and placed on a nearby empty table well out of anyone's reach. Ellington had sufficiently dried off. Mme. Couteau was finally able to, as she said, "get my wits about me." And Sam had apologized repeatedly, until the others threatened to search for another table if he mentioned the matter again.

Since they could not discuss their assignments, the conversation was sparse, which did not appear to bother anyone as they eagerly dove into their meal. Sam was especially quiet, and it had nothing to do with anything at the table. Once, he glanced at Ellington and noticed his old friend staring back, concern etched across his brow. *Can't hide anything from you.* He placed his fork on the table and eased back into his chair.

"So," Mme. Couteau said, taking the last bite of her dessert, "has anyone heard from Guy or Ms. Stürn? I haven't seen them in the dining hall this evening."

"Ate in," Mettenger replied.

"You can do that?" Sam asked.

"Apparently. I saw Laura before coming over. She and Guy decided to have their dinners delivered to their rooms. I guess so they could work on their assignments."

"Together?" Mme. Couteau said, surprised. "I didn't think they could tolerate each other."

"They can't," Mettenger replied. "Any discussion between the two of them would only be to discover what the other one knows. Certainly not to work together. Guy has hated her for a long time."

"Now, Otto, *hate* is such a strong word," Ellington cautioned.

"Believe me, old friend. He hates her. Always has. Guy's extremely devoted to Brighten, and she's made no secret of her efforts to find an alternate power source."

"He sees her as a threat?" Mme. Couteau asked.

Mettenger shook his head. "No, I wouldn't say *threat* exactly. He's so stubbornly devoted to the old ways. He won't consider any new possibility. No discussion. Nothing." He clapped his hands. "And that's all there is to it. No, not a threat. It's just that it's not *his* way, so he refuses to consider any good that might possibly come from any new development."

"You mean…new *power source*," Ellington corrected.

"Y-yes, yes…that's what I meant," Mettenger stammered.

As the Senior Manager finished off his dessert, Sam looked out the glass wall. The manufactured sky had dimmed, signaling the approaching end of scheduled daylight. The forest grew darker by the second, and Sam could already make out the faint glow of blue light that would soon surround Heis. Mme. Couteau had also been watching the changing scene.

"It is getting late," she observed. "I believe I will retire to my room, gentlemen. I still have work to do before bed."

Mettenger stood and helped her from her chair. "I believe I'll call it an evening, as well."

Ellington was about to join them when Sam poked him under the table.

"I think I'll have a cup of tea," Sam said, then looked at Ellington. "You?"

"Uh, sure. I can go for one."

"Well, suit yourselves," replied Mme. Couteau. "When you get to be my age, caffeine at night is not such a good idea. And I want to make sure I have everything ready for Sam tomorrow evening. Gentlemen," she said and turned to leave.

Mettenger followed her as Sam and Ellington called out their good evenings. Sam closely watched the two make their way out of the dining room. As soon as they entered the central lobby, he turned to Ellington.

"I'd like to talk to you about something if you have a few minutes."

"Why certainly, my boy," Ellington replied, noting the concern in Sam's voice. "What's wrong?"

"Nothing's wrong, really, but when I got to my room…"

"Your tea, sirs." A server appeared as if on cue and placed two cups of hot tea on the table. "Will there be anything further?"

"No, thank you," Ellington replied.

As the server walked away, Sam suddenly remembered something Kenneth had told him that morning. He looked about the room and scanned the ceiling.

"What is it?" Ellington asked.

"Probably nothing. But to be on the safe side, let's go somewhere else."

"But my tea."

"Well, take it then."

Ellington got his cup and joined Sam, who had already stood to leave. "Where are we going?" he whispered.

"To my room."

Upon entering the suite, Sam motioned for Ellington to be quiet, then searched the bath and bedroom. Satisfied, he signaled Ellington to follow him and together they walked silently down the hallway. Sam gazed around the wall and into the large, darkened room. Stepping inside, he activated the ceiling light. The room was empty. He wearily motioned for Ellington to join him.

"Impressive. So this is where the interviews are to take place?"

Sam nodded. He made his way to the couch, plopped down, and spread out as though he were about to take a nap. Ellington walked into the snug alcove and took a seat in one of the chairs facing Sam.

"I appreciate the opportunity to see your room, though I would have tomorrow morning anyway," Ellington said dryly, "but I don't think that's why you brought me here."

"Sensors," Sam said.

"Sensors?"

"They're all over as far as I can tell. Up in the ceilings. You can just make them out if you look close enough. Kenneth mentioned them. That's how they know whenever we might need help. We just speak, the sensors pick it up, relay the information, and, voilà, they appear."

"Amazing."

"Yeah, but I don't believe they have them in the rooms, at least I haven't found any that I can see. I guess they respect our privacy and have us use the intercoms instead. I didn't want anyone listening in."

"I don't understand," Ellington said, frowning. "What's this all about?"

Sam stared at the ceiling.

"I had a visitor after I got back from the afternoon session."

"Who?"

"Davidson."

"Really?" Ellington said, pleasantly surprised. "I'd wondered what had become of him. He seems like a nice fellow. Why did you have him over?"

"I didn't have him over. He was already here."

"You hadn't invited him?"

"No."

"He just showed up outside your door?"

"Not exactly." Sam sat up and looked across to Ellington. "He was already here...in this room...when I returned."

"In your room?"

"Yes!" Sam said emphatically. "In my room. Standing over there, by the window."

"That's not what I would have expected from him at all." Ellington frowned again as if trying to figure out this new mystery. "Have you told anyone else?"

"No, just you."

"Well, maybe we should alert Kenneth or Madhu. I'm sure they will not be..." Ellington stopped speaking when Sam shook his head.

"No good there. They work for him."

This news surprised Ellington. "They work for *him*?"

"You know," Sam said, a bit agitated, "this will go ever so much better if you don't repeat everything I say."

"Sorry," Ellington apologized. "Guess I'm...well, I'm not sure what I am, actually."

"Don't worry about it." Sam sighed. "I'm not sure what I am either."

Ellington leaned toward Sam. "Did he say *why* he was here?"

"Yes. That's the part I'm concerned about...not that I'm happy about finding strangers in my room, but the other is more important at the moment."

Sam settled back into the couch.

"Davidson said he came to make sure I understood about this report I'm to do. It isn't simply to gather information, sort it out, present it in an intelligent manner, and make it all pretty in a clever binder. He said he'd like...no, let me change that...he *wants* me to take this information and provide my own independent analysis and recommendations. *Mine.*"

"*He* wants? Our driver?"

"Yes, *he*…and you're doing it again.

"Sorry."

"Besides, I don't think he's merely a driver, at least not in the way I first thought. He seems to be much more involved."

"How's that?"

"The way he spoke, how he carried himself. Whenever he mentioned Kenneth and Madhu, it was always in terms of '*I* will have them' or '*I* will tell them.' He must be some kind of manager here."

"Well, that is certainly going to come as a shock to Williams." Ellington laughed.

"Yes, but you're missing the point," Sam replied curtly. "He wants *me* to analyze the information, comment on it, and make my own recommendations. Information from the Senior Managers, Ellington!" he exclaimed. "Not that I'm comfortable doing the same with you and Mme. Couteau, but we're talking about the Senior Managers."

"Sam," Ellington said, gently, "I've known you for quite some time. I'm sure you'll do an excellent job."

"But that's the very thing! We're talking about my job. What if Williams or Stürn or even Mettenger doesn't like what I prepare? What if my report makes them look bad? I haven't a chance. I'll be out on the street before I can clear my desk." He ran his hands through his hair as he looked down to the floor. "Ellington, I've got Ali and the kids to think about. I need this job."

Sam continued to stare at the floor as Ellington sat back into the chair. He was much older than Sam, but had never used that to any advantage. Sam was always very respectful of others, and especially of Ellington, even when they might not agree. They had a special relationship, a close friendship…one Sam treasured. He needed his friend, especially now.

"Sam," said Ellington, finally. Sam lifted his head. "Let's walk through this together." Sam nodded. "All right then. Did you explain your concerns…any of this…to Davidson?"

"Yes. Pretty much all of it, I think."

"And what was his reaction? He doesn't seem to be the cold-hearted sort."

Sam once again fell back into the couch. "He said not to worry, everything will be fine."

"Did he explain how he could know that?"

"No. He just said I could trust him."

"Do you?"

Sam thought about that. Trust was a scarce thing in Brigos Glen. He trusted Ali, of course. Several neighbors could be trusted for certain things, though not anything of the magnitude now facing him. There had been no one he felt he could trust during his time at New Power nor, for that matter, now at Glen Community, other than Ellington. Most were decent people, but their loyalties belonged to themselves alone, especially at work. If the opportunity presented itself and a choice had to be made between integrity on one side and their job on the other, the job would undoubtedly win out. Except for Ellington.

"I asked him how I could trust someone I didn't really know, and he said, 'By faith in the promise I keep.' So I asked how I could have faith in his promise when what he promised only came after my faith."

"Interesting," Ellington said. "I would never have thought of that. What was his response?"

Sam laughed. "He said, 'I brought you Ellington.'"

Ellington looked puzzled. "Yes, but he also brought Williams up here, too, and I'm not sure that works into his equation."

"No," Sam said, shaking his head. "I don't think that's what he meant. He didn't say he brought you along on this trip. He said he brought me *you*. And I've been thinking about that. I got a transfer from New Power to Glen Community. It's rare, though not unheard of. There was the administrative part, the waiting and all, but everything went incredibly smooth when I think about it. Then I'm given an assignment in central operations and my cubicle is just down from you…the only person who spoke a kind word to me the entire first year I was there."

"Well, there were others, certainly," Ellington said, a bit embarrassed.

"No," Sam replied emphatically. "No one. Not that first year. There are now but that's only because of you. You reach out and try to help others. I've always admired that, so I've tried to follow your example, I guess. Ali and the kids love you. You're like a part of our family."

Sam paused, then smiled.

"You're my friend, Ellington, and I don't believe I could do what I've been asked to do…if you weren't here."

Tears welled up in the old eyes.

"Yes, well," he stammered, "I don't think that's true at all. You have a gift for this reporting thing. I could never do it. And while it's clear you're emotional and apparently delirious, I thank you for those kind words. Very kind. And"—he coughed, trying to rid his throat of the painful lump—"and if I can be of any help and encouragement to you, I will."

Sam nodded. Everything about the day had been so tiring, especially the weight of his encounter with Davidson, which had been particularly draining. Though he honestly wanted to go over and hug the old man, he was exhausted and sat motionless on the couch. A nod would have to do.

"Well, then," Ellington said, regaining his composure, "was there anything else Davidson mentioned?"

"Yes," Sam replied wearily. "A warning. He told me this report is extremely important for the future of Brigos Glen…for the lives of everyone there. It will affect the entire system…the power distribution, the grid, existing usage, developments…everything."

"Sounds ominous."

"Gets better. He said the Senior Managers will try to slant their information to suit their own purposes…"

"Nothing new there."

"…but I'm not to let them do it, regardless of how angry they become. I'll have to dig for the truth—hold their feet to the fire—to get to the truth."

"And how will you do that?"

"No idea. Davidson wasn't particularly helpful there. He told me I'd have to find a way. 'Everything depends on it,' he said."

"Seems like he should have given you some guidance, some instructions. Something."

"Nothing," Sam replied. "Well, that's not entirely true. He gave me this."

He reached to the side of the couch and lifted a small, metallic object. It was rectangular, eight inches by four inches in size, a half-inch thick, and appeared to be one solid piece.

"And what is that?" Ellington asked, eyeing the object with considerable curiosity.

"He called it a sifer. It's what he wants me to use in preparing my report. Must be some kind of computer, but I've never seen anything like it. I can enter information and prepare everything with this. It even has a camera and mike so I can record the interviews, then play them back later. Watch this."

Sam moved his hand over the device and immediately the image of a condensed keyboard appeared across the top of the sifer. A holographic screen projected above it, showing Ellington's inquisitive face with great detail and true color.

"What is it you want me to see?" asked Ellington.

"This," Sam replied, gesturing to the sifer. "The keyboard and this floating screen."

Ellington looked more closely. "Sorry. I don't see a thing. Are you sure it's working?"

"*Yes*, it's working. Maybe I need to turn it around." He moved the device so Ellington could get a better look."

"No, still nothing."

"Are you serious?" Sam asked, exasperated. "This doesn't make sense. I must be doing something wrong. Here, let me try something else." But nothing helped.

"Well, don't worry about it, Sam," Ellington said, at last. "It isn't important for me anyway. It's for you to use. Does it do anything else?"

"Yeah. When I finish, all I have to do is tap right here." He pointed to the image of a tiny purple square that appeared at the bottom right corner of the device. "Then the report...*my* report... will be delivered directly to Lord Mohae."

"Mohae?"

"Yes. Davidson said it will be used extensively after we leave Heis."

Ellington looked stunned and for a moment said nothing. The device, the Center, this report, Lord Mohae coming—it was all so strange, so confusing.

"What could be at the heart of it all?" Ellington wondered out loud.

He gravely looked at Sam, as one with a terrible question he truly did not want answered. The words stuck in his throat, but he forced them out.

"For...what...purpose?"

"To determine whether to," Sam whispered, "...whether to terminate power to Brigos Glen."

CHAPTER 10

INTERVIEWS BEGIN

SAM GOT LITTLE sleep. All night he tossed and turned. When he did manage to get a few minutes here and there, he dreamed of his conversation with Davidson, the coming interviews, and the report that awaited him. Sometimes he saw Williams yelling at him, sometimes Stürn sitting there, refusing to say a word. Once Mettenger and Mme. Couteau were even trying to interview *him*. And each time he awoke with a start, sitting straight up in his bed with the same thought shouting in his head—*I can't do this!*

Ellington had been a huge help the night before, much more than he probably realized. They talked well into the evening about all that Davidson had said and what the report could mean for everyone back home. Whenever Sam questioned his ability to carry out this select assignment, Ellington was quick to encourage him. He reminded Sam of the many reports and analyses he had prepared over the years. He listed Sam's dauntless campaigns for caution and reason even when his superiors did not support him. Every terrifying doubt Sam conjured, Ellington wiped away with gentle confidence.

Sam struggled out of bed at 04:10. He desperately wanted to sleep, but it was impossible. His mind raced with every possibility for the day…too much for sleep to overcome. He took a long, hot shower, shaved, and dressed. An open suitcase sat on the neatly made bed near the rumpled one Sam had been using. Except for a few items, he had not bothered to unpack. He rummaged through the luggage and pulled out a fresh Glen Community shirt. A piece of paper, neatly folded, fell from the creases and onto the bed. He picked up the paper, opened it, and immediately recognized the handwriting.

> *Whatever you're doing, I know you will do your best. I am so proud of you. We miss you. Hurry home, but as long as you're there…knock their socks off!*

> *I love you,*
> *Ali*

"She must have done this when I was packing."

He smiled and wiped a tear from his eye. Suddenly his nerves were not so controlling, his concerns not so insurmountable, and the dread…though still lingering…not so consuming. He carefully refolded the note and placed it in his shirt pocket, then softly patted his chest over his heart.

Sam made his way to the dining hall. He had no idea if anyone would be there to serve him, but figured it was at least worth a shot for a cup of coffee. The lights were on, though dimmed. No one could be seen anywhere, which was expected. He walked over to the glass wall near "our table" and looked out. Everything was dark, though bathed in that strange blue light. He checked the time. 05:07. More than an hour before the kitchen would begin serving breakfast.

Then he got an idea. Looking up, he said distinctly, "I need coffee."

He waited, then heard a door open. Footsteps dashed across the room. He turned to see one of the servers coming toward him with a tray holding a single cup.

I could really get used to this.

The server quietly made his way to Sam and held the tray out for him to take the cup, which he did gratefully. Sam took a quick sip of the hot coffee and smiled. He looked at the server and realized he had not seen him before.

The man was Sam's height, short by what Sam had seen of Heis's standards. His complexion was similar to Madhu, though much darker. And there was not a single hair on his perfectly smooth head.

"Thank you," Sam said.

"You're quite welcome, sir. Can I get you anything else?"

"When's the earliest I can have breakfast? I've got work I need to do."

"Now, if you wish."

"Oh, I don't want to be any trouble."

"No trouble at all, sir. We thought you might come in earlier this morning, so we've been expecting you."

"Really?" Sam was surprised. "All right. That would be great." He turned to take a seat at the table.

"No sir, not there."

"But this is where I always sit."

"I understand, sir, but I have been instructed to take you to the private dining room for your meals today and tomorrow."

"Why?"

"I believe it is so you can carry out your work undisturbed…"

"From anyone who might try to influence the report," Sam added, completing the server's sentence.

"From anything at all, sir, even myself. We will be here if you need anything and all you have to do…"

"…is ask for help," Sam interrupted. "Yes, I know the drill. Thank you. I do appreciate that." The server politely nodded. "Well then, lead on."

Sam followed the server toward the door other staff used when entering and exiting the dining hall. He had assumed that since the kitchens were below, this must be a private way to move between the two floors. But before they reached the door, the server stopped in front of a large mirror on the wall. A sound came from within, like locks being released. Suddenly, that portion of the wall moved back two feet, then swung away to reveal a carpeted walkway spiraling downward.

As they stepped inside, the wall silently returned to its former position.

They walked down the gradual slope to the first floor, coming out into a broad corridor. To the left, Sam saw several doors with small round windows. *The kitchen?* They turned right and passed another dining room before coming to a door at the end of the hall.

The server stood motionless in front of the door for so long that Sam wondered if he had misplaced a key. Sam was about to ask if there was a problem when the door mechanically opened, revealing a large, dark room. Soft lights slowly came to life. The server entered with Sam close behind.

Paneled walls surrounded the room, with the exception of one covered with deep purple drapes. An oval, wooden dining table stood in front. Though eight feet in length, it had seating for only one. To the left, a pair of leather chairs angled toward each other with a small table in between. Along the opposite wall stretched a desk similar to the one in Sam's suite.

The server stepped up to the table and pulled out the solitary chair. Sam thanked him and sat down. The chair was far more elegant than those in the dining hall and far more comfortable.

"Sir, your breakfast will be ready shortly, and in the meantime, I will bring a carafe of coffee. We also have some pastries that have just come out of the oven."

Eyes wide, Sam looked about the beautifully appointed room. "So that I understand correctly, *this* is where I will have my meals for the next two days?"

"Yes, sir. This room has been reserved for your use, at any time you wish to use it. You may have your meals here, use it as a study, whatever you wish. And for the next two days, whenever you would like to return, simply ask. I will be glad to escort you."

"So I will need you with me each time?"

"Yes, sir. That is the only condition for the use of this room. Well, and that it is solely for your use. Now if you do not require anything further at this time, I will bring the coffee and pastries."

"Sure, that's fine." As the server reached the door, Sam asked, "Excuse me. If you don't mind, could you tell me your name?"

A bright smile burst across the server's face. "Tunde."

"Thank you, Tunde."

"Certainly, sir."

Sam watched Tunde leave, then took another look around the room.

Unreal. How did I deserve all this?

As he considered his unexpected good fortune, a rushing sound filled the air, not remarkably loud, yet constant...like steam escaping a teakettle. Curious, he searched the room for the cause until he finally spotted a vent in the floor near the drapes.

"Hmm. With all this, you'd think they could afford silent air conditioning."

After breakfast, Sam summoned Tunde to escort him from the private dining room. At Sam's request, the server took a different route, avoiding the dining hall entirely. He had decided it would probably be best not to run into any of the others before the interviews began, and by now, they would most likely be having breakfast themselves. A different hallway, a new staircase, another sliding door…and Sam was in the central lobby.

Tunde bowed and turned back toward the dining hall. Sam headed to the housing wing.

Upon entering his suite, Sam searched the rooms to make sure there were no surprise visitors. Satisfied he was alone, he went straight to the desk, opened the middle drawer, and removed the sifer. He then walked to the couch, sat down, and put the device on the coffee table. Sam looked about the room. *Where should everyone sit?* He considered several options, definitely deciding against the couch, though nothing else.

"I'll figure it out later. Ellington's first up and it won't matter with him."

Sam moved his hand over the sifer and it immediately sprang to life. The keyboard appeared, then the holographic screen. He typed:

First Interview:	B. Ellington
Location:	Heis Center
Time Allotted:	2 hours
Beginning Time:	07:00

He checked the time—06:30—and slumped back into the couch. The first interview had not yet begun and already he felt as though he had been working for hours. He thought of what might lie in store for the remainder of the day, picturing each person sitting in the room and telling whatever story they had come to share. He settled deeper into the couch. His eyes closed…

A tone sounded and Sam awoke with a jerk. It sounded again. He frantically checked the time. 07:02. He jumped off the couch and nearly knocked over the coffee table. He ran down the hall to the door, which promptly opened to a bewildered Ellington.

"Sorry, sorry," Sam said, still groggy with sleep.

"You look terrible!" Ellington exclaimed. "Did you not sleep at all? I thought we agreed last night there was nothing to worry about." He stepped in as Sam turned toward his meeting room.

"Yeah," Sam yawned. "No, I'm okay. Just fell asleep for a few minutes. But I'm fine. Come on back." He staggered a bit as he made way for Ellington to pass. "Go on. I'll be right there."

Sam hurried into the bath, turned on the faucet, and splashed cold water on his face. "Wake up, wake up, wake up," he mumbled, dragging a towel across his face. He looked in the mirror. Ellington's assessment had been correct. Baggy eyes, wild hair, a crease across his right cheek from falling asleep on the couch. He straightened himself up as best he could, then marched off to join his friend.

Ellington had taken one of the seats opposite the couch. The envelope he had been given was lying on the table next to a cup of coffee. Sam eyed the coffee suspiciously.

"Where did that come from?"

"What?"

"The coffee. I don't remember asking for any."

"Well, it isn't yours," Ellington said matter-of-factly. "It's mine. I brought it with me." He looked at Sam with concern. "Are you sure you're okay?"

"Yes, fine. I thought they'd…well, doesn't matter. You have your coffee," he said, and took his place on the couch.

"Would you like some? I'd be glad to get you some."

"No, not necessary. I've had a pot already this morning, and I don't really care for the stuff. No look, it's getting late. Let's go ahead and start this." Sam sat up and looked directly at Ellington. "So, what have you brought me?"

"Nothing," Ellington replied.

"Excuse me?"

"Nothing. Absolutely nothing."

"What?" Sam's head cocked slightly to one side. His eyebrows lowered. "I don't understand."

"I didn't either at first." Ellington picked up his envelope and shook out the contents. The only thing that fell out was a small piece of paper that dropped lightly to the table. He picked it up and read out loud, "Do what you do."

"Do what you do?"

"Do what you do."

"What does that have to do with the report?" Sam asked, a frown buried in his brow. "That doesn't make any sense. What am I supposed to do with that? I can't write, 'Do what you do.' If anyone's looking to cut off the power, that would be reason enough right there."

"Calm down, my boy. It's not for you, remember. It's for me. It's *my* envelope."

"That doesn't really help *me*, though," Sam replied. "I don't know what I'm supposed to do."

"But," Ellington smiled for the first time, "I know what *I'm* supposed to do."

"And what is that?"

"I've given this a lot of thought, Sam, and not just since I opened this envelope. Even back when we were first told about coming here, I wondered, *Why me?* And as Davidson gathered everyone else, the question became even stronger in my mind. The Senior Managers made sense. Mme. Couteau can add a great deal to anything we do here. And I felt you had an important role as well. Your assignment has borne that out. But what could an old fellow with no significant responsibilities in the Company—who will probably retire before too long—what could he possibly contribute? Then it occurred to me. I can help Sam."

"That would be great," Sam said, and he meant it. "But I'm not following you."

"I can tell you about the beginning in a way none of the others can. I was there, Sam, right there when it all happened. I saw it all. And I've known each of the others, some a very long time. Maybe in telling you more about them, I can help as you develop whatever questions you might have for them. I believe that's it, Sam. I want to encourage and help. It's what I do."

Ellington had made his case and sat back in his chair. He watched Sam closely, apparently waiting for some sign his young friend had understood and agreed with his conclusions. But Sam did not immediately respond. He sat there, deep in thought.

Is this a test? Sam thought back to when he had received the assignment. *Kenneth said this was my report and mine alone. I can sure use the help, but can I trust my feelings? Should I?*

Then he remembered something Davidson had told him—"I brought you Ellington."

That's it. It wasn't about last night. He was talking about today. A broad smile crossed Sam's face.

"Yes," he said confidently. "You're right."

"Ah, great. I'm relieved. For a moment there I was afraid you felt I'd gone round the bend." Ellington laughed. "So then, let's get started."

"Just a minute. Now I need some tea."

Sam stood up and headed for the front door.

"But where are you going?"

"Outside."

For the next two hours, Ellington described in detail how even *before* Last Day, the world had already become a dark place. The fertile soil of the valley proved well suited for raising a variety of crops. The air had been fresh and the water clean. The hills were deep green in the summer and snow-covered wonderlands in the winter. Spring brought beautiful flowers, and autumn displayed gold and red across the landscape. And the sky always seemed the most striking blue. But all this still did not satisfy the people of the Glen.

Pride and greed ran their course like a wild pandemic. Everyone wanted what the other had, or better. No one shared, but hoarded as much as they could whether they needed it or not. Wealth became a much-sought-after goal, then developed into an entitled expectation, and finally, a claimed right.

The people clamored for more and worked increasingly longer hours to achieve their success. But they failed to notice that the right they claimed was nothing but a carrot held by those in authority. Debt rose, families dissolved, and desperation grew until the only thing that mattered...was themselves.

Ellington painted a bleak picture. Never had Sam heard what his old friend so carefully described. He listened intently to details his schoolbooks had conveniently omitted. Teachers, politicians, village leaders, and even the media had used the curriculum to portray a very different history...one that Sam now understood was of their own choosing.

Ellington moved on to Last Day and in great detail told of the terror that had gripped the Brigons. He recounted the many days they struggled to stay alive, never knowing what had happened or why. Then he described the day Karis arrived, the work of the Yonders, and how light returned to Brigos Glen. Most of this, Sam already knew, but there was a passion in Ellington's voice that made everything come alive. The loneliness of the fires, the startling Voice, the months of hard work, the glow from the very first tower—Sam could see it all.

"Now, as for the Senior Managers," Ellington said, "the main thing for you to remember is this—not one can be trusted to tell you what you need to know."

"You think they're going to lie? Why would they do that?"

"Not necessarily lie, but we all see things a certain way. Even me. A man once told me that a single eyewitness testimony was bad enough because there was only one point of view, but several were even worse because there were so many."

"Meaning?" Sam said, looking rather puzzled.

"Meaning we often see things the way we want them to be, not the way they really are."

"Okay," Sam replied. "I get that. I'll be careful. Now, what can you tell me about Williams? He's next, so if you know anything that might help, I'm all ears."

Ellington thought for a moment.

"Guy Williams…he comes off as though he knows a lot, super smart, but it's more of a mask. He's afraid to think for himself and doesn't find value in those who do, so watch yourself there. But you can trust him to follow rules, even to a fault. The man may be arrogant and stubborn at times, but he doesn't break lines. As for history, he knows very little. Doesn't see the point in it. That may be useful, as well. He's very different from Otto."

"How so?"

"Well, for one thing, it's much easier to tolerate Otto." Ellington laughed. "Otto and I grew up together and, to a point, have a lot of the same experiences. Being my age, he's much older than Williams and he's seen what happens in a world where rules control everything and compassion is put aside."

"That's a good thing," Sam suggested.

"Could be. Should be, I guess. But as much loyalty as Williams has for rules, Otto has absolute disdain. He doesn't want to be tied down or hemmed in, always searching for something new. He has no regard at all for First Brigos, I can tell you that. Not old ways, old ideas…"

"Old friends?"

"Possibly," Ellington replied sadly. For a moment he gazed at the blue pattern in the carpet.

"What about Mme. Couteau?" Sam asked, bringing his friend back.

Ellington smiled. "Ah, Miriam Couteau." He said the name as though he were reading a file. "Now there's a story I'd like to hear, as well. She's a strong lady, been around a long time, knows a lot. But be patient with her, Sam, and kind."

"Well, of course. Someone her age…"

"Be patient and kind," Ellington interrupted, "because she has perhaps the saddest memories of us all."

Sam studied his gentle face. "And what is that?"

Ellington shook his head. "No, it would be wrong for me to say. This is for her to do, and I believe she will. But give her time, Sam. It will be very painful."

Sam wanted to pursue this further, but the expression on Ellington's face made it clear any such effort would be a waste of time. Besides, the session's allotted time was nearing an end.

"Okay," Sam conceded. "Then we have Laura Stürn. In all the years at New Power, I never met her or heard very much. Anything I should know?"

Ellington's countenance grew terribly grave. Sam had never before seen Ellington this way, and it startled him. Stürn had never behaved like Williams. In fact, she had stood up to him, unlike everyone else, and Sam rather admired that spark of defiance. And while not friendly like Mettenger, she nonetheless had been courteous toward him. He could see nothing to cause such a reaction in his friend, and yet something greatly alarmed him. The dread returned to Sam's heart, and he had no idea why.

"Sam," Ellington said, almost in a whisper. "She is dangerous. Be careful with her. Be *very* careful."

CHAPTER 11

SENIORS

A TONE SOUNDED at precisely 09:30. Sam got up from the couch and made his way to the front door. There stood Guy Williams, Senior Manager of First Brigos, in yet another expertly tailored suit. His left hand clutched a leather briefcase that hung by his side. Though Ellington's greatest caution pointed to Stürn, this was the interview Sam dreaded most.

"Good morning, Mr. Williams. Come in."

"Thank you, Mr. Mitchell."

"We will be in the back, down the hall there." Sam pointed toward the meeting room. He was about to lead the way, but Williams walked briskly past. *All right then*, Sam thought, and followed after him.

Ever since Ellington left, Sam had spent much of the time again considering where everyone should sit, especially Williams. Any arrangement with Sam on the couch seemed inappropriate, and he certainly did not want to begin the interview by offending the Senior Manager. The reverse with Williams on the couch would not work, far too casual for someone of such position. After much thought, Sam decided to use the chairs opposite the couch. He positioned them so they faced each other, still close enough for the coffee table to be of use if needed.

"We can sit..." Sam said, entering the room, but saw that his earlier planning had been wasted.

Williams walked directly to the desk and sat down. Sam watched as he methodically placed his briefcase on top of the desk, opened it with two clicks of the latches, and pulled out several thick folders which he placed on the desk. Carefully closing the briefcase, Williams spun the chair around to face Sam.

"Can I get you anything?" Sam asked, a bit taken aback by it all.

"No, Mr. Mitchell," came the perfunctory reply. "We have much to do and little time in which to do it, so let's begin."

Sam nodded obediently. He hurried to one of the chairs he had so carefully positioned and turned it to face Williams. He took his seat and waited for the Senior Manager to say something further. Then remembering the sifer on the coffee table, he reached out, successfully grabbed it without falling out of his chair, and placed the device on his lap.

"Now," Sam said, trying to regain control of the interview.

He glanced up, but Williams was not looking at him. His eyes were locked onto the sifer.

"Where did you get *that*?" he asked, nodding to the device.

Sam could not tell if Williams was angry, shocked, or both, but something about the sifer disturbed him.

"Oh, this? This is a..."

"I know what it is," Williams said, sternly. "*Where* did you get it?"

"Well...uh, Davidson gave it to me."

"Davidson? The driver...gave it to *you*?"

Sam's mouth drew tight, a thin white line across a reddened face. Williams was not upset about the presence of the sifer.

"*You* should not have that," Williams continued. "They are only for..."

"Well, I do have it," Sam snapped, "and I suggest that if you have a problem with that, you take it up with Davidson."

The tone of Sam's voice was surprising, even to Sam, and caught Williams off guard. He looked at Sam.

"You don't understand what this is, Mr. Mitchell," Williams said, in a much calmer manner.

"With all due respect, sir, I don't want to understand." Sam saw Williams stiffen, then remembered something Ellington had told him. "All I know is that this came with my assignment and my using it is part of the rules for these interviews."

He paused. The briefest sigh of resignation escaped from Williams. He looked squarely at Sam and nodded.

"Quite correct. How do you wish to proceed?"

Sam felt relieved. At least some control had returned. Struggling with Williams the next two hours was definitely not how he wanted to spend the rest of the morning. He did not answer Williams directly, but took a moment to fully activate the sifer. Only when the screen and keyboard were within his view did Sam look across to him.

"Why don't we begin with your assignment. What were the instructions you were given?"

Williams took the top folder from the stack on the desk, withdrew a single sheet of paper and read, "What have you done?"

Williams returned the sheet to the folder, carefully picked up the remaining ones, and handed them all to Sam.

"What are these?" Sam looked down at the neat pile, then back to Williams.

"Information. A complete description of what I've accomplished at First Brigos. Customer lists, financial statements, distribution charts, maintenance records…it's all there."

"Extensive," Sam said, feeling the weight of the folders.

"Certainly should be, Mr. Mitchell. That covers each of my twenty-four years as Senior Manager." The number rolled off his tongue with considerable pride.

"Pardon me for asking, but do you always carry these with you?"

"Of course not," Williams replied curtly. "But it seemed prudent to have them for this conference, if it proved necessary. It isn't as though I'm asked to attend a meeting in the Outlands every day. It was clear Brighten had something very important and I wanted to be prepared."

Sam carefully placed the folders on the coffee table.

"I'll look at these later. They'll be returned as soon as I've finished the report." He focused on Williams. "But for now, without going through this material, what do you see as the primary goal at First Brigos?"

"Maintenance," Williams shot back.

Sam squinted.

"Maintenance? Of the lines?"

"Of the system, Mr. Mitchell. As your time with the Company has been spent only with New Power and Glen Community, I would not expect you to understand, so if you will allow me, I'll explain."

"Certainly. Please do."

"First Brigos was the only branch ever truly established by Brighten Power Authority. The others came about over time, either through disagreements concerning the management of the Plan or simply misunderstanding it. More educated Senior Managers, like myself, spent a great amount of time and effort explaining what the Plan allowed and what it did not, but to no avail. Divisions occurred, resulting in the two factions we have today."

"Factions?" Sam asked. "Are you referring to the other branches?"

"They are not true branches, Mr. Mitchell. Have you ever read the Plan?"

"Yes, sir. It was part of my training at New Power, but I've read it several times since."

"Then you should be well aware there is only one operation mentioned for the distribution of power."

"Yes, but I don't recall it referring to First Brigos by name."

"It doesn't have to, Mr. Mitchell. First Brigos was first. It has sole right to distribute the power and, I might add, to interpret the Plan."

"Why to interpret the Plan? Do you not find it clear enough?"

"Absolutely clear enough. In fact, crystal clear. And that is why there can be only one interpretation. If it isn't in the Plan, it cannot be allowed. To do otherwise would be offensive to Brighten. One interpretation, one branch. It is Brighten that has ultimate authority here."

"It sounds as though you're trying to protect Brighten."

"Mr. Mitchell," Williams laughed. "Brighten is the owner of all the power. It gives its power to whomever it chooses and it chose First Brigos. Had it not been for Brighten after Last Day, you and I would not be sitting here now. I have no doubt that everyone in the Glen would have died or become savages. We owe our strictest allegiance to Brighten. That's why we at First Brigos are so adamant about maintaining the system in the exact manner as has been done over the past seventy years. The same procedures, the same protocols. To consider anything different causes unnecessary distractions and considerable disruption in the overall operation of the system."

"But Mr. Williams," Sam interjected, "I'm sure you are aware of the argument by some that Brigos Glen has grown considerably, both in area as well as population. And because of that growth, other ways to use the power and reach more people should be considered. Many, myself included, are far removed from those early days when it was necessary to closely follow certain procedures and strengthen the new connection with Brighten. What would you say to that?"

"I don't have to say anything, Mr. Mitchell," Williams replied, coldly. "Above all, we must look to Brighten. Above all, we must follow the letter of the Plan and…if it isn't in the Plan, it *cannot* be allowed."

"So, if I understand you correctly," Sam said, as respectfully as he could, "there can be no new developments…"

"If it isn't in the Plan…"

"Or expansion into new territory."

"…it *cannot* be allowed."

Sam thought for a moment.

"Would you shut everything down that Glen Community and New Power have been doing? Prevent power from reaching the areas they have developed?"

"Yes. There is no choice in the matter."

"Without any consideration?"

"Nothing to discuss."

"What about the people who now live and work in those areas?"

"They can always come to First Brigos, of course."

"But you won't go to them?"

"It isn't in the Plan."

For the remainder of the interview, Sam kept his questions solely to matters concerning branch operations within the First Brigos district. There was no point going further into Williams's impressions of the other branches or their activities. He adamantly believed in only one way of doing things—the First Brigos way—"The way it has always been done," as he stressed throughout the interview.

But at least Sam had no problem getting information from him. Williams was more than willing to discuss anything and everything about the operations of First Brigos, which he maintained proceeded strictly in accordance with the Plan. Only two areas caused him any hesitation—the branch's headquarters and its emergency fund.

The headquarters were located in the Thomas Complex, named after the Chief Elder who, as Williams phrased it, led the village out of the dark times and into the light. The Complex consisted of three interconnected buildings spanning an entire block in Old Brigos. The actual structures preceded Last Day by several years, but the interior…especially the executive offices…had been completely and elaborately renovated. Sam suggested this might be considered "new development," but Williams defended the expenditures as necessary for First Brigos to honor and reflect the significance of Brighten Power Authority, especially being its only true branch.

The emergency fund would never have been mentioned had Sam not questioned the resulting increased cost of maintaining the Thomas Complex. Williams assured him no concern at all existed due to the more than sufficient resources of the fund, which had grown exponentially over the years. The amazing growth, Williams explained, resulted in large part because First Brigos had taken a firm position against new developments, expansion into new territory, and providing new customer services. As Williams presented the details, Sam entered into the sifer, "People needed help, First Brigos made money."

The interview ended promptly at 11:30. Sam had asked all the questions he could think of, and Williams had provided more information than he could ever need. Still, Sam was certain that even if he had made another request, Williams would nonetheless have held him to the two-hour limit—rules being rules—and that would have been the end of it.

After Williams left, Sam used the hall sensor to request that Tunde meet him in the central lobby. Though only a short distance from the suite, Tunde was already there by the time Sam arrived. Together, they slipped through a hidden doorway and silently made their way to the first level corridor and the private dining room.

"I'll have your meal brought immediately, Mr. Mitchell."

"Thanks, Tunde."

After Tunde left, Sam entered several notes into the sifer. He had been so involved in the interview, he kept forgetting to make much use of it. Now it was important to get his thoughts down before he forgot those, as well; and with three more sessions to go, Sam knew there would be far too much critical information to rely on memory alone.

As he made his last entry, a small purple dot flashed in the lower right corner of the projected screen.

"OK, what did I do?"

He looked at the keyboard, then over the entire device, but found nothing related to it. He stared at the pulsing light, then reached out and touched the holographic image. Immediately the light steadied. A message appeared on the screen.

"Very good session, Sam."

Sam thanked Tunde for the meal, but had little appetite. He picked at his food and forced a few bites. With fifteen minutes before the next session, his plate remained full. He eventually gave up and returned to his suite, where he tried to clear his mind in preparation for Otto Mettenger.

Since Sam also worked at Glen Community, he was familiar with his Senior Manager's public image. The man had seemed nice enough from a distance, the only way Sam had observed him prior to the last few days. Often appearing at public functions, Mettenger was the epitome of the glad-hander—always smiling, always eager to meet new people, and since the man seldom remembered those he met, they were always new. But despite such pleasant appearances, Sam decided he needed to be extra careful regarding his own demeanor and especially the questions he would ask the Senior Manager.

Davidson may think everything's going to be okay, but he doesn't have to work for Mettenger. He could easily have me fired when this is over.

He nervously paced about the room. Twice he rearranged the chairs, only to return them to their exact former positions. He even thought about hiding the sifer in case Mettenger might have the same reaction as Williams, but finally decided not having it there could be the bigger risk if Williams later mentioned it to him. After more pacing, Sam checked the time and was surprised to discover that it was already 12:45.

"Hmm. He's late. Well, this will probably be a short one anyway," Sam said, hopefully. Then he resumed his pacing.

Time dragged by. At 13:00 Mettenger still had not appeared. At one point, Sam decided to go look for him. But he changed his mind, certain that as soon as he left, Mettenger would arrive to an empty room and everyone would think it his fault for not being there. Sam took a seat at the desk and anxiously watched the minutes slip away.

Not until 14:00—a full ninety minutes past the scheduled time—did Sam hear the familiar tone. He leapt from the chair and rushed to the door. There at last stood Otto Mettenger. Upon seeing Sam, he simultaneously slapped him on the back and shook his hand. Sam suddenly felt like a contributor at a campaign rally.

"Good to see you again, Mitchell. Has it been going well? Did old man Williams give you a hard time?"

Sam thought it strange that Mettenger would refer to his peer as "old man Williams," considering he was by far the elder of the two.

"Uh, no sir. It went fine."

"Well, glad to hear it," Mettenger said, rather robustly. "Now, where are we to have this thing, anyway?"

"Down the hall there." As Williams before him, Mettenger took off without waiting. "Sir, do you realize the time?" Sam called after him.

"Time?"

"Yes, sir. Your session...*our* session...was to have begun an hour and a half ago."

Mettenger stopped and turned around.

"Now, son, you're not going to get hung up on a bunch of rules? I would've thought we had taught you better than that."

"But there's the later session with Ms. Stürn and…"

"You're not telling me anything I don't already know, but we have a job to do…right?"

"Yes, sir."

"And it's a very important one, right?"

"Yes, sir."

"Well, I'm sure what we need to do here is what Lord Mohae would want us to do. So why don't we get to it?"

Sam did not care to use what little time remained belaboring the point. He would have to work faster, and there was his own thirty-minute break he could use as well.

"All right, sir. Let's get to it then."

"Now you're talking." Mettenger laughed and slapped him on the back again.

They walked into the meeting room and, to Sam's pleasant surprise, Mettenger asked where he should sit. Sam pointed to one of the chairs opposite the couch, and as the Senior Manager took his seat, Sam sat in the chair across from him.

"Wow, look at that," Mettenger exclaimed, noticing the sifer. "That's a nice one. Mine's much older. Probably time to get a new one."

"You have one of these?"

"Sure," Mettenger replied. "Each Senior Manager has one."

"Maybe you can have this one after the report has been filed."

"Nah, doesn't work that way. They're optically encoded. I've no idea how they manage it, but it has something to do with a person's retina."

"So it won't turn on without a recognition scan?"

"Better than that. Have you seen the keyboard and that floating screen?"

"Yes."

"Well, you're the only one who can. This sifer is synced up with only *your* individual retina. Whether it's working or idle, you're the only one who knows. No one else can see. It's only a shiny piece of metal to anyone other than you. Amazing bit of technology there. And pretty handy for notes, reports, presentations, Company communication…"

"Company communication?" Sam thought about the message he had received.

"Yeah. Years ago, after completion of the first phase of system construction and the Yonders had returned home, all communication between Farside and Brigos Glen came through these. It was mainly instructions and orders from Brighten back then."

"I'm not sure I understand. What do you mean…*first* phase?"

"Well, Williams would argue the point I'm sure, but after Brighten got everything started with the Plan, Olasom Contracting stepped up and led the way for expanding the system. New training methods, new protocols. Olasom was really responsible for the growth of Brigos Glen. That's what I call the second phase of system construction."

"And Mr. Williams doesn't agree with you, I take it."

"Absolutely not. He's married to that Plan. Tied to the past. If it were up to him, we'd all be crammed in the old village, living on top of each other with nothing to look forward to. Those old ways of doing things are a joke. You know, he wears a *suit* to work every day. Can you imagine that? I don't even own a tie." Mettenger laughed.

"So, you don't see any value to the old ways?" Sam asked.

"No, not if you want to do anything worthwhile. Not if you really want to get out there and reach more people, give them room to grow and show them a better way of living. That's what we're all about at Glen Community." Mettenger paused as if on cue in a marketing campaign. "You know, it's funny."

"What's that, sir?"

"There was only one thing in that big envelope for me, and it was perfect—one sheet of paper with just one question. Any idea what it could be?"

"Maybe, what have you done?" Sam said, cautiously.

"No, no," Mettenger cried out, obviously pleased that Sam had not guessed. "Not have *done*, but are *doing*. What are you doing? That's what it asked, and that's what we're all about. The *doing*. We don't let ourselves get stuck in old routines like First Brigos. We do things…new things. We make a difference."

Mettenger then launched into a list of the new developments he had authorized over his tenure as Senior Manager. New commercial centers, new residential housing, new parks. He described with great satisfaction how the neighborhoods and village shops of yesterday had given way to apartment complexes, gated communities, and the slick, new retail centers of today. As he rambled, Sam typed into the computer, "New developments—30% occupancy. Retirement centers—crowded."

"Sam," Mettenger said, out of breath, "surely you understand. We have to keep up with the changes that are bound to come. In fact, we must anticipate them. And these changes require a broader distribution of power, one that even I will admit stretches our resources at times. But Sam, that's why we follow the information Olasom gave us all those years ago. I've got nothing against the Plan. The Plan's great, but there's more to this than just the Plan. And what Olasom was telling us was about the creation of more power."

Sam frowned. "You mean like what New Power's been working on?" Sam squirmed a bit in his chair.

"No, Sam. That's something completely different. I'm not for what they're doing at all. I'm talking about the creation of more power that will come from Brighten and be given to even more people. That's the vision, and we are focused on it. We are committed to this next generation."

Sam let out a sigh of relief. Mettenger did not subscribe to what his former employers claimed as the "Enlightenment of New Power." In his first ten years with the Company, Sam had seen the idea of a new power source become their obsession. Through constant propaganda, they sought to bring as many as possible in line with their views. Still, something Mettenger said troubled him.

"But…" Sam cautiously chose his words, not wanting to offend his Senior Manager. "If your focus and commitment are on this next generation you've mentioned, what happens to the current generation?"

"Current generation? It's all *current*, Sam," Mettenger said, and for the first time, in a condescending tone.

"No, I'm sorry," Sam replied. "Not that kind of current. Current, as in the present. What happens to the present generation? If everything is about the next, if all your resources and attention are there, who will take care of the present generation? Who will maintain it and make sure it is operating properly? There are lives depending on that, as well."

"Lives in the current generation?"

"Yes," Sam said emphatically, more so than he had intended.

"Lives, even in the current generation, can join us, Mr. Mitchell," Mettenger said, irritated. "They can join us in our mission…our *calling*…to build a new world."

"Lives like Mme. Couteau? She lives in Hopewell, Mr. Mettenger. It's an old retirement community. Run-down. Barely functional."

"That is Miriam's choice."

"To be forgotten?"

Stunned by Sam's question, Mettenger became like stone in his chair. His irritation transformed into embarrassment. He stared at Sam. The question had cut through the space between them like an invisible knife, dividing and defining the two men. Silence filled the room. Sam looked at his watch.

Mettenger began. "What you've got to understand…"

"I'm sorry, sir," Sam interrupted. "It's already 14:52…well past the time for your session. I'm afraid we need to close so that I can prepare for the next interview."

"What? You can't end this whenever you wish, Mitchell!" Mettenger's voice rose with indignation. "*I am Senior Manager of Glen Community.*"

"Mr. Mettenger, please. It's just that I have to make sure I'm ready for Ms. Stürn. You were late for your interview and…"

"See here! You don't have the authority to tell me when I must come and when I must leave."

Mettenger spoke with defiance, but if this was meant to back Sam down, it failed. Sam remained calm, watching his Senior Manager, who stared back at him.

"Next week, I will certainly not have such authority," Sam said, his words carefully measured, "as I may also not likely have a job. But today I do have that authority, as well as a responsibility to carry out and a report to write. And now I must ask you to leave, or I will have you removed. I'm sorry," he said, not feeling a bit sorry, "but *your* time is over."

Sam did not see him to the door, not that Mettenger gave him any opportunity. The Senior Manager stormed out. Despite the man's actions, Sam could not tell if he were truly angry or just ashamed. He had seen the way Mettenger acted toward Mme. Couteau. He always showed sincere respect, even affection, for the elderly lady. It made no sense that he could be so courteous earlier, and yet so callous now. But there was no time for Sam to think on it. The tone had sounded.

Laura Stürn had been a Senior Manager less time than the others—only ten years—but her history with the Company was widely known. She had quickly risen through the ranks of New

Power, gaining a well-deserved reputation as a formidable negotiator. Never outmatched, she always knew as much, if not more, about any given situation than those on the other side of the table.

Her opponents found it a grave mistake to underestimate her abilities. It was she who convinced Guy Williams years earlier that First Brigos would greatly benefit from New Power remaining a completely independent branch. Together, she had argued, they could effectively work to keep a rein on Otto Mettenger and his new developing trends. But Williams did not realize that before the ink had dried on their agreement, Stürn had brokered another. She persuaded Mettenger that with New Power by its side, Glen Community could better stand up to First Brigos and expand even farther into the valley. A second alliance was formed.

New Power never sought the permission or blessing of either branch. There was no need. Neither paid it much attention. Stürn's hidden alliances encouraged First Brigos and Glen Community to monitor each other, rather than the activities of New Power… activities designed to develop a viable alternative to the power that came from beyond the mountains. Though the pursuit of an alternate source had not originated with her, she had long ago become an ardent supporter of the position and, within the branch, frequently voiced her opposition to anything that would hinder future independence from Farside's control.

Stürn developed the propaganda campaign "Freedom from Farside" and fed her superiors a steady diet of it. As a result, her popularity, both within New Power and with their customers, grew rapidly. When the previous Senior Manager abruptly resigned—for reasons he refused to disclose—she was swiftly installed as the new leader.

Since then, she had become much bolder, no longer concealing her search for a new power source. Williams vehemently denounced the operation, but she was two steps ahead of him. New Power responded with a carefully crafted apology.

We regret that our research to develop a secondary power source may have caused alarm. That was certainly never our intent. To date, our best efforts have produced only a poor alternate, far below the quality and strength of that supplied by Brighten Power Authority. However, in times of emergency, particularly to prevent shortages for First Brigos, this lesser substitute could be diverted to the other branches for their use.

Williams soon ended his attacks and made no further comments. But the alliances had been permanently weakened.

Few in First Brigos regarded her as much more than a nuisance they had to tolerate. Most in Glen Community were equally divided between those who casually supported the idea of an additional power source and those who simply did not care. But within New Power, Stürn's actions were celebrated as the dawning age of New Power…the beginning of a new order. And Sam had heard such proclamations every day for the last five years he was there.

"Please sit wherever you like," he said, as they entered the meeting room.

"Thank you, Sam," she replied, in a polite, businesslike manner.

Stürn took the chair in the corner, just to the right of the desk. She adjusted the open coat of her pinstripe suit and gave the sleeves a quick tug. Then she settled in the chair, her envelope on her lap. Sam was surprised she had chosen that particular chair. Now armed with at least the appearance of authority, he could sit at the desk—a position Williams had quickly taken for himself. Stürn apparently had no problem with the arrangement, and Sam felt grateful, even appreciated. He picked up the sifer from the coffee table and took his seat.

"I hope this is not a distraction," he said, motioning to the device.

"Not at all. Why should it be?"

"Well, Mr. Williams seemed very upset about me having it. Mr. Mettenger was fine, but apparently these are normally reserved for Senior Managers."

"Nonsense," Stürn said, sounding like a harsh schoolteacher. "I assumed you would have one. The report is to be issued directly to Lord Mohae, and what other means would be best suited? I certainly do not have an issue with it, if that's what you're wondering."

"Good," Sam said, nodding. "I'm glad to hear that. Well, if you're ready, I suppose we should begin."

"I'm ready." She smiled.

Stürn took her envelope, carefully opened it, and took out several sheets of paper.

"I've brought the assignment, as well as a few notes I've made, which you are more than welcome to have after our session."

Sam noticed it was nothing like the stack of folders Williams had produced. He let out a slight sigh.

Stürn grinned. "Let me guess. Guy gave you a bit more."

"Quite a lot, actually." Sam laughed, and pointed to the stack on the table.

"Oh my," she said. "Well, that's Guy for you. I imagine, though, that Otto did not burden you with the same."

"No," Sam replied. "He didn't bring anything at all."

"Really?"

"No, we just talked."

"Well, we can do whatever you feel is best. I am at your disposal."

The corners of Sam's mouth turned down as he tried to suppress a grin. He nodded, just once but emphatically. Sam already felt encouraged. Stürn did not seem interested in asserting her authority through power plays, as had Williams. And unlike Mettenger, she apparently took the interview seriously.

Just as it should be, he thought. *Ellington was being way too cautious about this.*

"Why don't we begin with your assignment. What was it exactly?"

Stürn took a sheet of paper and handed it to him. Printed in bold letters was, What will you do?

"Interesting," he said, laying it on the desk. "How do you interpret that?"

"I believe it's straightforward," she replied confidently. "It's about the work we've been doing at New Power and the directions that work will take us."

"Such as the new developments at Glen Community?"

"It's far more than that, Sam. It's a new way of life. One that is not dependent on others."

"Such as Farside," he added.

"Exactly!" she replied with great enthusiasm. "That's *exactly* it."

Sam instantly recalled Davidson's warning that power from Brighten could be terminated. He drew a hand to his chin, one finger resting on his lips. Then he made a loose fist in the air as though he had captured a thought.

"But there are those, I'm sure you're aware," he said carefully, "who feel such actions are disrespectful, perhaps even offensive to Brighten."

"Nonsense," she said again. "This would never be a threat to Brighten. Besides, who do you think is strongly encouraging our efforts?"

"You don't mean Brighten?" Sam asked, surprised.

"No, Sam. I would not expect anything of the sort from Brighten. It's obsessed with its own authority, trying to dictate everything in the Glen. No, I'm talking about QolCom."

Sam's fist opened, palm up. "I'm sorry, but I don't follow."

Stürn paused and took a deep breath, as though she were about to reveal a great secret.

"QolCom is the communications agent for Farside. It is every bit as significant as Brighten, and I believe even more so than

Olasom. Just like them, it is a Yonder institution. But unlike them, its purpose is to provide us information so that we can think for ourselves, make our own decisions. So that we can be truly free—free of any foreign influence and control, free to do as we please…finally free from the darkness forever. Wouldn't that be wonderful, Sam?"

"Yes," he agreed, not entirely sure what he was agreeing to.

"Of course, it would. This is not *against* Brighten, Farside, or any of the Yonders. This is *for* us! We've spent an eternity living off the goodwill of someone else. We've become beggars. It's time we pulled ourselves up and stood on our own two feet. It's time we help ourselves, Sam."

"I guess I can see that," Sam said, hesitantly, "but I'm not sure where QolCom comes in. It just sends out information concerning the Plan."

"At first, that's what everyone thought. Just reminders of what the Plan dictated, as well as those instructions we got from Olasom. But that was never all there was to it. In fact, that wasn't even the important part. QolCom provides its own guidance apart from the other two. QolCom urges us to freedom and shows us what we can accomplish."

"But I always thought QolCom worked *with* Brighten and Olasom. This sounds more like it's doing its own thing."

Stürn sat back in her chair and offered Sam a sympathetic smile.

"I know how hard this can be to understand, Sam. It took me many years to come to terms with it, myself. It's so foreign to what we've always been told was the truth. But that was to keep us in our place, to keep us from growing and becoming responsible, thinking people once again. We were never meant to be someone's slaves. The time of Brighten and Olasom is coming to an end, and we've got to be ready to take over."

As she said "take over," a shiver ran down Sam's back. Something in her voice unnerved him. Her words made sense, her cause sounded more than reasonable. There was no arguing about the depth of her passion. Yet, Sam found something deeply unsettling. Her face lit up with a strange excitement, and her stare pierced him to his soul. Feeling a desperate need to break the connection, he glanced down and noticed the sifer had somehow activated. Visible only to him, the screen floated in space between Sam and Stürn. Across the image, words came into view, "Has she read the Plan?"

Startled, Sam glanced from the screen to Stürn, but as Mettenger had indicated, she could see nothing at all.

"Is there a problem?" she asked.

"Uh, no, everything's fine," Sam said, regaining his composure. "It all makes perfect sense." Stürn beamed her approval. "I do have one question if you don't mind…you know, for the report."

"Certainly, what is it?"

"This seems to have been important to Mr. Williams and Mr. Mettenger, and I was wondering where you stood on it. Do you feel that everyone should read the Plan?"

Stürn laughed. "Sam, you are insightful. That's *exactly* what's wrong with First Brigos and Glen Community—their misplaced devotion to something that no longer applies to this day and age. I had those horrid lessons as we all did in school, but when I became an adult, I put those childish chains behind me. I've never read the Plan per se, but I know what it's about and that's all I need to know. It isn't necessary to read that ancient thing. It serves no purpose but to fetter our minds and prevent us from achieving all that we can. Freedom, Sam. That's what life is all about."

Sam nodded politely.

CHAPTER 12

INTERVIEWS END

"FOUR DOWN, ONE to go."

Sam picked at the food Tunde had brought him. He did not feel like eating. The last three sessions had been more stressful than he had imagined. Tension gripped his body even now as he recalled each encounter.

As expected Williams proved difficult at times, though he had been respectful and certainly provided a lot of material for the report. On the other hand, Mettenger, the one Sam had been certain would be the easiest, completely surprised him. He had brought nothing of substance—none of the paperwork he had seen at dinner the day before, no data, no projections, not even a chart or two—only wide-eyed excitement for whatever might be in store around the corner.

And then there was Stürn...well prepared, very courteous, even deferring at times to his position as recorder. But now as Sam recalled her interview, he could not escape the possibility that she had been far more interested in furthering an agenda than assisting with the report.

Yet each of them had brought one thing in particular to their interviews. Judgment. They viewed one another with disdain, never missing an opportunity to condemn a fellow Senior Manager. Each believed himself or herself to be the sole voice of reason and truth as to everything concerning the management of the power system in Brigos Glen. Still, there had been something even more with Stürn. Sam could not put his finger on it exactly, but every time he thought about that last session, Ellington's warning rang in his ears, growing louder and more urgent.

"Enough!" Sam slammed his fork onto the table. "I can't think about this right now."

He marched to the desk. There sat the sifer, exactly where he had left it. He had not used the device since returning to the private dining room. And yet, the screen once again hovered above. "Be patient." Sam angrily stared at the floating words.

"Who's sending these messages?"

Mme. Couteau arrived at 18:45 along with Kenneth, who had her arm wrapped around his. She seemed weary and walked with great effort.

"Thank you, Kenneth," she said. "You have been such a dear."

"My pleasure, Mme. Couteau, and if Mr. Mitchell would let me know when your meeting is over, I will be glad to escort you to your room."

"Oh, yes, certainly," Sam replied.

As Kenneth turned to leave, Sam took her by the arm and helped her inside.

"Are you not feeling well?" he asked, concerned. "I'm sure we can do this some other time if that would be better."

"No, I'm fine, Sam. It's these old bones of mine. Everything goes in spurts these days. One minute I feel wonderful and can get around with no problem at all, then my joints begin to freeze." She let out a slight groan with her next step. "Arthritis can be a terrible thing, Sam. If you should have the option, elect not to have it." She chuckled.

Sam noticed her thick wool cardigan. "And let me know if it's too cool in here."

"It's quite pleasant, but thank you. I will."

They carefully made their way down the hall and into the meeting room.

"My, this *is* nice," she exclaimed. "They weren't exaggerating."

"They?"

"Ellington and Otto," she replied. "I even overheard Guy and that Ms. Stürn talking about it. I believe they're all a bit jealous. I know I am." She laughed.

"Well, I'll gladly give it to you," Sam said with a grin, "if you would like to prepare the report."

"Oh, no, my dear." She laughed again. "It would certainly not be worth that. No, you were the one chosen for that task and I do not envy you at all. I will do what I do best, and that is to sit, have some tea, and prattle on for hours."

"We have only the two." Sam smiled.

"Well, I'd best get started then. Could I sit there, if you don't mind?" She pointed to the couch.

"Absolutely."

As Sam walked her over to the couch, she bumped into the coffee table.

"Oh, I'm so sorry. Did I knock anything over?"

"No, no, you're fine."

Sam's eyes darted from Mme. Couteau to the table. He frowned, puzzled. He guided her around the empty coffee table and helped her down to the couch.

"Thank you, dear. I don't see as well as I once did. Everything is fuzzy. I see shapes and lights all right. It's the details I sometimes can't quite make out. But I hide it well."

"Yes, you do," he replied, with genuine surprise. "I had no idea."

"It isn't that difficult, really. Most people don't notice an old woman bumping into things."

Sam waited, expecting her to laugh again, but instead she silently settled onto the couch. He excused himself and went outside to ask the sensor for hot tea, which was promptly delivered in a bright orange cup. Sam hurried back to the meeting room and placed the cup on the coffee table.

"Your tea," he announced. Mme. Couteau reached out and took it with no problem at all. "How did…I thought…"

"I can make out colors fine," she explained. "I'm not blind. I just can't see." She laughed again.

As Mme. Couteau sipped her tea, Sam took a chair opposite her. He activated the sifer and entered the session information as he had for each of the interviews. With that accomplished, he looked across to Mme. Couteau, contentedly holding her cup.

"I guess we should begin as I have with the others. That seems to have worked well enough."

"Tell me what I can do, dear."

"All right. Could you tell me about your assignment?"

He waited patiently as Mme. Couteau took another sip of tea, then carefully returned the cup to the table. She folded her hands across her lap and gazed into the fabric of her plain brown dress.

"That's an interesting thing," she said. "I had this large envelope…like everyone else, from what I could gather…but there was only a single sheet in it. Thank goodness the writing was large or we would not be sitting here. Even then, it was a bit blurry, but I could make it out. Only it didn't make much sense to me, and I'm afraid I may not be of much help to you."

"Why? What did it say?"

"Only this—Tell him about Lord Mohae."

"That seems straightforward enough."

"Yes," she replied, bothered. "But you see, I know next to nothing about him."

"Hmm. That *is* odd. Maybe this will be a short interview." He laughed, but Mme. Couteau did not join in. Sam sensed her frustration. "Why don't you tell me what you do know. Anything at all will be helpful."

He tried to sound encouraging, but with no beneficial effect on her. She sat on the couch, silent and still, and thought.

"He's very old," she said, at last.

"You've met him?"

"No."

"Then how do you know he's very old?"

"Stands to reason, doesn't it? He is the author of the Plan and we received that from Karis seventy years ago. So even if he wrote it as a young man, and I don't believe that was the case, he should at least be about my age, and I'm ninety-two."

"So he might be older than *you*?"

"Well, you don't have to say it like that," she teased, "but yes, I believe so. At least, that's how it all seemed back then. Whenever Lord Mohae's name was mentioned, all those Yonders would get very serious. You know, in a deeply respectful way. And when his orders would come, well, you've never seen men suddenly snap to attention like that. It always looked to me as though they were in the military. Whatever the orders would say, that is exactly what they would immediately set out to do…no questions asked."

"Did he ever come to Brigos Glen?"

"Not that I know. We thought he might early on. There was word he would come to inspect the initial work after the Yonders laid the lines across the mountains, and again when the training center was built. But no one ever saw him. That was back when all the work was being done by the Yonders, and we pretty much stayed in the village. After they returned to Farside, there's not much left to tell, really. From time to time, he would send various communications from Farside, which the system managers would then announce to everyone in Brigos Glen. But eventually that stopped."

"The communications from Lord Mohae?" Sam asked, typing away on the sifer.

"No, the announcements," she corrected. "Sometimes we were told they were about operation matters that did not concern us, other times they said they were too complicated for us to understand. The managers would occasionally issue their own interpretations, but after a while even that stopped, especially when the branches formed. It's been a long time since I've even heard him mentioned. I thought he had died."

"You said something about a training center. What was that? I haven't heard of a training center before."

Mme. Couteau bit her lip and glanced about. She pulled her cardigan close, as though a chill had suddenly swept into the room.

"Nothing to it, really. Just a place. Doesn't exist anymore. Wasn't needed after the work was turned over to Brigons." She spoke quickly, never looking in Sam's direction.

Sam checked his sparse notes. He had written very little, and even that did not seem helpful for the report. No one else had mentioned Lord Mohae in their interviews, so nothing could be drawn from them.

Why have her tell me about this guy if she doesn't know anything?

"Are you sure there wasn't anything else on the sheet? The assignment, I mean."

"Yes, that was all there was." She picked up her cup and sipped more tea. "I'm sorry I couldn't be of more help."

"Oh, that's OK." Sam sighed. "It's not your fault. I'm kinda stumped here. Somehow this has something to do with the report, but for the life of me I don't know what it could be."

"Well, I'm sure you'll do fine," she replied, sounding a bit grandmotherly.

"I'm not so sure."

"It's only a report, Sam. It's not like it's the end of the world."

Sam frowned and glanced over his shoulder toward the hallway. Turning back, he leaned forward. "Can I tell you something? You cannot mention this to anyone. It must remain a secret."

Mme. Couteau fell silent. She placed the cup on the table as though she were about to stand and bid him good evening. Instead, she sat back, once more folded her hands in her lap, and gazed at the young recorder.

"Yes," she said firmly. "I promise not to share this with anyone."

"OK, here goes." He nervously looked around the room, as if someone might be listening. "I met with Davidson yesterday."

"You, too?"

"Uh, yeah. I guess he was making the rounds."

Sam had no idea what she could be talking about, but that was not important. He continued before she had a chance to say anything further.

"He talked to me about these interviews and the report. I think he felt he was trying to help, and maybe he was...I don't know... but he told me something about the report."

Sam hoped she could somehow understand the depth of his concern. She reached over and put her hand on his.

"Go on. What did he say, Sam?"

"Before he left, he said the report would be used to decide if power to Brigos Glen would be cut off."

"No!" she gasped, snatching her hand back.

"That's what he said," Sam replied. "So that's why I've been worried about all this. I've got to do this right. Lives are depending on it."

He looked at the elderly lady and fear leapt into his heart. Her face had grown terribly pale and her hands trembled.

"I'm sorry, Mme. Couteau," Sam begged. "I shouldn't have said anything. I don't know why but I thought you should know. I'm so sorry."

"No," she said, shaking her head. "You did right, Sam. I'm glad you told me."

"But I've upset you." Sam's face flushed. He quickly rubbed the back of his neck. "Listen, there isn't anything else we can do here. I'll have Kenneth take you back to your room."

"Wait." Mme. Couteau closed her eyes and sat perfectly still. "There is something more," she said, forcing the words to come. "This may take a while."

Sam paused. "I have time," he replied, gently.

All was quiet.

After a moment, she took a deep breath and sighed. "I told you I had never married, and that part was true. What I did not tell you was that I had been engaged…once…a year before Last Day. His name was Edgar. He was a few years older than me and had moved from a small town in the south. I forget the name of it now. He came to Brigos Glen to work with an agricultural engineering firm while he finished his doctorate. My family had a very successful farm at the time and Edgar would visit us each week to take soil and plant samples. At least that's what he told my father," she said, smiling. "In time, we were seeing each other quite often, and one thing led to another. He proposed in the middle of a cornfield."

Mme. Couteau looked straight at Sam, but he knew she saw a treasured memory instead. Then her smile faded.

"The wedding would have been on Last Day. So, of course, that didn't happen. It was a terrible day, Sam."

"I can imagine," he replied.

Her eyes narrowed and she shook her head. "No, you can't."

Sam searched for something comforting to say, but she went on. "Everything was dark. People were screaming. I can still hear them some nights. My father got my mother and me into the cellar. We had a generator, so we weren't without light like almost everyone else."

"And Edgar?" Sam asked.

"*Edgar*," she said, amused, "somehow made his way through the chaos, through that pitch black darkness, and found his way to our farm. Took him all day, there was so much confusion. When he got there, he began yelling and beating on the walls. Father had to go get him before he tore the house down." She laughed.

"After things got under control, he and Father would help others who had truly suffered. Every day they reported to the Elder Council and offered their services, which, of course, they were only too glad to accept. Then one day the Council asked Edgar to be part of something special they were putting together—four groups to go out and see if they could find anyone else who had survived that horrible day. Father wanted to go, too, but the Elders felt he was too old. Edgar joined without any hesitation. When the time came, he and his team were assigned to search beyond the eastern range. The poor boy had never even been camping," she said sadly. She paused and wiped a tear from her cheek. "That was the last time I saw him. They never made it back."

Sam quickly handed her his handkerchief, then with his hand wiped his own eyes. He had read about this lost group, but had never known anyone connected with it. Pretending to enter a few notes into the sifer, he waited as Mme. Couteau regained her composure. After a few minutes, she returned his handkerchief.

"Thank you."

"I'm very sorry," Sam said. "It must be difficult carrying a memory like that."

"That's the funny thing," she replied. "I had not thought about Edgar for a very long time, not until Davidson came to my room last night. He asked me how I was doing and if I needed anything. Then when I told him everything was fine, he asked if I would come with him. He said he had something special he wanted to tell me. He has always been so polite that, of course, I said yes and thought we would go to the dining room. But he took me outside."

"Outside? You mean, outside the building?"

"Yes, to that nice garden you and Ellington have talked so much about. Most of it is a blur to me, but I do see the colors and it sounds lovely. We walked out there and, Sam, I could see it all very clearly. Something about that blue light helped my sight. I don't know what it was, but I could see…and it was so beautiful, just as you had said. I could hear a little waterfall and feel a cool breeze. It was wonderful.

"Davidson took me to a bench and we sat there for the longest time, enjoying the garden. Then he told me a story about Lord Mohae. He said it happened long ago. Last Day had come and gone. The world had grown dark, except for Beannachd."

"Beannachd?"

"That's what they call Farside. It's the true name of the Yonders' home."

"But what do you mean that it wasn't dark? I thought what happened on Last Day was on a global scale."

"I don't know, Sam. To be honest, I didn't ask, but I don't believe Davidson would have told me if I had. There was something more important on his mind…something he wanted me to know."

She paused and gathered her thoughts.

"One day Lord Mohae was walking through the foothills on the other side of these mountains. He found a young man lying among some rocks. The man was unconscious and badly hurt, but still alive, though only barely. He had lost a lot of blood. Lord Mohae had him taken to Beannachd and cared for. The young man awoke, but just once, and only long enough to tell him what had happened. He and three others had been searching for survivors and in the darkness had stumbled over a cliff. The other men died in the fall. The young man was terribly injured, but somehow managed to drag himself as far as his strength would allow, trying to find anyone who could help his village. Before again slipping into unconsciousness, he begged Lord Mohae to help them. A few days later the man died.

"Lord Mohae was so moved by the man's bravery and compassion for his people, he drew up a plan to rescue the man's village. When it was finally ready, he sent for his chief commander and instructed him to travel beyond their homeland, cross the mountains, and seek out this village the young man so dearly loved. When he found it, he was to ask its leaders one simple question."

"Would you like some help?" Sam murmured.

Mme. Couteau nodded.

"Karis?" Sam asked.

"Yes."

"And the young man…"

"Edgar." She smiled, not in sadness, but with pride. "He had made it, after all."

"Amazing," Sam said, almost to himself. "Did Davidson tell you what they did with Edgar? With the body, I mean, and I understand if this is too personal."

"It was a beautiful thing, Sam." She smiled. "Davidson said that Lord Mohae instructed the Yonders to carefully wrap the body and place it in a wooden casket. They carried it far into the mountains, into the gap between Chokmah and Sunesis. They laid him in a deep grave which they filled with smooth, round stones. Near the grave were two streams and Lord Mohae had the Yonders dig new channels, diverting the streams so they would come together above the grave before continuing over the stone ledge of a thirty-foot waterfall he had them build."

Sam could see everything being played out in his mind. Then it suddenly dawned on him.

"You mean *our* garden?"

Once again Mme. Couteau's eyes filled with tears. All she could do was nod and smile.

It had been some time since Kenneth had come to escort Mme. Couteau to her room. Sam had watched them leave, filled with both profound sympathy and deep compassion for the lady. Now he understood why this interview had been scheduled last. Mme. Couteau had brought everything together and given it meaning. This was not about the branches or their operations or even about the Plan. He had been listening to the Senior Managers spin their tales of division and ambition, but now he realized the truth. Even with the great distance between Brigos Glen and Beannachd, the two were each a part of the same story.

He stretched out on the couch to consider what all this could mean and fell fast asleep.

CHAPTER 13

THE REPORT

THE INTERVIEWS PROVED to be considerably draining, each more than the one before. But the session with Mme. Couteau easily surpassed them all. Though strangers only days before, Sam had grown quite fond of the lady from Hopewell. His heart broke as he watched her relive those old memories. The thought of her physical condition pained him even more. But the lack of care and attention she had received filled him with anger.

Mme. Couteau had lived with arthritis and poor vision for many years, unable to pay for the medical treatments that could give her considerable relief. No one offered to help. First Brigos sat there with millions in a fund that did nothing but collect interest. Glen Community used all its resources in pursuit of tomorrow, at the cost of today. New Power had no place for those who could not join its march toward a new order.

Fitful dreams made for a restless night, leaving Sam as exhausted as when he first fell asleep. It was 09:15 when he finally awoke, 10:30 before Tunde brought him back to the private dining room. Breakfast awaited him, and for the first time in the last two days,

Sam discovered he was ravenous. He dove into the food. He even had seconds, which Tunde gladly served.

"Can I get you anything else, sir?" Tunde asked, as Sam finished off the last bite.

"No, that's been more than enough, but I will take more coffee. It may be difficult to stay awake today."

Tunde left for the kitchen and in short order, returned with a large urn. He carefully set it on the table, then filled Sam's cup. After making certain Sam had everything he needed, the server turned to leave.

"Tunde."

"Yes, sir?"

"There is one other thing, if you don't mind."

"If it is within my means, I will be glad to see to it."

Sam hesitated. "I know this may sound silly, but can you do something about the noise?"

"The noise, sir?"

"Yes. It's coming from the air conditioning over there." He pointed to the floor vent in front of the drapes. "I know it doesn't seem like much now, but after a while, it really gets to me and I'd rather not listen to it all day."

"And where is this coming from?"

"Just there." He pointed to the vent again.

Tunde walked over and bent down toward the vent, listening carefully. Then he smiled and nodded.

"Ah, yes. I understand now. It isn't the air conditioning you hear." He stood and drew back the drapes. "It is this."

The walls sparkled as light danced into the room. Behind the drapes was a large picture window and on the other side, water plummeted from a great height, crashing into a small pool. Amazed, Sam stepped up to the window and stared out, looking directly through a waterfall. Beyond he could make out the shapes of trees, flowering plants, and a stream carrying water from the pool toward the nearby forest.

Sam looked up and smiled. Somewhere above him was a peaceful grave. "Edgar," he said softly.

"Sir?"

"Nothing. I was thinking of someone." Sam looked back to the waterfall.

"If the noise will be a problem, perhaps we can move you to a quieter room," Tunde offered.

Sam shook his head. "No, I've changed my mind. I believe this is going to be fine after all."

The morning crept into the afternoon, but the afternoon did not seem to move at all. For three long hours Sam worked on the report, or tried to. Nothing was coming together. All he had to show for his efforts was a single paragraph...and not a very good one at that.

He had decided to forego lunch—despite Tunde's urging that he at least have a salad and perhaps soup—but Sam wanted to waste no time. Yet the harder he worked, the more difficult the task became.

By 12:00 he was frustrated. By 13:00, exasperated. And by 14:00, completely lost. He tried one approach after another. He had collected a great amount of information, but he had no idea what to do with it or what this Lord Mohae might want. His only guide was Davidson's warning for Brigos Glen. He thought about his family and recalled Ellington's vivid description of the suffering and chaos after Last Day. The possibility terrified him.

Are we about to repeat it all? And will it be my fault?

Shortly before 15:30, Sam sat motionless at the desk. He had stared at the sifer for hours and entered nothing. His mind was cluttered. His body ached. He ran stiff fingers through increasingly wild hair, then slumped back into the chair. He stared again at the blank screen and sighed.

"Maybe some tea would help," he suggested to the sifer.

"Couldn't hurt," came the imagined reply.

Moments later the door eased open and footsteps crossed the room.

"Thanks, Tunde," Sam said wearily, still focused on the sifer. "Put it anywhere, will you?"

The cup rattled in its saucer as it touched the table.

"I don't know what to do, Tunde."

"I have an idea."

That was not Tunde. Sam spun in his chair and gaped at the gray-haired man.

"Davidson! What are you doing here?"

"Would you like some help?" Davidson asked. "If so, I have an idea."

"What? Well…" Sam sighed. His frustration dissolved into resignation. "Yeah, I would, in fact. If you have *any* idea, I'm all ears. I've been beating my brains out trying to get this done and so far, nothing."

Davidson nodded, gently.

"Come with me. Let's take a walk." Then as an afterthought, he added, "You can bring your tea if you wish."

Sam did wish. He grabbed the cup and followed Davidson out of the room.

They walked down the corridor back to the spiral passageway that would return them up to the dining hall, but Davidson continued on. Farther down was a plain, metal door. Sam followed him into a narrow, empty room. On the opposite wall stood another door. Davidson opened it. Immediately Sam was blinded by a rush of light. Hand above his brow, he carefully crossed the threshold.

With each step, he could see more clearly. A breeze caressed his face. Water splashed into a pool.

We're outside!

For several minutes, neither said a word. Sam wandered over to the waterfall and felt the cool spray. He gazed at brightly colored flowers hugging one side of a stream and deep green reeds skirting the other. He dared to touch them, thrilled to find they were real. Everything was so incredibly beautiful, many times more than it all appeared from the dining hall. He looked over the top of the waterfall, searching for the glass wall near "our table." As he stepped back for a better angle, Davidson called him.

"Come, let's talk."

Davidson led him to a courtyard. A short wall of tightly fitted stones surrounded a lush grass lawn. Nearest Heis, dense ivy traveled up wooden trellises to an arched arbor. Vines and flowers intertwined, providing shade from the bright light. Underneath, two chairs faced each other, with a small table in between. Davidson motioned for Sam to sit and then took the remaining chair.

"I understand you are having a difficult time with the report."

Sam grinned. "I would ask how you know that, but you probably wouldn't tell me." Sam waited, but Davidson made no comment. "Well, yes," Sam admitted. He placed his cup on the table. "I am having a difficult time...a *very* difficult time, actually."

"What do you think is the problem?"

"Thoughts, images, too much data...some of it, all of it...I don't know. I start to write, but there's so much to deal with. And when I read back over it, it's terrible. None of it is good enough."

"Why do you say that, Sam? You've prepared reports before."

"But not like this."

"What's different?"

"You know what's different!" Sam exclaimed. "Everything. It's all different. There's a lot riding on this. It's got to be perfect. People could lose…" Sam could feel his emotions getting the better of him. He stopped and regained his composure. "I want to do this right."

Davidson silently studied the young Brigon. In contrast to the storm raging inside Sam, he seemed perfectly at ease.

Sam nervously looked away. *Should I be talking?* He leaned slightly forward, searching for something…anything…but nothing came to mind.

After a few minutes, Davidson's gaze briefly left Sam as he glanced at the cup on the table.

"Would you like more tea?"

"What?" Sam asked in surprise. "Tea? Uh, no. No, thank you."

"Was it satisfactory?"

"Sure, it was fine."

"Would you say it was the best tea you've ever had?"

"Well, uh, no. It was fine, a little bitter perhaps… Listen, I don't mean to offend you." Sam spoke rapidly, trying to change the subject. "I thought we were talking about the report. I should probably get back to it. There's so much to do and Lord Mohae…"

"So the tea was not perfect?" Davidson interrupted.

"No!" Sam said emphatically. "It was delightful, very good, but not the best I've ever had and certainly not perfect, but it did its job. Okay? I don't see what this has to do with anything right now."

Then suddenly Sam's eyes brightened. His shoulders relaxed. It had to do with *everything* right now. The report was like the tea. It did not have to be perfect. It only had to do its job. Sam eased back into his chair. Embarrassed, he looked away.

"Sam," Davidson said gently, "why do you think you were chosen for this assignment?"

Sam shrugged. "I've wondered that, myself. I don't know, really. I guess because I've had a lot of experience with reports."

"There are many others who have much more experience writing reports, Sam. You've been with the Company now fifteen years. That's admirable, but there are also many more people with much more time. Some, like Mr. Ellington and Mr. Mettenger, have worked in the system longer than you've been alive. But they weren't asked to write the report. No one else in Brigos Glen was asked to write the report. Only you. Out of hundreds and hundreds of people, *you* were the one chosen. Why? Do you know?"

Sam's lips tightened. He grimaced as he considered Davidson's question. Then he shook his head. "I *have* thought about this," he said hesitantly, "and to be honest, I have no idea. My first reaction was that there had to be a mistake. Ellington has been very encouraging and said he didn't believe that was the case, but after today…"

"There's been no error of any kind, Sam," Davidson said confidently. "You, and only you, were chosen for this. The reason will become clearer in time. But understand there are no expectations that you will write the perfect report, nor are there any demands that you do so. There is only one thing that is expected, and that is—at the appointed time, a report be sent to Lord Mohae from *you*."

"But how do I begin? What do I say?" Sam rubbed his face, then looked directly at his host. "I get so confused that I can't think of anything to write, and then I worry…"

"Don't." Davidson's warm eyes embraced Sam. "Your desire means more than you can possibly imagine, and it has not gone unnoticed."

"Thanks," Sam replied. "But I still need some direction, something to get me started." He paused. "I would like some help… if you're willing."

Davidson beamed. "I am willing, and I have an idea."

Davidson returned Sam to the private dining room and left him to his report. They had been outside a long time, and Tunde soon arrived with dinner. Twice Sam begged off so he could continue working. By the third time, Tunde had become more insistent.

"If I can have just one more hour," Sam bargained, "I'll gladly eat every bite of whatever you desire to bring me."

That satisfied the server. He returned promptly on the hour, and refused to leave until Sam had made good on his promise.

For the next several hours, Sam worked at a feverish pace. He took the folders he had received from Williams and emptied them onto the dining table. Looking through the piles, he selected several documents, which he arranged in neat stacks. He studied his notes, especially those from his session with Mme. Couteau. He reviewed the video recordings, which the sifer—he happily discovered—had automatically made of each interview session. Sufficiently refreshing his memory, he sat at the desk and prepared an outline for the report. So much time had been lost he did not want to waste another second, and now, at last, he knew exactly what he wanted to do. He typed as fast as he could, constantly checking the accuracy of the data. Soon the report took shape.

At 20:11 he slumped back into his chair—eyes closed, arms dangling on either side, legs stretched out under the desk. Sam took a deep breath and let out a long, satisfied sigh. The report was finished. After all the interviews and frustration…after all the anxiety and self-doubt…after all the hard work…the report was finally finished.

Sam heard the door open, but was too tired to move.

"Sir?" Tunde murmured.

"Yes," Sam replied, without moving a muscle.

"Are you all right, sir?"

"Oh, yes." Sam grinned. "I am quite all right."

"The report is completed, then?"

Sam came alert and faced the server. "Indeed it is, my friend. Completed, proofed, and ready to go."

"I had been hoping. So it is an even better time to give you this."

One hand had been behind his back. Now he carefully brought it around to reveal a plate displaying an enormous slice of something white and fluffy.

"What is that?"

"It has many names and is made in many ways. We call it Lakhayea, something to be shared among friends. Five layers soaked in coconut cream, vanilla bean icing, with nutmeg sprinkled on top. It is rich. I recommend you have it with espresso."

"Sounds great." Sam laughed. "Does it have any calories?"

"It would be best not to think about that," Tunde said with a broad smile.

Another server entered the room, carrying a tray with a silver pitcher and a small cup. Tunde cleared a space on the table, where the server set the tray. As he left, Tunde poured espresso into the cup and handed it to Sam.

"You keep that one," Sam objected. "I'll take mine in this," and handed him his teacup from the afternoon.

"No, sir, this is for you…to celebrate the report."

Sam smirked, playfully. "Tunde, I thought you said this was for friends. Can't be friends by yourself. Please join me."

"But, sir…"

"It would mean a lot to me if you would."

Tunde grinned. "Certainly, sir, if that is what you truly wish."

"It is."

Tunde filled Sam's cup with hot espresso, then cut the cake into two equal slices. Sam used his saucer, letting Tunde have the plate. He held his cup high in the air.

"To the report and to friendship," Sam toasted.

"Yes, sir…to the report and to friendship."

Sam took a bite of the cake which, as he later told Ellington, had to be the sweetest thing he had ever put in his mouth. Immediately, he followed it with espresso and was very thankful for the strong flavor. Together, they formed a perfect blend.

"This is wonderful, Tunde."

"Thank you, sir. I made it myself. I'm glad you like it, and I'm glad you were able to finish the report."

"Me, too. But you can thank Davidson for that."

"Why is that, sir?" Tunde took another bite of his cake.

"He helped me. Told me what I needed to hear. If it weren't for him, I don't think I would've written a single page."

"If you do not mind my asking, sir, what was it he told you?"

Sam smiled. "'Write as though you are writing for yourself.' That was it. Simple. I'd been trying so hard to write something that would please others, I could not focus on what I thought was important. So, I wrote the report I would have wanted to read."

"That was very clever," Tunde said, with a slight grin.

"Thank you."

Sam spun around and activated the sifer. The holographic screen appeared, displaying the completed report. In the bottom right corner of the image was a single word—Send. Sam sighed, then looked at the tiny purple square that appeared on the sifer.

"Now all that's left is to get this to Lord Mohae…wherever he is."

As he pressed the virtual button, Tunde said softly, "He is here."

CHAPTER 14

BREAKFAST WITH FRIENDS

MORNING CAME QUICKLY. Sam could not remember the last time he felt so refreshed and rested. The automated alarm sounded as usual, but he did not mind. He even thanked the nice lady for waking him, then bounded out of bed. He took a hot shower, feeling even more relaxed, and as he toweled off, the pleasant recorded voice reported the day's schedule.

"The time is 06:00. Breakfast will be served until 08:00. You may return to the dining hall if you wish. No meetings are slated for the morning. At 11:30 in the private dining room, you, Mr. Ellington, and Mme. Couteau will have lunch with Lord Mohae. The final general session for all attendees will begin at 15:00 in Conference Room Twelve. Dinner will be served during the regular hours."

Sam stirred.

"What? Did you say…lunch with Lord Mohae?"

"Would you like me to repeat the schedule?"

"Oh right, you're not a person. Yes, repeat the schedule," he said, overemphasizing the words as he gave the command.

Sam listened carefully and this time he was certain. He would be having lunch with Lord Mohae. He sat on the edge of the bed and looked at the sifer, left on the dresser the night before. The work of the device had been about the report. Since the report was meant for Lord Mohae, the sifer had come to symbolize him. Now Sam stared at it as though it were Lord Mohae himself.

"This should be interesting. We'll finally meet at last. I hope you like the report."

Sam knew exactly where he wanted to be this morning. The news of lunch with Lord Mohae was certain to be the topic of conversation at breakfast. Sam hurried into the dining hall. The glass wall shone with the new day's manufactured light and the world outside was as beautiful as ever. He quickly made his way to "our table," where Ellington and Mme. Couteau were already waiting.

"If it isn't our long-lost Mr. Mitchell," Ellington said with a laugh. "Welcome back, my boy."

"Thanks. It's good to be back," Sam replied, just as cheery.

"And how did everything go yesterday? Well, I hope."

"Actually, most of the day was a bust."

"But the report...?" asked Mme. Couteau.

"Prepared and sent. Yes, ma'am. Late last night. Davidson gave me an idea of how to go about it and after that, everything went pretty fast."

"Davidson?" Ellington asked, surprised.

"Yeah, he's pretty helpful when he wants to be." Sam smiled at Mme. Couteau, but she made no reply. Her glazed eyes wandered about in Sam's general direction. "Are you all right, ma'am?"

"Oh my, yes," she replied heartily. "Couldn't be better."

"Hmmf." Ellington snorted. "She's having trouble with her vision."

"Vision?" Sam asked, warily.

"Yes, quite a bit of trouble today," Ellington replied.

"It isn't as bad as he makes out," she insisted.

"I found you sitting at the wrong table."

Mme. Couteau made no reply.

Sam broke in. "Well, we certainly couldn't have that. I mean, this is *our* table after all." Mme. Couteau smiled again. "So what have the two of you been up to in my absence? I'm sure it wasn't as fun as interviewing Senior Managers and writing lengthy reports, but then not everyone can have such a good time."

Ellington was the first to answer. "Not much, really. Kenneth showed me around Heis yesterday morning, and we had a nice chat after lunch. He's a Yonder, of course, which was no surprise, but he's quite knowledgeable about Brigos Glen. They must have an extensive history of the village over there in Beannachd. That's what they call Farside."

Sam nodded politely, not letting on he already knew.

"We talked about a lot of things, especially the day Karis came. He really enjoyed that part. He thought it was hilarious that we have our Marturia celebration. You know, I think he must have known Karis."

"Really?" Sam replied. "That was a long time ago. He doesn't look old enough."

"Yeah, I know, but I get the feeling they don't age like we do. He does look young...maybe older than you...but young to me. He seems to have been around for a while."

"I get the same feeling about Davidson," Mme. Couteau said.

"Davidson?" Sam asked, pretending to know nothing of her meeting.

"Oh, I've already told Ellington. You don't have to keep going on as if you don't know." She laughed. "I may not be able to see you very well, but I can hear the struggle in your voice."

"Thank goodness. I'm not very good at keeping secrets anyway."

Ellington slapped him on the back. "No, you're not, but it has been quite entertaining to see you try."

Before Sam could make a defense, the servers arrived, and his attention immediately diverted to the ample breakfast laid out before him. The others must have been quite hungry, as well. Little conversation passed among them as they enjoyed their morning meal. It was some time before Sam noticed that Mettenger had not joined them.

"Where's…?" he tried to ask. A mouthful of food successfully prevented him from completing his question, so he pointed with his fork to an empty chair.

"Otto?" Ellington answered. "Good question."

"What do you mean?" Sam mumbled, his mouth still full.

"Haven't seen him. No one has. Not since his interview with you. Madhu checked on him and said he was fine. Just wanted to be alone. Didn't come to dinner either, and then stayed in his room."

Sam could not hide his concern. He took a deep breath and glanced out the window.

"It had nothing to do with you," Ellington quickly added.

"I'm not so sure."

Sam did feel responsible. He remembered how everything had played out during the brief interview. He could still see Mettenger's shock and indignant anger as the interview came to an end. Mettenger certainly was not the man Sam had once thought him to be, and he had not expected such an emotional reaction.

"Sam," Ellington said, in a fatherly tone, "I don't know what happened in the interview or what may have been said, but Otto's a big boy. He can take it. I'm sure he wanted to be by himself to think things over. And trust me, he's got a lot to think over."

Sam nodded. He knew Ellington was right. Sam continued to see Mettenger as a powerful Senior Manager and himself as just an employee—perhaps a short-term employee after the interview, but still, just an employee. In the end, he believed Mettenger would have nothing to be concerned about, being more than capable of defending himself from anything Sam had written in the report.

"Maybe he'll turn up for lunch," Ellington said.

"Lunch," Sam said with a start. "Hey, did you get…"

"Yes," Ellington interrupted.

"Me, too," Mme. Couteau added. "Sam, do you have any idea why Lord Mohae would want to meet with *us*?"

"No. I was hoping one of you might."

"Not a clue there," Ellington said, with a shake of his head. "We were discussing that very thing when you arrived. This morning's schedule announcement was the first we'd heard of it."

"I wonder if it's about the report," Sam said.

"I don't see how it could be. Neither of us have any idea what it might contain."

"Perhaps it has something to do with the Senior Managers," Mme. Couteau suggested. "None of them were invited."

"I don't think so," Sam replied. "The two of you know a lot, I'm sure, but I don't, not really, and what I do know went into the report. If that were the reason, I wouldn't be needed at all."

"Then it will have to remain a mystery until lunch, I'm afraid," Ellington concluded. He looked around the empty dining hall. "Of course, I suppose the others could be having breakfast with him and talking about *us*."

After breakfast, Mme. Couteau, with considerable assistance from Ellington, returned to her room for a rest. Sam decided to stay a bit longer. After ordering scones and tea, he gazed outside, hoping to find Davidson walking about the garden. He would somehow get his attention and signal that he would join him. But either Davidson was not there or he could not see him.

Sam sat there for almost half an hour. He was about to leave when Mettenger walked into the dining hall. He looked haggard, as though he had not slept in several days. Sam instantly returned to staring out the huge window, sitting very still in the hope that Mettenger would not notice him. But it was not long before he heard footsteps coming his way.

"Mind if I join you?"

Sam turned around. Mettenger looked even worse up close.

"Uh, no. No, sir. Please do."

The Senior Manager sat down heavily. Sam could not help feeling sorry for him.

"Have you had any breakfast?" Sam asked.

"No. I haven't eaten for a while. Not much of an appetite."

"Why don't we get you something? You look like you could use it."

Mettenger smiled. "In a minute, perhaps. But there's something I need to do first. Something I need to get off my chest."

Great. Here it comes, Sam thought. He braced for another tirade.

"I..." Mettenger paused. He frowned and looked very sternly at Sam. "I would like to apologize."

"Apologize?" Sam asked, surprised.

"Yes, apologize...for my behavior at the interview. It was completely inappropriate and I had absolutely no right to treat you that way. I should not treat anyone that way, but certainly not you."

"It's OK, really."

"No, it isn't. I was late for the interview and should not have been. I don't pretend to understand what all of this has been about or what it could be for, but it's obvious this is very important or Lord Mohae would not have sent for us. You were given an assignment and I certainly did not make it easy for you. And for that, I'm sorry."

"Thank you, sir, but it really isn't necessary."

"It is to me, Sam. What you said, even the questions you asked... they were things I needed to hear. They got me thinking about Glen Community, how I've managed..." he peered far beyond Sam and the dining hall, "...and a number of things I heard years ago from a dear friend, but had forgotten." He glanced at the table. "Ellington's a good man."

"Yes, he is." Sam relaxed. "And thank you, again. I do appreciate that. I'm willing to move on, if you would like to."

"Nothing better. That would make me very glad. I feel a burden has been lifted."

Sam thought for a moment and frowned. "You do realize," he said cautiously, "the report was finished and submitted yesterday. I can't change anything now."

"Yes, I understand and would not want you to. Whatever you put in the report, I'll own up to. No, that's not why I've come to you. I hope you will believe me when I say that."

Sam nodded. "I do."

"Good! Then if you don't mind, I'd like to order breakfast. I'm starved."

It was almost 08:00 when Mettenger placed his order, but the servers took no notice of the time. They promptly brought everything he requested—the Grand Brigon omelet with four eggs, a stack of pancakes dripping with warm syrup, sausage links, back bacon, and hash browns, with a side of spiced apples.

For the next two hours they talked about the village and especially the operations of Glen Community. Sam shared a few ideas for improving the protocol to determine which developments received priority treatment. Mettenger listened with great interest, even offering to continue the discussion upon their return home.

Afterward, Mettenger retired to his room for what he jokingly described as "a ridiculously long nap." He looked relieved, even happy, though he admitted to having reservations about the session with Lord Mohae later in the day.

"Doesn't matter," he told Sam. "We will move forward and whatever happens, happens. I haven't heard from him in a long time, but that's probably my own fault. I trust Lord Mohae."

Sam remained in the dining hall. He thought about returning to his room until lunch, but there was nothing for him to do there except sit and wait. So he spent the rest of the morning sipping wonderful tea, nibbling on a scone or two, and watching the streams flow together.

At 11:15 Ellington and Mme. Couteau rejoined Sam in the dining hall. The two had no idea where they would be having lunch, but their messages directed them to the dining hall for their escort. As they waited, Sam told them of his second breakfast with Mettenger. Ellington was delighted and had Sam describe in detail everything he could remember. Mme. Couteau was also glad that "he has at last come to his senses," as she declared the situation.

They decided to wait at "our table" for the escort, and it was clear Mme. Couteau's sight had grown worse. She bumped into a chair, even with Ellington guiding her, and was able to take her seat only by feeling her way down. Sam tried to get her to say something to Kenneth in the hope there might be something for her at Heis, but she would not hear of it.

"Sam, you're such a dear, but we have to accept our age. I've lived a very long time and, yes, I have my aches and pains, but this is simply a part of life."

Her reaction did not satisfy Ellington, who insisted he would not go further into his twilight years without a fight. He had just launched into a monologue on the quality of life and the value of living each and every day—which Sam had heard often over the last five years—when three servers approached the table.

"Tunde!" Sam exclaimed as soon as he saw them. "I was hoping to see you again. Will you be taking us to the private dining room?"

"Yes, sir," Tunde replied, with a broad smile. "Today I will also have Santos and Mikhail to assist me." The two men immediately went to Mme. Couteau and helped her from her chair. "Madame, would you like a wheelchair? They are very comfortable."

"I will walk," she said stubbornly.

Tunde led them along the same path he had originally taken Sam. Through the door at the wall with the mirror, along the spiral passageway to the lower level, down to the end of the corridor, and finally into the beautiful private dining room where Sam had spent so many hours the last two days. Everything remained exactly as before, except the dining table now had place settings for four. Santos and Mikhail assisted Mme. Couteau to one of the chairs and, upon making her comfortable, exited the room.

"Lord Mohae has asked that we delay lunch to allow him time to speak with you first. If you should need anything in the meantime, I will be glad to bring it."

"Could I have some tea?" Mme. Couteau asked. "Iced tea, if you have it."

"Yes, Madame. We will have that to you shortly. Mr. Ellington? Mr. Mitchell?"

"No, thanks," Sam said.

"Nothing for me, either," Ellington added.

"Lord Mohae will join you momentarily." Tunde turned and left the three to themselves.

Ellington looked about the room, impressed. "And there I was, worried you were in a dungeon, beating out that report." He grinned. "You really had it bad here. How did you survive all this?"

"I toughed it out," Sam replied. "You know, you can joke all you want, but I didn't get a chance to enjoy this room. A lot of work was going on in here. It was very hard and…"

"Excuse me, Mr. Mitchell," interrupted Tunde, who had slipped back in and stood in the doorway.

"Yes?"

"After dinner, would you and your friends care for more dessert and espresso as you had yesterday?"

Sam nodded.

"Very good, sir."

As Tunde left, Sam glanced at Ellington, who was laughing softly.

"OK," Sam conceded, "except for that."

They waited in the room for almost twenty minutes. Ellington continued his inspection of the room, while Sam described every detail to Mme. Couteau. He drew back the drapes and revealed the beautiful waterfall. Ellington watched in amazement, expressing surprise that it was the same one they could see from the dining room. Though Mme. Couteau's weakened sight provided only a blurred image, she delighted in hearing the water splashing outside.

"I can see it all in my mind," she assured her friends. "And it is breathtaking!"

Sam and Ellington eventually took their seats, one on either side of Mme. Couteau. Moments later, the door opened and a man entered. Sam and Ellington had been looking out the window and their sight had not adjusted to the dimmer light of the room. Eyes widened with anticipation, but they still could not make out who he was.

"Tunde?" Sam asked, hesitantly.

"No, Sam. It's me. It's time for our lunch."

As Ellington squinted to get a clearer look, Mme. Couteau leaned toward Sam.

"I don't understand," she whispered. "Why is Davidson here?"

CHAPTER 15

LORD MOHAE

DAVIDSON TOOK HIS seat at the dining table. Sam and Ellington just looked on, too stunned for words. Had it not been for Mme. Couteau, they might not have spoken at all. Impatient that no one was answering her questions, she took matters into her own hands.

"Davidson," she said directly to the blurry shadow. "That is you, isn't it?"

"Yes, Madame. Good morning, or what is left of it." His tone was friendly and comforting.

"I don't understand. I thought we were to have lunch with Lord Mohae."

"That is correct."

"When will he be arriving?"

"But he is here, Madame."

Mme. Couteau let out an exasperated sigh. "I'm sorry, but my eyesight has been troubling me the last two days and I can't see very well. Is he going to speak or will someone at least point me in the right direction?"

"Davidson's the only one in the room," Sam whispered to her.

"But…"

"Madame," Davidson interrupted, "I am Lord Mohae."

Mme. Couteau's mouth fell open, but no words followed.

Sam shook his head. "But how can that be? You told us your name is Davidson. I've heard Kenneth and Madhu call you that."

"Lord Mohae is more of a description, Sam. It is how the Brigons have known me, but it is not my name."

"So Davidson is your name and 'Lord Mohae' is just a title," Sam replied, still confused.

"Yes and no. Davidson is a name I enjoy and what I have chosen to be called by each of you and the Senior Managers. My true name is very complex and you would not be able to pronounce it.

"But it would be wrong to view Lord Mohae as *just* a title. It is one of deep respect and honor given to me by the Yonders, and is very rich in meaning and purpose. But please, call me Davidson."

"You said it was given to you by the Yonders?" Ellington broke in.

"Yes."

"So, you're not a Yonder?" he asked, rather excited.

"No," Davidson calmly replied.

"I knew it!" Ellington exclaimed. "You don't look much like Kenneth and the others." He turned to Sam. "I told you he was different. Said it from the start."

"Yes, you did." Sam nodded, then looked back to Davidson. "Where are you from, if you don't mind my asking?"

"It isn't that I mind your asking," he replied patiently, "but it is not possible for you to understand at this time. All you truly know is Brigos Glen and, to be honest, not much of that. Your world has always been subject to the darkness. Trust me that you simply could not understand." He gestured to everyone in the room. "None of you could."

"Will we ever understand?"

"Yes, when the sun returns."

Sam grimaced. He preferred outright answers rather than these vague responses. He especially did not like being told something was beyond his understanding. He had always been smart enough to figure out anything he set his mind to. This was not satisfactory.

"When the sun returns?" Sam echoed the words, but in a manner that showed his impatience. "How do we know if the sun will ever return? I've never seen it. Almost no one in Brigos Glen has ever seen it. How can you be so sure *anyone* will ever see it again?"

"Because I will provide the way."

Sam was stunned by Davidson's simple response and found himself at a loss for words.

Davidson continued. "I will do so at a time that I, and I alone, will choose. It is not the correct time now. Everything is not yet right, but when it is, you will be amazed." He smiled warmly, and Sam's irritation faded. "As for now, I want you to get ready for that day. It is coming. It is most assuredly coming, and it will be like nothing you or anyone else has ever seen before."

Sam was not sure why, but he believed him. He believed every word of it. Sam glanced at Ellington, who sat there smiling and nodding. Then a thought occurred to him.

"How many Lord Mohaes have there been?"

"One, and one only."

"You wrote the Plan?"

"Yes."

"But that was seventy years ago," Ellington interrupted. "You don't look even close to that now. No offense, but how could you have been the one who wrote the Plan?"

"Appearances can be deceptive. You know that. My age is not important, but I am much older than you realize." He leaned back in his chair and glanced at his three guests. "We have more to discuss, but first we should go ahead and eat. The time for the session will be here soon."

As he finished speaking, Tunde, Santos, and Mikhail appeared carrying trays loaded with food. They placed them on the table and poured whatever drink was chosen. Sam asked for especially strong tea. He felt he needed it, given the most recent events of the day. After everyone had been fully served, Tunde bowed to Davidson and again to Mme. Couteau, Ellington, and Sam. Then the servers silently left them to their meal.

Sam said little during lunch. There were so many things he wanted to know, but dared not ask, at least not yet. Davidson had specially set this time aside just for them, so Sam would wait until he could be alone with his host. In the meantime, he ate the fine food before him and politely listened to the friendly conversation at the table.

Davidson, for his part, seemed very interested in Mme. Couteau's health. He particularly asked about her vision and the pain in her hip. She gave the same answers Sam and Ellington had heard before and, as with them, failed to convince Davidson that she was "just fine."

"It concerns me that these were not corrected," Davidson said. "The technology has been in Brigos Glen for a long time."

"That is true," Mme. Couteau sighed. "But the cost of such care is prohibitive. I can't afford the surgeries on my modest income, and there certainly isn't enough in my savings."

"Money is not the issue," Davidson said sadly.

"True enough," Ellington agreed. "The Elder Council should have taken care of this. It's their responsibility to provide for everyone, especially good people like Mme. Couteau here."

Davidson shook his head.

"You don't agree that something should be done for people like Mme. Couteau?" Sam asked, surprised. "They need the help more than most."

"I do not agree that it is the responsibility of the Council."

"Who then?"

"Neighbors. The people who live around Mme. Couteau and see her each day. Those who should care about others. *All* the people of Brigos Glen. Mr. Ellington. You." Davidson paused. "Before you met Mme. Couteau, did you seek to meet her needs?"

"Well, no," Sam replied, defensively. "But I didn't know her then."

"But there are others, many others, even in the complex where you live. Have you checked on them, learned what needs they may have, or made any effort to help them?" Davidson asked gently.

Sam did not know what to say, but Davidson gave him no time to answer.

"It is easy to expect someone else to do what should be done, to turn away from those who need help—all the while with the conviction that one must live his own life, follow her own dream."

"You don't agree, I take it."

"Not at the expense of others, Sam. Life is not about what you wish for, it's about what you do. Fulfillment is not found in caring for oneself, but in using oneself to care for others."

"You make us sound selfish," Sam objected.

"Some are," Davidson said firmly. "Some aren't. Take Mr. Ellington here." Ellington's eyes lifted. "He could have moved up the corporate ladder years ago. And he could have retired altogether. But he stayed—not for any gain to himself, but for the benefit of those around him, and regardless of where they lived or worked."

"Thank you, sir," Ellington said, embarrassed. "But I'm not all that. There have been times I could have done more, as well. I've made plenty of mistakes along the way."

"Yes, but you have tried." Davidson looked at the humble man. "That means a great deal." He glanced back at Sam. "You have learned much from him."

Sam's not-so-stellar reviews over the few years flashed before his eyes. He could hear the coarse reactions of his superiors, feel the weight of their discouragement. Davidson seemed supportive, giving no indication of either criticism or condemnation.

"And you're okay with that?" Sam asked, suspiciously.

"Very. In fact, I expect it."

"Yeah…well, that's fine here, but Carrington, my supe…"

"He's not a part of the Company," Davidson interrupted.

"No, see you're confused," Sam corrected. "He's been at Glen Community for more than twenty years."

"Mr. Mitchell!"

The words burst from Davidson. Sam froze, not daring to say another word.

"He is an employee of Glen Community. He has walked those halls a long time. But…he is *not* involved in the work of the Company, and never has been."

Nothing about this made any sense. Sam had known Carrington for the last five years. He might not be friendly…ever. He might be more interested in clocking his time and getting a paycheck than in anyone who worked under him, or even in the work of Glen Community, for that matter. But he had a position there. He even had a service pin.

"There is more to the Company," Davidson continued, "than these branches, and there is more to being involved in the Company than merely being a branch employee. It is very important that you understand this. Employment has nothing to do with it. There are people scattered all about Brigos Glen who have never worked a day in their lives for any of the branches, and yet they are most definitely involved in the work of the Company."

This did not help Sam at all. He wanted to understand but was now more confused than ever. He glanced at Ellington and Mme. Couteau. Neither offered any help. He looked again at Davidson.

"All right. If it has nothing to do with the branches…if all the devotion they've demanded and that we've given all these years doesn't add up to anything…then what's it all about? What does it mean to be involved in the Company? And for that matter, who is the Company then?"

Sam waited. All this about the Company obviously held great importance for Davidson, but Sam could not put the pieces of the puzzle together. And Davidson was in no hurry to provide him a clue, much less an answer. He thoughtfully looked at Sam. Finally, he stood.

"Come. The hour has arrived."

By the time Sam walked into Twelve, the Senior Managers had already arrived and were seated. Unlike their prior meetings, none of them sat together. They appeared to have intentionally avoided it, not wanting even the appearance they might know each other. They sat on different rows—Stürn on the second, Williams at the very back, and Mettenger in between—with no one directly behind another. Santos and Mikhail assisted Mme. Couteau to a seat on the front row, the opposite side from Stürn. Ellington sat next to her, with Sam immediately behind, as he had done before.

The room held an uneasy silence. Sam wanted to see if Ellington had gleaned any more out of that last conversation with Davidson than he had, but that would have to wait. There had been no opportunity on the way and now was not the time, especially for a private discussion. Every sound seemed so amplified he feared even his heart could be heard.

He glanced around the room. Stürn sat like a statue, staring straight ahead and stoic as ever. Williams had an open folder across his lap and intently studied whatever documents it held. He appeared upset, but then, he always seemed that way. And last, there was Mettenger. No smiles this time. He stared down into loosely clasped hands. Sam searched the tired, drawn face. Concern intertwined with tenderness...a new look for the old Senior Manager.

At 15:00 precisely, a door opened. Kenneth and Madhu entered and proceeded to their usual places in front. Sam spotted the wooden lectern, all alone in the middle of the stage. His heart beat faster. He glanced again at Stürn, Williams, and Mettenger.

Do they have any idea?

"Welcome," Kenneth said. "This session will be our final time together in Twelve as this conference is coming to a close. We would like to thank each of you for your attendance and participation these few days. I hope your stay at Heis has been pleasant and especially that it will prove productive for you after your return to Brigos Glen. While you are still with us, if we can be of service, please do not hesitate to let us know."

Madhu stepped forward.

"Lord Mohae will be joining us in a moment. As each of you are well aware, this is a most extraordinary event. Lord Mohae does not make appearances. However, he has a special message regarding Brigos Glen, and rather than sending it through the usual means, he has chosen to speak directly. *No* questions or comments will be allowed during this time."

Was that a warning? Sam glanced at the Senior Managers and was surprised to find Williams nodding his acceptance. Mettenger sat quietly, remaining much as before.

But Stürn's body tensed. Her jaws locked. Her eyes narrowed as she glared at the messenger.

"This evening," Madhu continued, "Lord Mohae will meet with each of you. I cannot give you a specific time, as that is at his sole discretion, so please make sure you are available. We will come for you as Lord Mohae directs."

This latest news must have eased Stürn as she seemed somewhat calmer than moments before. Williams continued his nodding, but now Mettenger had taken on the countenance of one who had received the appointment for his own execution. Sadness appeared to fill him, and he slumped into his seat. Sam once again felt sorry for his Senior Manager.

I wonder what's in store for him.

The lights dimmed and a single blue light shone down on the lectern. Madhu made a slight nod to Kenneth and they separated— Madhu to the right of the stage, Kenneth to the left. They turned in unison toward the lectern and bowed.

Sam stood with the same solemnity and bowed toward the stage. At any other time, he would have thought such actions overly dramatic and nothing he would ever consider doing. But now it all seemed right and natural. He wanted to do this, felt compelled to do it. After a moment, Sam lifted his head and noticed everyone else doing the same.

The scene had changed.

Beyond the blue light, well behind the lectern, stood a solitary, dark figure. At first it did not move. Anticipation filled the room. Then the figure stepped out of the shadow and into the blue light that quickly brightened. Within seconds, the figure came into sharp focus, and Davidson stood before them.

Stürn gasped. Williams dropped his folder, sending a shower of graphs and charts across the floor. Mettenger sighed.

"Be seated," Davidson said. His voice echoed throughout the room.

Sam glanced at Williams. For a moment, he continued to stand, obviously stunned and in a great struggle. Sam guessed there must be a thousand questions he desperately wanted to ask, perhaps even a few objections to raise. But in the end, Williams reluctantly returned to his seat and remained silent.

Davidson looked about the room, pausing on each person. He offered no smiles or friendly nods. Neither was there any anger or sternness in his face, only utter and absolute seriousness. He commanded their full attention.

"I summoned you to Heis." He paused, as if allowing each word to sink deeply into their understanding. "I summoned you to Heis just as I summoned the Brigons long ago, but they refused. Instead, they chose to live in a darkness of their own design—and to their own destruction."

His words were startling. They were not carried by emotion. They did not fill the room as a shout of condemnation. They simply came as undeniable fact, and sadness filled his voice.

"Years ago when the clouds came and you could no longer find the sun, a man came to me. He had traveled a great distance and through many dangers. Those who set out with him had died, and he was alone. But he valiantly continued, even beyond Chokmah and Sunesis. I found him and took him to Beannachd. His last words in this world were a plea to help the people of Brigos Glen, the people he had grown to love."

Mme. Couteau turned around toward Sam and, with glistening eyes, smiled. Though he knew she could not see him, Sam smiled back and without thinking, patted his chest. Somehow she understood and smiled even more.

"It was then," Davidson continued, "that I sent Karis. The Brigons were a miserable people, barely surviving. Yet pride already had a firm hold in your land. Even as they accepted help, they grumbled and murmured with discontent. But help was provided, nonetheless. The Yonders came and worked diligently. Some Brigons eventually joined them and together they worked side by side. Those were your heroes, though no one recognized them.

"Brighten Power Authority extended its operations from beyond the mountains and light returned to Brigos Glen. But in time, that was no longer enough. The Brigons wanted more. They wanted to control the power that was not theirs. They wanted the Authority. The Plan had been provided to your Elders, but few bothered to read it, and many of those ignored its instructions. Olasom came and established a place among you, to teach you how to spread the light throughout the valley. But your leaders found no profit in it."

Sam sat motionless. Davidson spoke of things he had never heard. This was not what he had been taught in school as a child or in the many training classes he suffered through as an adult. This was not the approved history—Brigons and Yonders happily working together so Brigos Glen could pull itself up and once again be an independent village. Everything had always sounded so positive.

"Senior Managers!" A noticeable sternness rose in Davidson's voice. "What have you become? You have set about creating your own kingdoms. New Power, Glen Community. Yes, even First Brigos. I had nothing to do with these. I established *one* branch... *one* to serve...*one* to make certain everyone had access to the light. But you have allowed division to grow and thrive. You look with disdain upon each other, claiming yourself as the only one worthy. Yet each of you has failed."

Davidson carefully eyed the Senior Managers. Then he locked in on only one.

"First Brigos!" Davidson called out.

Williams snapped to attention. He leapt to his feet, ignoring the folder that immediately joined the papers on the floor.

"More than any other, you have devoted yourself to following the commands I laid out in the Plan. You sacrificed greatly as you made every effort to honor and respect the Plan. Over these many years, while others wandered away to follow their own desires, you have stayed true to your calling and to Brighten."

Williams appeared pleased and smugly looked at Mettenger and Stürn.

"*However*," Davidson continued, "you have failed the Company."
The blood drained from Williams's face.

"For all your laborious studies…for all the hours you held your employees accountable for memorizing every passage, every line, of the Plan…you have failed to understand the purpose of my commands—and without understanding their purpose, it is impossible to know how to apply them.

"You have followed, but followed blindly, until all that you now see are rules. You no longer seek the will of Brighten. You refuse to consider the lessons of Olasom. You ignore the messages of QolCom. And in the process, you have enslaved the very people I came to free."

Tears rolled down Williams's cheeks. He had great difficulty holding his head up to look into Davidson's penetrating gaze. This was not the same man everyone had seen the last few days. For the first time, Sam understood that this often belligerent, usually arrogant, and always irritating man did care about his work, and especially about his relationship with Brighten Power Authority.

Then Davidson gently added, "I did not send the light for you to cling to it, but to give it away." Williams nodded and wiped the tears from his face. "Be seated."

As the shaken man returned to his seat, Davidson's focus fell directly on Mettenger. Sam immediately felt a knot in his stomach. After seeing what happened with Williams, he wondered if this poor man would survive at all.

"Glen Community."

Instantly the Senior Manager rose to his feet and to Sam's surprise, Mettenger did not seem afraid. He was certainly not his once jovial self, but he appeared to have more resolve…ready to accept whatever Davidson might cast his way.

"You have helped a great number of people," Davidson said. "I have been very pleased that you did not mire yourself in one place…geographically or mentally. Through your efforts, the system has greatly expanded and more light has been brought into Brigos Glen. But you, too, have failed the Company.

"Just as it is impossible to know how to apply the commands of the Plan without understanding their purpose, so it is also impossible to fulfill that purpose when you no longer know the commands. Glen Community has been the victim of its own obsession, dutifully following the instructions left by Olasom to share the light, but ignoring Brighten and the Plan.

"These commands exist for a reason, and that reason is to further the purpose of the Plan. But in your rush to bring light to where once there was only the darkness, you have not passed down my commands or instructions, leaving your people untrained, unfit, and unprepared."

Mettenger looked down at the floor, his broad shoulders sagged. As Williams had been thoroughly crushed by Davidson's judgment, Mettenger was just as thoroughly ashamed. He sadly nodded with every statement Davidson had made. He continued nodding, though Davidson had stopped speaking. He stood there for some time before Davidson spoke, again in the gentle manner as he had ended with Williams.

"As you have ignored the Plan, so you have ignored me. The distance between us has grown great. It is time to return. Be seated."

Mettenger sat down. Tears welled up, and he buried his face in his hands. Sam looked at Ellington, who also had tears. He reached down and patted Ellington's trembling shoulder. Still watching Mettenger, Ellington nodded his appreciation.

Then something Sam could never have expected occurred. Williams rose from his seat, moved to Mettenger's row, and sat next to him. He put his arm around his fellow Senior Manager, whose face remained hidden in his hands. Williams drew him close and quietly spoke to him. Sam strained to hear but could not catch a single word. The message seemed to encourage Mettenger. He wiped his hands on his pants and, with reddened eyes, raised his head.

Forgotten in all this was Stürn. Sam glanced across the room to find what reaction she might have to such a scene. But there was none. She looked exactly the same as when Sam had entered Twelve. Stoic. Unmoved. Staring straight ahead. She had reacted to absolutely nothing, and for an instant, Sam wondered if she might have died from the shock of it all.

He looked back to the stage and was startled to find Davidson looking directly at him. *What have I done?* Sam tried to appear apologetic, though he had no idea what he could be apologizing for. Then Davidson turned to Stürn, and Sam realized Davidson had wanted to make sure he had Sam's full attention. He did.

"Laura Stürn."

Unlike with the others, Davidson called her name specifically, leaving no doubt that everything had changed...and changed drastically. He glared at her with an intensity that frightened Sam. Stürn gasped, but quickly regained her composure. She remained in her seat and locked eyes with Davidson, defiantly never once looking away. "Yes, sir," came her cold reply.

"Hear me now," Davidson warned. "Your life and the lives of those who follow you depend on correctly understanding what I am about to say."

"I will do my best."

Her voice was void of emotion, mechanical. Sam half-expected fire to literally leap from Davidson's eyes and thoroughly consume the Senior Manager, leaving her a smoldering pile of ashes. Everyone in the room sat absolutely still. Not a breath could be heard as they waited anxiously.

"There is no new power!" His words rolled like thunder. "You claim to follow the messages of QolCom...to be its agent for the people, calling them to a life of freedom. But you have no part in the Company. You have no knowledge of Brighten. You have no understanding of the Plan, its commands, or its purpose. Olasom and its instructions have no meaning to you. Without such knowledge and understanding, there can be no wisdom to interpret the messages of QolCom. You do not seek freedom for your people. That is a lie to manipulate those who hear what they want to hear. What you seek is independence, power, and control. What you seek…is *my* authority."

Sam could not take his eyes off Stürn. Any second, he expected an angry outburst, passionately denying the charges that had been thrown at her feet. But there was nothing. No outburst. No denial, of any kind. No emotion. She stared at Davidson in absolute silence. Enormous tension filled the air, and Sam felt any minute the room would explode.

Then with a few words, Davidson took it all away. The tension, the pressure, the silence. His face softened into genuine sadness.

"Why have you betrayed the Company? There is still time."

Stürn's frozen face instantly fell and shattered, as one whose dark secret—so carefully hidden—had suddenly been discovered. There was no remorse or shame as had been so evident with Williams and Mettenger, just the pronounced expression of shocked indignation. Without a word, she angrily gathered herself and marched out of Twelve. The door slammed shut. Madhu made a move to follow, but Davidson signaled to let her go.

Sam closely watched the scene before him—part audience, part actor caught in a tragic play. Mme. Couteau, eyes squeezed tight, slowly shook her head. Williams seemed in shock. Mettenger leaned over and whispered. Williams silently nodded. Ellington simply stared at the door, as if expecting Stürn to return. The door remained closed.

What will he do now that he's lost a Senior Manager? Sam turned back to the lectern. Immediately his jaw dropped. The stage was empty. Davidson had left.

Kenneth stepped forward.

"Dinner will be served at the appointed hour. In the meantime, I suggest you relax as best you can and get some rest. There is still much to be done this evening before the conference concludes."

CHAPTER 16

A NEW TASK

THE DINING HALL seemed a strange refuge, but it offered calmness and order.

Sitting behind the glass wall, Sam did not hear the soothing sounds of the garden. No matter. He could see leaves moving with the wind and water flowing off the stone ledge. Beautiful flowers graced gentle streams. The stately forest stood guard beyond. He longed to be there. No one strolled along the path. No animal stole among the thicket.

That's why it's so peaceful. No one to mess it up.

For almost two hours, Sam and Ellington sat at their table, neither saying very much. The events of the day, especially those in Twelve, had left them emotionally numb. Once filled with anxiety and tension, they now felt empty…physically spent. And their day was not over.

Mme. Couteau had not joined them. Insisting she was fine, she retired to her room to rest before dinner. But Sam thought she looked exhausted and encouraged her to take her time. He was worried, and he told Ellington as much. She no longer appeared to have times of even moderate sight—he questioned whether she could see at all now—and her walk had noticeably slowed, requiring more assistance.

Sam checked the time. He and Ellington had agreed to wait for Mme. Couteau before ordering dinner, and it was getting late.

"Do you think we should check on her?"

Ellington had been silently staring toward the garden. The sound of Sam's voice abruptly returned him to the dining hall. A tired old hand rubbed a furrowed brow.

"I'm sorry, my boy," he said wearily. "What was that again?"

"Mme. Couteau. I was wondering if maybe we should go check on her. It's been a while."

Ellington looked at the time. "Oh my, I had no idea. Perhaps we should. She's likely taking a long nap, but I wouldn't..."

"Mind if we join you?"

They turned to find Williams and Mettenger walking toward them.

"If it's all right," Williams added.

"Please do," Ellington answered. He motioned toward the empty chairs. "There's plenty of room."

Mettenger took a seat, but Williams remained standing. He gazed out the glass window.

"Astonishing," he said, just above a whisper. "Have you been able to see this all along?" He spoke to no one in particular, fixated on the garden below.

"Yes, sir," Sam replied. "You couldn't see it from your table?"

Williams shook his head. "No. I couldn't see many things."

"Where's Miriam?" Mettenger asked Ellington.

"Resting. We're expecting her for dinner."

"It's getting late. Shouldn't she be here by now?"

"That's what we were thinking, too," Sam said. "And she didn't look well when she went to her room. I was wondering if we should do something."

"I suppose we could." Mettenger pursed his lips as he considered the idea. "I'm not sure. Ellington, what do you think?"

"Well, I…"

Before Ellington could offer an opinion, Williams called to one of the servers.

"Excuse me. Could you check on Mme. Couteau? We had expected her by now, and we're a little concerned."

"Certainly, sir," the server replied and hurried off.

When Williams turned back to the table, everyone was looking at him.

"What? Seemed more expedient than sitting around talking about it."

"True," Ellington agreed, somewhat reluctantly. "We should probably go ahead and order, in case Kenneth or Madhu or whoever comes to get one of us for the next meeting."

They gave their orders to the nearest available server and within a short time, the meals had arrived. No one had asked for much, though it had been several hours since their last meal. The trauma of the general session still lingered, and more meetings lay ahead. Conversation was kept to a minimum, with only an occasional word as to Mme. Couteau's absence.

Sam could not summon even a modest appetite. He picked at his salad for a while, then gave it up altogether. He sipped his tea and looked outside to the garden. He imagined himself wandering among the flowers, walking beside the stream, sitting in the coolness of the courtyard…until he felt a tug on his sleeve. Ellington nodded toward the entrance of the dining hall. The server sent to check on Mme. Couteau had returned.

"Sir?" the server said, approaching Williams. "I apologize for my delay. Mme. Couteau was not in her room, and it took some time for me to locate her."

"What's the matter?" Ellington asked. "Is she all right?"

"She suddenly fell ill, sir. Madhu found her sitting on the floor outside her room and alerted Lord Mohae."

"I should have checked on her earlier," Sam scolded himself. "Where is she now?"

"She is in medical services. I understand that she is doing much better, sir. I believe she will be fine."

"Will we be able to see her?" asked Ellington.

"Not for a while. Lord Mohae directed special treatment for her and that is being done at this time. She should be up and about in a few hours."

"Special treatment?" Mettenger said. "What kind of special treatment?"

"I do not have that information, sir."

"Is Davidson..." Sam thought better of using such familiarity with the server, "...uh, Lord Mohae, I mean. Has he been with her?"

"He was a moment ago, sir, but I believe he had been there only a short time. For the last two hours, he has been in a closed meeting with Ms. Stürn."

All four at the table looked at each other in surprise.

"I wouldn't have wanted to be there," Ellington said, under his breath.

"Sirs," the server said, "I will be glad to let you know of any updates I may receive."

"Thank you," Williams replied.

"Yeah, thanks," echoed Sam.

"There is one other thing," the server added. "I was given a message to deliver to Mr. Williams and Mr. Mettenger."

The men looked up, concern etched on their faces.

"Lord Mohae would like to see you now."

"Both of us? Together?" Mettenger asked.

"Yes, sir."

"Where?" Williams asked.

"I will be glad to show you the way."

Time crawled by. The kitchen closed, though servers graciously continued to wait on Sam and Ellington. Neither was hungry. Despite frequent offers, they asked only for a bit more to drink.

"How about some strong black tea this time?" Ellington suggested.

"Definitely. I could use the caffeine." But more than the caffeine, he sought the comfort of something familiar in this most unfamiliar place.

Soon, a small pot, made of the finest china, sat upon the table. Sam cradled a cup in his hands. The tea flowed down his throat and warmed him. He felt calm, even renewed.

Outside, day had long ago bowed to night, and the blue light once again flooded the garden. It felt like forever since Williams and Mettenger had left, though in reality, only an hour had passed. Ellington appeared calm enough. He sat at the table, cup in hand, patiently waiting. Every now and then he would close his eyes and hum a little tune.

Sam's composure, however, deteriorated rapidly. He walked around the dining hall…paced back and forth along the black glass wall…sat for a brief moment…then resumed the routine from the beginning. Once he thought someone had called his name. He rushed into the central lobby, but no one was there. Dejected, he returned to the table and slumped into his chair.

"This is driving me crazy."

"Do tell," Ellington said, with feigned surprise. "And why is that, my boy?"

"Why? Doesn't this bother you, all this waiting?"

"And why should it? I have no idea what I'm waiting for. It could be something most unpleasant. In that case I would like to slow its arrival as much as possible. If on the other hand, it should turn out to be quite wonderful, then I can enjoy the longer experience rather than having it all come and go more quickly. Either way, creating deep ruts in the nice carpet here will not hasten or delay whatever is to come."

Sam sighed. "You're impossible."

"Just a matter of perspective. Why worry about what we don't know what to worry about?"

"What? Oh, I'm sorry," Sam said sarcastically, "for a moment there I thought that was going to make sense."

"What I mean is…"

"No," Sam whined, "please don't tell me. I really don't want to know. I just want to get this over with."

"But, my boy…"

"No, seriously."

"But…"

"Excuse me, sir."

Sam jumped in his chair and knocked over his cup of tea.

"Kenneth!" he shouted.

"Yes, sir," replied the Yonder, with a short bow.

"Stop doing that," Sam said, his hand pressed against his chest. He took a deep breath and looked at Ellington. "We really must put a bell around his neck."

Ellington smiled, then turned to Kenneth.

"Is it time?"

"Yes, sir."

"Who?"

"Lord Mohae would like to see both of you, sir."

"Ah, as with Guy and Otto."

"Have they survived?" Sam asked Kenneth.

"Excuse me?" he replied.

"Sam's a wee bit worried," Ellington explained.

"That's understandable, sir. I would be, too, if I were in his position."

Kenneth took Sam and Ellington to the conference wing and led them down the familiar corridor. As they approached the stairway to Twelve, Sam leaned toward Ellington and whispered, "Why do we need an escort?"

Kenneth looked over his shoulder. "We will not be going to Twelve this evening," he said, and briskly strode on.

"Where then?" Ellington asked, hurrying to keep up.

"Lord Mohae will meet with you in his chambers. He has concluded his meeting there with Mr. Williams and Mr. Mettenger, as well as that earlier with Ms. Stürn."

"Where are they now?" Sam asked.

"Mr. Williams and Mr. Mettenger have returned to their rooms, sir."

"And Ms. Stürn?"

"She has returned to Brigos Glen."

Sam glanced at Ellington, who merely shrugged. Obviously he was not affected one way or the other, but Sam could not help but wonder what had happened with Stürn…and what might be in store for them, as well.

Kenneth led them into a narrow passageway. There were no windows or doors, just long blank walls. They continued for several minutes with nothing but their footsteps breaking the silence. Eventually they came to a massive wooden structure. A great tree had been deftly carved into dark mahogany. Leaf-covered boughs extended like arms from one side of the passageway to the other. A thick canopy touched the ceiling, and the tree's broad trunk, with furrowed bark, stretched down to roots that buried deep into the floor.

Kenneth stopped a few feet in front of the carving, with Sam and Ellington close behind. No one said a word. They stood there, motionless as the tree before them. Then suddenly, the carving moved with a loud crack. Sam and Ellington jumped back, but Kenneth stood his ground. The tree split from the very top of the canopy all the way down the trunk and through its roots, breaking the carving in two. Each half turned on hidden hinges and slowly swung out to reveal a large, oval room. Kenneth wasted no time entering. As Sam and Ellington quickly followed, the great wooden doors closed tightly behind them.

The room spanned forty feet across, twenty feet from the back of the carving to the opposite wall. At the widest point on either side stood a single door. Madhu appeared beside the one to Sam's left. Kenneth took his place beside that to the right. Otherwise, the room was completely empty…no couches, no chairs, no furniture of any kind.

Sam looked nervously about the room and wondered if they should be doing something, anything. He opened his mouth, but it was Madhu who spoke.

"Lord Mohae."

The far left door opened and in walked Davidson. Upon seeing Sam and Ellington, he rushed over and hugged each of them.

"Welcome," he said, warmly. "It has been a difficult day, but we have a few more things to discuss before it's done. Come with me."

They followed him past Madhu into a study. Shelves filled with old books completely covered one wall, and on the opposite hung ancient maps and charts. A beautifully paneled wall stood directly before them and to either side, small round tables with a thick book on each. The one on the right lay open and Sam immediately recognized it as the Plan, but that on the left remained closed. Sam took a step toward it.

"Do not go near *that* book, Sam," Davidson said. His voice, though not unfriendly, made it clear this was not a suggestion. "What lies there is not for your eyes."

Sam nodded and stepped back.

There were three chairs in the study, two turned to face the third. Davidson motioned for Sam and Ellington to sit in the two chairs, while he took the remaining one. They obediently took their seats and waited anxiously for whatever might happen next.

"I have already met with Mr. Williams, Mr. Mettenger, and Ms. Stürn," Davidson said solemnly. "I have extensively discussed their operations, management, and the directions they have taken... especially those in the last few years. As I stated this afternoon, I do not approve of many decisions they have made. They have forgotten and sometimes ignored the calling of their position.

"As a result, the people of Brigos Glen have become severely divided and arrogant. Seeking their own desires, they use the light but do not cherish it. They foolishly follow the branches they have made, yet have no true knowledge of the Company. They have lost their gratitude for life, while abandoning the one who saved them. For seventy years, I have provided the Brigons many opportunities to set things right, but they have failed to do so. I cannot allow that to continue."

Fear instantly seized Sam. Images of Ali, Mark, and Molly flashed in his mind. Before he realized what he had done, he leapt from his chair and paced about the room, his hands desperately, firmly clasped together.

"But, sir," he cried out, "you can't cut off the power."

"I can do whatever I want," came the calm reply.

"But you can't," Sam insisted. "It wouldn't be right. Not everyone is like that. They don't realize what's going on. No one's ever told them. There *are* good people. I've met many of them."

Davidson frowned slightly.

"Well, *some*," Sam corrected himself, "but there can be more. I'm sure of it!"

"I have to agree with Sam, sir," Ellington added. "I don't pretend to know as much as you about the people in Brigos Glen, but I do believe there are many good hearts there. They just need some guidance and encouragement. Sometimes what they need is a friend."

"There aren't many friends among the Brigons," Davidson said, somewhat dispassionately.

"That's true." Ellington nodded. "But there are some." He glanced at Sam. "And as for the others, they can learn by our example. I believe we can make a difference...*if* you will give us the chance."

Sam walked behind Ellington. With both hands firmly taking hold of the top of his friend's chair, he leaned toward Davidson.

"Please, sir," Sam pleaded. "Give us a chance."

Davidson looked at the two men before him, but remained silent. Sam searched his face for the slightest sign they had been able to move him. Then slowly, Davidson relaxed. Sam could see him softening, perhaps with some ancient compassion that had been there all along. He waited for a word of hope.

"Today I have dissolved First Brigos and Glen Community, and removed Mr. Williams and Mr. Mettenger as Senior Managers."

Such action did not especially surprise Sam. He had thought something such as this might be in order. But something much more important concerned him. Grasping Ellington's chair even tighter, he asked, "And termination of power?"

"And termination of the power," Davidson echoed, "will not occur at this time."

Sam let out a joyful sigh of relief, but his elation was short-lived.

"However," Davidson continued, "it will come...one day."

"When?"

"At a time only I will know. Until then, I will allow the Brigons ample time to prepare." Then Davidson's voice became noticeably gentle, even comforting. "Don't worry, Sam. The Company will take care of its own."

"But what about the others?" Sam's thoughts once again turned to his wife and children. "Not everyone works for the Company. What will happen to *them*?"

Davidson sighed. "You still don't understand, Sam."

"Sir," Ellington said, "I'm not sure I do either. Could you help us?"

And for the first time all day, Sam saw Davidson smile.

"Yes, my friend. Listen carefully, because this will affect both of you, now and for the rest of your lives."

Such words did nothing to relax Sam. His legs soon ached with tension as he stood behind Ellington.

"For many years, now," Davidson said, "the Brigons have focused on power. How to use it, how to maintain it, how to control it. But it isn't about power. It has never been about power. Mr. Ellington, do you recall the words that came out of the darkness those seventy years ago?"

"Like it was yesterday. '*Would you like some help?*'"

"Yes. That wasn't an offer of power. That was an offer of love. The desire was to show compassion and give help to those who desperately needed it. And the goal was to set an example so that one day they would do the same…among themselves and with those beyond Brigos Glen."

"For the Yonders?" Sam asked.

"There are others, Sam…many others, just like you. Some are in the same situation. Some worse. Some better. But they all need help."

"So there *were* other survivors," Ellington said, more to himself than anyone else.

"The light that has been shared with you has been shared with them, as well. But this is the most important part." Davidson paused and looked intently at the two men. "I am not speaking of what comes down from your towers. That is temporary and, as I have said, will one day end.

"I am speaking of a different kind of light. It is caring for each other, encouraging each other. It is putting selfish desires aside to help someone else. It is standing with each other, even through disagreements. It is friendship. True light is all this, and much more. Those who have it belong to the Company. This is the light I want you…the two of you…to share with the people of Brigos Glen. Will you do that?"

Sam's grasp on Ellington's chair eased as he rocked back. He joined Ellington in nodding silently to their host. This was certainly not what he had expected to hear…and for that, he was exceedingly thankful.

"What will become of Guy and Otto?" Ellington asked.

"The Plan calls for only one branch and from this date forward, that is to be made clear throughout Brigos Glen. Mr. Williams and Mr. Mettenger understand the situation and have pledged to work with the new Senior Manager I have selected."

"And Ms. Stürn?"

"I have given her…an opportunity. She has returned to Brigos Glen to consider it. We will wait to see how she responds."

"And if she refuses?"

"She and all who follow her will be banished."

As Sam considered what would happen to them, it suddenly occurred to him what else Davidson had said. The knot in his stomach returned.

"You mentioned a new Senior Manager," Sam said, hesitantly.

"Have you selected one?" asked Ellington.

"Yes to you both, but I have not yet made that known." Davidson smiled broadly. "However, I will do so now. I want you to be the new Senior Manager of True Branch."

Sam felt his heart skip a beat. Never could he have expected such an incredible offer, especially to one so young compared to the others. He did not come close to having the breadth of their knowledge and experience.

"I…I don't know what to say," he stammered. "This is…I just don't know."

Davidson looked at Sam with great warmth and compassion.

"Sam," he said gently, "I was speaking to Mr. Ellington."

For the next hour, Davidson and Ellington discussed the changes to be made in Brigos Glen. Sam stood off to the side, pretending to look at the books that lined the wall. He was still terribly embarrassed and humiliated by his grand assumption. Davidson had been gracious, and no one had laughed at his foolishness. But Sam could not have been more shocked had Davidson doused him with ice water. At least he could hide in silence.

Ellington, for his part, had immediately protested Davidson's selection. With great vigor and conviction, he pointed out one reason after another that showed him to be an inadequate, even dangerous, choice. He rattled off the names of several others he argued were far more qualified to take on such a vital position.

"And I am far too old for this. Besides, I'm just an engineer. No one is going to listen to me. I've never headed up anything in my life. Suppose they want to know by whose authority I've become Senior Manager. What am I to say? They don't know who you are."

And on it went. But for every reason, every thought, every excuse Ellington threw at him, Davidson replied with clear instructions. At last, Ellington reluctantly weakened.

"Sir, I'm afraid I won't know what to do," he finally admitted.

"I will tell you."

Davidson handed him a sifer similar to the one in Sam's room.

Those messages were from you. Sam smiled to himself.

"I'm not sending you out alone. Mr. Williams and Mr. Mettenger will also be with you. They understand what they must do and will be of great help to you. Draw on their knowledge, learn from their experience. They will be very valuable in establishing the new structure. And Sam will be there, as well."

The mention of his name caught Sam's attention. He put down the book he was holding and looked at his friend. Ellington nervously stared at the floor.

"It'll be fine," Sam said. "How many times have we been called into the Supe's office in the last five years? Twenty? We can handle whatever they throw at us. And everybody in the division loves you. You know that. Besides, what's the worst that can happen? We get fired? I figure we're in a better position now than we've ever been."

"Yeah, I know." Ellington sighed. "I just don't want to make a bigger mess than what we already have."

"As long as you listen to me," Davidson replied, "you won't."

Ellington took a deep breath. "Well, then, let's do it...I guess."

Sam walked over and patted him on the back.

"Senior Manager Ellington," he said, with a laugh. "Not bad."

"This is good," Davidson proclaimed. "Now then, with that settled, Mr. Ellington, there's someone who has wanted to meet you ever since you arrived at Heis. I believe he might be of special assistance to you. Would that be all right with you?"

"Certainly," Ellington said, puzzled.

"Then come with me."

As they followed Davidson out of the study, Ellington eyed Sam with a questioning look. Sam answered with a slight shrug and shook his head. Once in the oval room, Davidson signaled Kenneth, still guarding his assigned door. Kenneth turned on his heel, opened the door, and stepped into a dimly lit room. Sam vainly peered inside.

"He is ready to see you," Kenneth said to someone there. Turning back, Kenneth nodded to Ellington and smiled.

A tall man rose from a chair and methodically made his way to the door and into the oval room. Ellington could not see clearly and squinted to get a better look. Then suddenly his face shone with joy and disbelief. Tears filled his eyes.

"Is it really…" were the only words Ellington could manage.

The stranger walked up to him and firmly shook his hand.

"I've heard so much about you all these years," he said. "You've done an excellent job, and I understand you have a tough one coming up. Would you like some help, Brian?"

"Karis?"

Sam looked on as the two entered the other room. He had never seen his friend so excited. Ellington seemed like a little kid again, one who had just met his hero. So many times Ellington had told him of that fateful night when Karis came to Brigos Glen and first appeared to the Elders. He had been a child at the time. Curious to see who this stranger might be, he broke free of his mother's hand and pushed his way through the crowd until he was almost to the fire.

He heard adults talking, arguing, and shouting. Then came that unmistakable Voice…strong, resolute, inspiring in an odd sort of way. It kept asking if they would like some help. Ellington desperately wanted to see the kind man who owned that singular voice. With one great effort, he shoved past the last few who stood in his way…only to find himself tumbling out of the crowd.

"I fell flat on my face, right in front of everyone," Ellington had told him. "I lifted up my head and the first thing I saw was this mountain of a man. He never said a word, but there was this kindness about him. I was so embarrassed. As soon as I could get myself up, I ran back into the crowd. But I didn't leave. I stayed and listened to everything he said. I don't know what it was, but that very night I decided I wanted to be like him and help anyone I could."

Sam could see the entire scene play out in his mind, as he had so often before. As Kenneth closed the door to the room, Sam turned to Davidson.

"Was that really him? Karis?"

"Yes."

"But he would have to be…"

"Quite old." Davidson nodded. "You seem to be terribly concerned about age," he added, with a grin. "Yonders live a very long time, and he's in excellent health. Come, they have much to talk about…and so do we."

With renewed apprehension, Sam silently followed him back to the study. He was about to take his seat, but Davidson continued to the paneled wall.

"Come here a moment. I'd like to show you something."

With a wave of his hand, the panels slid apart, revealing a wide, darkened window. Sam joined him and looked outside. The blue light shone as it had each night, but then began to fade. With each second, Sam became more puzzled. *How can we see anything without the light.*

"What is it you…"

"Look closer."

As the blue light of Heis grew fainter, a new, golden light appeared in the distance. The more one faded, the brighter the other became. Finally no blue light remained, and all Sam could see was a brilliant sphere of light sparkling far away in the darkness.

"What is that?" Sam asked, just above a whisper.

"Beannachd." Davidson spoke as though it were a precious treasure.

"The home of the Yonders," Sam said.

"You are the only Brigon to have seen it."

"But Edgar, Mme. Couteau's…"

"He was never able to open his eyes. Had he done so, he would have been instantly blinded. The only reason you can see it now is because of the great distance. There are no roads between Heis and Beannachd, just a narrow path, and it would take several weeks for you to reach it."

Sam looked at Davidson, who continued to gaze out the window.

"Why did you want me to see this?"

"One day I will bring Beannachd to your valley."

"The entire city?"

"Yes."

"But how? Is that even possible?"

"That does not matter, but it will be done. When it occurs, your people must be prepared. Anyone who is not prepared…who does not belong to the Company…will not survive. But those who do will live a life they have never known. One of peace. One without worry."

"That sounds wonderful," Sam murmured.

"Sam, that has been the purpose of the Plan from the very beginning. Beannachd was never meant to merely exist, just as Brigos Glen was never meant to merely survive. The purpose has always been to bring the two together and allow the power here to transform the world there. All that has ever occurred has been in preparation for that day. There is much more I will share with you in the days to come, but remember what I have told you. There will be a time when this knowledge will give you the strength to carry on in your assignment."

"My assignment?" Sam asked. "What do you mean? I'm done. I've already prepared the report. I sent it to you."

"And I'm sure it was a good one."

"What?" Sam exclaimed. "You didn't read it?" He gaped at Davidson.

"No."

"But I put in all that time. You made me have all those interviews. And you didn't read the report?"

Sam stood there, shocked. He thought about the effort he had given…all the hard work…all the concern and worry…for a report Davidson never read.

"I don't believe this," he wailed. "So you didn't have my information when you were making your decisions?"

"I already had that information."

"But…then what was the point of it, all the agony you put me through?" Sam demanded.

"The report wasn't for me," Davidson replied calmly. "It was for you."

"Me? What for? What good is it to me?"

"To remember, Sam. I want you to remember all that has gone on before this day. I want you to be able to recall how the Brigons were thrown into darkness and brought back into light. I want you never to forget the way the Brigons embraced Karis and the Yonders…only to put aside such kindness as they sought to satisfy their own lust for power and control."

"But why?" asked Sam, now more subdued.

"Because you are the recorder. I want you to share it with the Brigons—to prepare a people who can stand against the darkness. There will come a day when the darkness will grow worse, and if they do not stand together, they will have no hope."

Sam stared at Davidson. He had no idea what to say. It all sounded so strange, so fantastic…and not in a good way. Davidson turned and looked into his eyes.

"I want you to be my voice to your people. Tell them what I tell you. Share with them what I share with you. They will not always want to hear what you have to say, but you must say it, regardless. Their very lives are at stake here. Do you understand?"

Sam nodded.

"Will you agree to do this?"

Fear and dread washed over Sam. He suddenly wanted to run away. This would be more difficult than anything he had ever done, perhaps even dangerous. He thought of Ali. What would she say? Then something stirred deep inside, and he knew. This was what he had been called to do. This was why he was here…not just at Heis or in Brigos Glen. This was his purpose in the world. Finding confidence he had never known, Sam stood tall.

"Yes," he said, firmly. "I will."

Davidson nodded.

"We will talk once more before you return home tomorrow. I suggest you get some rest tonight. You are going to need it."

CHAPTER 17

THE ANSWER

REAKFAST HAD NEVER been so lively. From the moment Ellington arrived, he could talk of nothing but his time with Karis. In great detail, he described the ancient Yonder—what he looked like, how he dressed, his mannerisms, even his laughter. He told them each thing they discussed, which was almost exclusively about Karis's time in Brigos Glen and what had happened in the village since he had left. Williams and Mettenger listened to every word…but not Sam. Though he politely nodded every now and then, his thoughts were elsewhere.

Mme. Couteau had not been able to join them. Ellington was noticeably disappointed and mentioned he wanted to share his recent experience with her, especially since she had been so much a part of those early days. But Kenneth assured him she was doing well and would see them later in the day.

Sam ate little of his breakfast, noticed by no one except Tunde. With everyone engrossed in Ellington's tales, Sam was glad to see his friendly face.

"You should try to eat more, sir. It will be a long journey home today. I can bring you something different if you wish."

"Nah, that's okay. I'm not really hungry. Just have a lot on my mind."

"It is not good to have too much on one's mind." Tunde removed Sam's half-full plate. "It can distract from what is truly important. Take me, for example. I have my job here and do it as well as I can. I follow the instructions given me each morning and assist others as I am able. But there are so many things around me that can affect what I do. The chefs may not cook the meals properly. A guest may arrive late." He smiled at Williams, who was far too involved with Ellington to notice. "There may be fewer or more guests than were planned for. But I cannot worry about such things. Others have those responsibilities, and I have mine."

"Do you ever have other guests here? I mean, besides us."

"I am told more will be arriving tomorrow."

Other survivors! "Where are they from?"

"I do not know, sir." Tunde smiled. "That is not my job."

Tunde brought Sam a cup of tea as the conversation among the others raged on. At Williams's suggestion, their attention turned to Ellington's new role as Senior Manager and what thoughts he might have for the structure of True Branch. But rather than launch into any ideas he might have, Ellington asked for those of the former Senior Managers. He patiently listened as each, in turn, described what changes Ellington might consider. Davidson had spent considerable time with both, laying out his vision for True Branch. Since then, Williams and Mettenger had been discussing what should and could be done to carry out Davidson's instructions.

As Sam silently drank his tea, he closely observed the two men. Days before, he would never have believed such cooperation possible, expecting either Williams or Mettenger to seize control. But now they were working as a team—offering suggestions to Ellington and listening to what the other might have to say on any particular point. More importantly, each genuinely acknowledged Ellington as the leader.

Will wonders never cease?

Sam finished off the tea and excused himself from the table. He was not really a part of the conversation and decided his time would be better spent packing. The discussion stopped only long enough for a few quick goodbyes. He walked into the central lobby and found Madhu waiting for him.

"Mr. Mitchell, did you have a satisfactory breakfast?"

"Yes, as always."

This one had not been all that satisfactory, but Sam did not feel like getting into a protracted explanation.

"Very good. So you are finished then?"

"Yes, I was on my way back to my room."

"Lord Mohae has instructed me to take you to the garden instead, sir. I believe he would like a word with you."

"If it's only a word, that won't take long." Sam laughed.

"I would not know, sir," came the deadpan reply. "Now, if you would follow me."

"Yes, of course."

No sense of humor. Sam shook his head.

A warm breeze mingled with the flowers that waved to Sam as he entered the garden. Madhu led him to the courtyard where Davidson was already waiting.

"Lord Mohae," Madhu said with a solemn bow.

"Thank you, Madhu. That will be all."

Madhu bowed once more, then quietly left.

Sam looked around the garden. "I'm going to miss this place."

Davidson made no reply. He strolled to the empty chairs and motioned for Sam to join him. As Sam slid into his chair, Davidson studied him a moment.

"Your eyes are a little red this morning. Did you not sleep well?"

"It was a little difficult." Sam instinctively reached up to his eyes. They were dry and stung as he rubbed them. "I had no problem falling asleep, but staying there was a different story."

"Worried?"

"I don't think so. A lot happened yesterday—with Ellington, me, everyone really. A lot to take in. And I guess it's also not knowing what's going to happen next."

"Hmm. Before you came here, did you always know what was going to happen next?"

Sam laughed to himself. "Well, no, but at least then I didn't know what was going on." He paused. "That's all changed now," he added soberly.

Davidson nodded. "Yes, but it has been a good change, Sam. And through you, many others will also experience that change."

A slight frown crossed Sam's brow. "May I ask you a question?"

"Certainly, Sam. Always feel free to ask me anything." Then he added, "But don't expect to always like my answer."

"Fair enough," Sam said with a nod. "Well, I've been wondering…if you want to get the Brigons to change, to understand whatever it is you want them to understand…why not come to Brigos Glen and speak with them? Or bring them here to Heis. It would take longer, but this place is amazing. I'm sure they would listen."

Davidson leaned back. Hands together, resting against his lips, he closed his eyes. He seemed deep in thought. Then he let out a long, heavy sigh and looked out across the garden. Sam was taken aback by the intense sadness in his face.

"That's OK, sir, you don't have to…"

Davidson held up his hand.

"First, to bring them here is not possible. For all that Heis is, this facility will not change a heart that does not wish to be changed. Ms. Stürn, unfortunately, is a reminder of that truth.

"As for the other…many years ago, long before you were born, when the system was first established, Olasom Contracting relocated to Brigos Glen. It was an ordinary building, constructed to look like any other in the village. Nothing glamorous. Nothing really to call attention to itself. In time, it became the center of the training and instruction for the Brigons. But a problem arose.

"Many Brigons did not want the training and instruction. Some had already developed such a devotion to Brighten that they viewed Olasom's efforts as interference. Others, many of whom were Ms. Stürn's predecessors, believed they could best take care of themselves and refused to follow instructions from anyone. There were also a few who were angry that Olasom had not established a power source in Brigos Glen, especially one they could control. All of these tried to disrupt the training sessions, but they failed. Despite their efforts, even more people attended. They were outraged. Then, one very sad day, they destroyed the training facility."

Davidson looked far beyond the forest, as though he could see the angry mob. "She was there," he said softly.

"Who?"

"Miriam Couteau. She had run after them, pleading with them to consider what they were doing. But no one listened. She stood there weeping as the walls were torn down."

His voice trailed off to a whisper. A moment passed, then he glanced at Sam and smiled. "A few days later, they found the building had been rebuilt. But it was only there for a brief time. Olasom focused its attention on a core group of Brigons, and once they had what they needed to watch after the system, the entire building was removed from Brigos Glen and taken to Beannachd."

"And the training and instructions?" Sam asked.

"Everything had always been given verbally, but several in the group wrote it all down. You have seen some of it in your own training. And now you also have the broadcasts from QolCom, though far too few ever listen to them."

Davidson leaned toward Sam.

"The Brigons have what they need. The Plan from Brighten. The Olasom manuals. QolCom's communications. That is where their true learning lies. Some hearts have grown cold, Sam. They refuse to see. They refuse to listen. But there are others who will. Some need to be awakened, some to be reminded. And that is what you will do."

"I hope I can," Sam said softly.

"You will."

Davidson's confidence was comforting. Sam appreciated the encouragement, but something still nagged at him.

"I'm confused."

Davidson sat back in his chair. "About what?"

"In the interviews, the Senior Managers…well, *former* Senior Managers…they all had their favorite. For Williams it was all about Brighten. For Mettenger, it was Olasom. And Stürn…all she was interested in was QolCom. They talked about the Company, but what they really meant was just one of those operations. And yet, I've heard you talk about the Company, too.

"I know you're Lord Mohae, but I don't honestly understand what that means. I guess what I'm really asking is, who's in charge of all this? When I go back home, people are going to ask. What do I tell them?"

Davidson nodded. "You have good insight, Sam. There have been many problems over the years because people did not understand. What do you know about how businesses are structured?"

"Well, some are owned by one person. My dad had a small business for a while. He pretty much ran everything. And there are partnerships where people go into business together."

"What about corporations?"

"They have shareholders who own them. There's usually a board of directors that creates the agenda, I guess, for how the corporation is to run, sets goals, and that sort of thing. Then the officers provide the leadership to hopefully meet those goals."

"That's good," Davidson said. "Brighten Power Authority, Olasom Contracting, and QolCom are corporations. While they work together in the system, they have their own individual operations and purposes. This is all the Brigons see, and what they see is all they know. But let me tell you what they do not see and what they do not know."

He left his chair and squatted on the ground. Sam followed and watched as Davidson took his finger and made three circles in the dirt, each of equal size and none touching another. Next, he drew lines from the center of each circle, bringing them to a common point.

"These circles represent the three corporations of Beannachd," he explained.

In one he wrote the initials BPA, the next OC, and the last QC. Then he returned to his chair. Sam studied Davidson's drawing. They looked like three balloons tied together. He scratched the back of his head.

Davidson continued. "Remember how you described a corporation? There is usually a board with a number of directors, several different officers, and many shareholders. Brighten, however, has only one director, one officer, and one shareholder…and to make it even simpler, one person holds all three positions. The same is true with Olasom and also QolCom."

Sam studied the drawing again. "But these three lines…"

"Are lines of authority," Davidson said, finishing his thought.

"And they all come to the same place?"

"No. They all come *from* the same place."

Sam glanced at Davidson.

"Yes, Sam. That one person who is the sole officer, director, and shareholder for each of these, is the same for them all. And I am that one person. When you hear from QolCom, you hear from me. When you see the work of Olasom, you see me. And when you receive power and light from Brighten, it is my power and my light that you receive. You asked me once, 'Who is the Company?' Now you should understand."

Sam's eyes opened wide. Davidson nodded.

"I am."

The central lobby was unusually crowded. Sam had not seen so much activity since he arrived four days earlier. Packed bags formed an orderly line in the middle of the room. Madhu and Kenneth gave directions to several of the servers from the dining hall. And not far away, Williams, Mettenger, and Ellington continued their discussion from breakfast.

Sam had spent the remainder of the morning with Davidson, as well as two hours of the afternoon. On returning to his room, he found his suitcase already packed and a note saying departure would be in ten minutes. He was more than ready to go home, but it all seemed so sudden. Now he stood in the lobby, feeling rather lonely. Sam leaned against a wall and looked around the room. Someone was missing.

"Kenneth, where is Mme. Couteau? Is she all right?"

Kenneth promptly walked over.

"Yes, sir. She is well. I expect her momentarily." As he turned to rejoin Madhu, he suddenly stopped. "Here she is now."

Sam looked across the room and saw Mme. Couteau entering the lobby from the housing wing. Santos and Mikhail were with her, but she was walking confidently without their assistance.

"Hello, boys," she called out to Ellington, Williams, and Mettenger. "Hi, Sam." Today she had an infectious smile, and it quickly spread. Everyone hurried over to greet her.

"Miriam, how are you?" Ellington asked. "We've missed you."

"I'm doing wonderfully, Brian. These gentlemen have taken excellent care of me. My hip is feeling so much better and since the procedure…"

"Procedure?" Mettenger interrupted. "What procedure? We weren't told about any procedure."

"For my eyes, dear. Davidson suggested it, and though I explained I could not afford such a thing, they did it anyway. And now, I can see again. Everything is so clear. It's amazing."

"That's great, Miriam," Ellington said, cheerfully. "Really great! I'm sorry you missed some time here, but I'm glad you've come to join us for the trip back. You really had us worried."

Mme. Couteau glanced at Kenneth, who shook his head.

"No, Madame. I have not told them."

"Told them," Sam said. "Told them what?"

Mme. Couteau's smile faded. She looked compassionately at the four men.

"I did not come to join you," she said gently. "I came to say goodbye."

"What do you mean *goodbye*?" Sam asked. "You're coming home with us."

Bewildered, he looked for support, or at least an indication this was a joke. Neither came. The others stood there, silent. Mme. Couteau shook her head.

"No, Sam. I've been offered the opportunity to stay here. My room, food, anything I may need…all free. A gift from Davidson. It's very lovely here, and I have wonderful memories I thought were long forgotten. But this place…this very special place…has brought them all back. I have a peace here that I haven't known for a very long time."

"But Miriam," Ellington stammered.

"It's all right, Brian. This is what I want to do. I'm ninety-two years old. Life had become difficult. All my old friends are gone. I don't know how much longer I may have, but it would be nice to spend that time here. And you certainly don't need me. You have more than enough help." She took his hand in hers. "This is what I want."

Ellington nodded sadly, accepting the decision without another attempt to dissuade her. Sam wondered if he would ever see her again. Deep down he knew the answer. He brushed away a tear, then walked over and hugged this noble woman.

"Goodbye," he whispered through the hurt in his throat.

Then the others joined in, saying their goodbyes and wishing her well. Though she would undoubtedly be happier here, it was clear no one wanted her to remain behind. Putting their own desires aside, to a man, they promised to respect her wishes. As the last embrace ended, the patio lift arrived, and Santos and Mikhail began loading the luggage.

"Gentlemen," Kenneth called out, "the transport is ready for you. Madhu will serve as your driver to the gates of Brigos Glen. Other transportation will be there waiting to take you to your homes."

"So Davidson will not be…" Ellington began.

"No, sir. Lord Mohae will not be accompanying you on the return."

"Pity," Ellington replied. "I had hoped to see him again before we left."

The men lined up to shake hands with Kenneth and express their thanks for all his efforts. As Sam waited his turn, Tunde raced into the lobby.

"Mr. Mitchell, I am so glad I caught you. You were about to leave this."

He hurried to Sam and handed him a large, square box. Sam eyed it carefully, then shook his head.

"I'm afraid this isn't mine."

"No, sir. It is definitely yours."

"I really don't remember…"

"It *is* yours," Tunde insisted.

Sam laughed to himself. "If you say so," he said, rather skeptically. Tunde seemed so certain that Sam decided not to press the point. *Besides, I can find the real owner later.*

"And thank you, sir," Tunde added. He smiled from ear to ear. "I hope we see each other again someday."

"Me, too," Sam said. He reached out and shook the server's hand. "Me, too."

"It is time," Madhu announced.

He boarded the lift, followed by Ellington, Williams, and Mettenger. Sam remained long enough to give Mme. Couteau one last hug, then hurried on.

As the last suitcase was brought on board, Sam thought of all that had happened over the last several days. The assignments, all those interviews, and the report. The discussions with Ellington and the meetings with Davidson. The lonely hours in the private dining room. Then he remembered Tunde and the box he held in his hand. Sam gave it a shake and heard something slide about inside. He removed the bit of tape holding the top in place, but before he could open it, Ellington walked over.

"You okay, there?" asked the new Senior Manager.

"I'm fine. Just tired. It's been a long five days."

"Yes, it has," Ellington sighed. "You seemed pretty down back there. I have to admit, it was getting to me, too. You sure you're all right?"

"Yeah, I'm sure."

Ellington noticed the box.

"What do you have there?"

Sam lifted the top and peeked inside. Then he looked at Ellington and smiled.

"Lakhayea."

"Oh, yes," Ellington replied, looking down at the white icing. "I don't know it by that name, of course. We always called it Friendship Cake. It's an old tradition, given as a symbol for the beginning of a lasting friendship, a way of saying, 'Welcome' and 'We're here for you.' I haven't seen one in quite a while. Where did you get this?"

The platform shook as the lift prepared for its ascent to the surface. Sam and Ellington grabbed the nearby railing.

"Whoa," Ellington laughed, regaining his balance. "We're off then." Completely forgetting Sam and the box of cake, he excitedly looked at the circle of manufactured sky above them.

But Sam did not follow his gaze. He glanced back to the lobby one last time. Kenneth had already returned to the business of the day, giving orders to the servers, who hurried off with new assignments. There were Mme. Couteau and Tunde, smiling and waving goodbye. Sam waved back and forced a grin as best he could. As the doors of the lift closed, he saw someone standing alone in the back of the lobby.

Davidson looked directly at Sam and nodded, then softly patted his chest.

KEYS TO *THE COMPANY*

UTHOR'S NOTE—THE FOLLOWING is a brief key of certain references and names. It is not meant to be complete, nor an explanation in terms of the development of the story. That will have to wait for *Inside the Company*. When a word is referenced, it may be identical to or derived from the translated word. Regarding character names, few have any particular meaning, but those that do are noted. The primary intent is to show the diversity within the family of God.

Beannachd: The Scot Gaelic word for blessings. There are variations among the dialects, but generally it is pronounced **Bey-*uhn*-nahk** with the last syllable being more guttural.

Brighten Power Authority: From within a bright cloud overshadowing all on the mountain, God displayed His power and authority at the transfiguration of Jesus. (See Matthew 17:5) Bright 'n Power, Authority.

Brigos Glen: Brigos is adapted from "brig," a place of confinement. I wanted to project a certain image—a long, broad glen surrounded by towering mountains, high enough to shield the

glen from the effects of the meteor striking the planet. I decided
to include Glen in the name to reinforce this image each time the
name is mentioned. It also reminds me of the glens of Scotland,
such as Glen Coe, though the mountains of Brigos Glen would be
much taller.

Chokmah: A Hebrew word for wisdom. "Blessed are those who
find wisdom, those who gain understanding" (Proverbs 3:13).

Davidson: From Son of David, a Hebrew phrase with several
meanings. "Hosanna to the Son of David! Blessed is he who comes
in the name of the Lord!" (Matthew 21:9).

Farside: The name given by the Brigons for the homeland of
the Yonders. Its general meaning is as explained in the chapter.
However, I also chose it because of the cartoon series The Far Side,
where nothing is ordinary, normal, or as we assume.

Friendship Cake: A traditional gift in parts of the world to
someone who moves into a neighborhood or community. Also
known as Friendship Bread, it symbolizes the beginning of a
relationship with the hope of developing a strong lasting friendship.
The act (preparing, baking, delivering) is symbolic of giving oneself
for the benefit of another, a way of saying "Welcome" and "We are
here for you."

Heis: A Greek word for one. "I and the Father are one" (John
10:30).

Hopewell: From good hope. "May our Lord Jesus Christ
himself and God our Father, who loved us and by his grace gave
us eternal encouragement and good hope, encourage your hearts
and strengthen you in every good deed and word" (2 Thessalonians
2:16–17).

Karis: From a Greek word for grace and pronounced *kah*-**reece**.
"For it is by grace you have been saved, through faith—and this
not from yourselves, it is the gift of God" (Ephesians 2:8).

Lakhayea: A combined word taken from the Aramaic for bread
(*lakhmoa*) and life (*khayea*). "I am the bread of life" (John 6:48).

Last Day: The last day the sun rose. This day ushers in the age of darkness that will be broken only when the sun returns.

Lord Mohae: An acronym from LORD, Maker Of Heaven And Earth. "My help comes from the LORD, the Maker of heaven and earth" (Psalm 121:2).

Marturia: A Hebrew word for witness, one whose purpose is to tell others something. "There was a man sent from God whose name was John. He came as a witness to testify concerning that light, so that through him all might believe. He himself was not the light; he came only as a witness to the light. The true light that gives light to everyone was coming into the world" (John 1:6–9).

Miriam Couteau: From Miriam, a reference to Moses' sister, one who at times was strong and at times weak. "I sent Moses to lead you, also Aaron and Miriam" (Micah 6:4b).

Olasom Contracting: An acronym of One Like A Son Of Man. "In my vision at night I looked, and there before me was one like a son of man, coming with the clouds of heaven" (Daniel 7:13).

QolCom: From *qol,* a Hebrew word for voice. "Moses spoke and the voice of God answered him" (Exodus 19:19b).

Sifer: From the Arabic word *sifr,* which refers to the numeral 0 and carries the idea of a beginning. It is the beginning of the Arabic numbering system and is critical in the beginning of each set of ten, i.e., 10, 20, 30, etc. Based on *sifr* is the Hebrew word *cepher,* which generally means a writing or book, and the English word *cipher,* a secret method of writing.

Sunesis: A Greek word for understanding. "For this reason, since the day we heard about you, we have not stopped praying for you. We continually ask God to fill you with the knowledge of his will through all wisdom and understanding that the Spirit gives" (Colossians 1:9).

Thomas: The Chief Elder. This name is taken directly from the disciple Thomas and is meant to reflect his bravery and caution.

(On the basis of my own study, I have an entirely different view than most about this courageous man.)

Twelve: The reference here is strictly biblical and there are many applications...twelve months, twelve thousands, twelve rulers, twelve sons, twelve tribes, the Twelve (disciples). It carries the idea of being complete, sufficient, and enough.

Yonders: The name given by the Brigons for those who came from beyond the Great Peaks. It has no other meaning than that as explained in the book.

The Company contains many references to specific Bible passages. For example:

1. The way to Beannachd requires passage through Chokmah and Sunesis, or the way to Blessings requires one to pass through Wisdom and Understanding. "Blessed are those who find wisdom, those who gain understanding" (Proverbs 3:13).

2. The Council of Elders arrives at the boundary of the Outlands, demanding they also be taken to Heis, but Davidson refuses. When asked why, he says, "Because I don't know you." "Not everyone who says to me, 'Lord, Lord,' will enter the kingdom of heaven, but only the one who does the will of my Father who is in heaven. Many will say to me on that day, 'Lord, Lord, did we not prophesy in your name, and in your name drive out demons and perform many miracles?' Then I will tell them plainly, 'I never knew you'" (Matthew 7:21–23a).

3. In order to reach Heis, the travelers must first enter the Outlands through a narrow gate. "Enter through the narrow gate. For wide is the gate and broad is the road that leads to destruction, and many enter through it. But small is the

gate and narrow the road that leads to life, and only a few find it" (Matthew 7:13–14).

4. The travelers learn that Davidson told the truth when he said he was the only way they would have to reach Heis. Later they discover he is the same one known as Lord Mohae, who saved the lives of the Brigons in the early times after Last Day. "I am the way and the truth and the life. No one comes to the Father except through me. If you really know me, you will know my Father as well. From now on, you do know him and have seen him" (John 14:6–7).

5. Heis is a special place, built in the pass between Chokmah and Sunesis. "By wisdom a house is built, and through understanding it is established" (Proverbs 24:3).

6. At Heis, there is constant light (the blue light at night and the vivid light during the day), which none of the travelers can explain or figure out. The light at Heis comes ultimately from Lord Mohae and Beannachd. "Through him all things were made; without him nothing was made that has been made. In him was life, and that life was the light of all mankind. The light shines in the darkness, but the darkness has not understood it" (John 1:3–5).

7. Davidson brings the travelers to Heis so they may join together, fulfill the responsibilities they have been given, and become united as one. "I appeal to you, brothers and sisters, in the name of our Lord Jesus Christ, that all of you agree with one another in what you say and that there be no divisions among you, but that you may be perfectly united in mind and thought" (1 Corinthians 1:10). "As a prisoner for the Lord, then, I urge you to live a life worthy of the calling you have received. Be completely humble and gentle; be patient, bearing with one another in love. Make every effort to keep the unity of the Spirit through the bond of peace" (Ephesians 4:1–3).

8. *The Company* is an allegory that provides an explanation of the Trinity—one and only one God revealing Himself in three different and unique expressions as He alone chooses. In this story, there is Brighten, the symbol of power and authority—the Father; Olasom, the symbol of the teacher who came to lead the Brigons to a new life—the Son; and QolCom, the symbol of the unseen counselor who guides them in spreading the light—the Holy Spirit. The Trinity confuses many who believe each part is completely separate and distinct from the others. In Brigos Glen, a similar confusion is present as there appear to be three separate businesses, though each is referred to as "the Company."

This leads Sam to ask, "Who is the Company then?" Davidson finally reveals the answer: "When you hear from QolCom, you hear from me. When you see the work of Olasom, you see me. And when you receive power and light from Brighten, it is my power and my light that you receive. You asked me once, 'Who is the Company?' Now you should understand...I am." "Moses said to God, 'Suppose I go to the Israelites and say to them, "The God of your fathers has sent me to you," and they ask me, "What is his name?" Then what shall I tell them?' God said to Moses, 'I AM WHO I AM. This is what you are to say to the Israelites: 'I AM has sent me to you'" (Exodus 3:13–14). "'You are not yet fifty years old,' they said to him, 'and you have seen Abraham!' 'Very truly I tell you,' Jesus answered, 'before Abraham was born, I am!'" (John 8:57–58).

STARTING
THE COMPANY

WHY DID I write *The Company*? Here's how it all began.

For thirty-one years I had a very active and interesting law practice. My clients came from many different backgrounds and countries, and many with religions, philosophies, and views of life very different from my own. One day, a young man came to see me. Born in India and schooled in England, he had become a successful businessman in the U.S. He was also a devout Hindu.

Inside the conference room, a small pewter statue stood prominently on my bookcase. The statue was of two male figures, each in the everyday dress common to the Middle East of two thousand years ago. One figure, seated and leaning slightly forward, intently watched the second who was kneeling and washing his feet.

"I know what that is!" my client exclaimed, pleased with himself.

"You do?"

"Yes, yes. For a time in England, I went to an Anglican school and I remember them talking about this. That's a disciple washing Jesus' feet."

"Oooh, so close. It's actually the reverse," I explained.

Judging from his expression—very similar to that of a deer caught in the headlights of an oncoming car—he did not understand. So, for the next several minutes we talked about how Jesus came as a servant, demonstrating the way He wants us to live in our relationship with God and each other.

Then my client leaned back and said, "You know, your religion and mine are very much alike. Both seek peace and tranquility, and both have many gods."

I was a little stunned by that and my first inclination was to say, "Well, that's just silly." Instead, God thumped me on the back of the head and I replied, "There's a difference in *where* we find peace and tranquility, but why do you say I have many gods?"

"Because you do. There's the father god, the son god, and this other spirit god. You have three gods."

My young client had no clue about the Trinity, but at that moment I realized something about myself even more surprising. Now you must remember I was his attorney and, borrowing a line from *A Christmas Carol*, this must be distinctly understood, or nothing wonderful can come from what I am about to relate.

Legal documents are often confusing to anyone other than a lawyer. (Yes, even I have the ability to write complex documents that no one can understand.) Therefore, it was my job to provide a clear explanation of what they mean. As a Christian, I have a similar responsibility. Yet, with someone willing to listen, I didn't have a way of describing the Trinity. I wasn't doing my job and felt totally inadequate.

That experience launched me on a quest to find an explanation of the Trinity, one that we can more easily grasp...at least to a point. Some aspects of God we can't understand, in part, because we will never experience anyone like Him. When we speak of the "three omni's"—omniscience, omnipotence, omnipresence— nothing else compares. Also, we understand only as much of God's nature as He allows us to discover. Left to our own intelligence and cleverness, our minds cannot wrap around the fullness of who God is.

After much thought, I decided to work within the structures of business and corporate law I knew so well. The result was an explanation, not *the* explanation, of course, as there are still many questions. Even so, I've found that it does help us see a bit more of who God is. It has also been very helpful in my conversations with those who do not share my faith but are willing to listen.

The Company began as an allegory to offer this explanation and provide a better understanding of the Trinity. However, to my surprise, the story went far deeper into many other areas of the Christian walk. It was as though God were saying, "This is merely a first step on the path I've set for you, a path that will lead us to grow closer with every day."

Remember Sam's story. Consider all that God has ever said to you, and continues to say, as He leads in your own amazing adventure...sometimes alone with Him, sometimes with others. My hope and prayer is that each day you will know Him better, rediscover His love for you, and find that wherever you may be in life, good times or bad, He is standing right by your side.

Take care & be God's,
Chuck Graham

ABOUT THE AUTHOR

CHUCK GRAHAM IS Founder and Executive Director of Ciloa, an international ministry devoted to sharing God's encouragement with the world. Ciloa, which stands for Christ Is Lord Of All, actively teaches others how to become effective encouragers and provides encouragement through its Internet resources at www.Ciloa.org and weekly issues of "A Note of Encouragement" for which Chuck serves as both editor and principal writer.

For thirty-one years he practiced law, working with American and international clients, many of whom are denominations, churches, ministries, and other Christian organizations. In 2010 Chuck left his practice in order to devote more time to Ciloa and writing. He continues to work with churches, ministries, businesses, and individuals in matters of Christian encouragement, mediation, and reconciliation, frequently speaking on such topics.

Chuck is the author of *Take the Stand* (Broadman Holman Publishers), *A Year of Encouragement* (Xulon Press), and *Another Year of Encouragement* (Xulon Press). He is married to his high school sweetheart, Beverly, and they have three grown children, two of whom are married, and all live in the Atlanta, Georgia, area.

COMING SOON —
THE RISE OF
NEW POWER

CHAPTER 1

THE BREACH

THE NIGHT SEEMED darker than usual.

A young sentry stood at his post, nervously eyeing the perimeter. A single light tower shone down on a nearby guardhouse, the only habitable structure in the entire desolate region. The light was weak and provided little comfort. The sentry spun to look behind him. A tall fence, crowned with coiled razor-sharp wire, stretched to either side of a small gate before disappearing into the thick blackness.

Inside the building an older man, heavily armed and wearing a similar uniform, sat behind a large metal desk. He monitored the scene outside through carefully positioned windows. To his right, he could see the faint glow of a village faraway. Before him, just outside, stood the sentry…fidgeting in the night air, his back to the gate, scanning the landscape toward the village.

The guard's old swivel chair squeaked as he leaned back. "Recruits." He sighed. Jumping to his feet, he marched to the door and snatched it open with an irritated jerk. "Anders!"

"Sir. Yes, sir!" The sentry snapped to attention.

"What do you think you're doing?"

"Sir. Guarding the perimeter, sir."

"Son, do I look like an idiot to you?"

"No, sir!"

"Who do you think I am?"

"Sergeant Randolph Raines, sir. Lead Officer of the Eastern Gate, Outlands Boundary."

The sergeant eyed the young man from his polished boots to his crisp, neat cap. He turned away to look toward the village.

"Anders, how old are you?"

The sergeant's gruff tone had become more friendly and far less military. The sentry eased a bit.

"Twenty, sir."

"Twenty?" Raines laughed. "I've been pulling boundary duty longer than you've been alive. Most of it at the Eastern Gate. It's always night here, you know. Not like back in the village. At least they have their pretend days. Looks like it's morning there now. See the lights getting brighter? Not here, though. No mornings, no days…never…just night." He paused a moment. "This your first boundary assignment?"

"Yes, sir, but I passed all the training…first in my class."

"Excellent," Raines said with a grin. "And what did they train you to do, son?"

"Command structure, service protocols, weapons use…"

"Combat and survival?" the sergeant interrupted.

"Yes, sir. Extensive training in each area."

"Where? In the Outlands?" the sergeant asked, with obvious doubt.

"No, sir. No one's allowed beyond the boundary, but we studied field exercises."

"In a classroom, Anders," Raines said in disgust. "You can't learn about war in a classroom. You've got to be in the environment… experience the Outlands, breathe it all in, feel the darkness close in on you like a coffin." He spit at the ground. "A classroom. And did anyone explain to you why you're standing here, why we're at this forsaken half-acre of the world?"

"To guard the perimeter, sir."

"But for what purpose? Did they ever mention that in your air-conditioned classroom?"

The sergeant looked at the young sentry...still at attention, still looking straight ahead. But Anders remained silent.

"I didn't think so."

"I...I assumed it was to restrict access to the Outlands, sir."

Raines's lips grew tight and his eyes narrowed.

"No. We're not here to stop someone from getting out." The sergeant's voice betrayed a deep concern. "We're here to stop someone from getting *in*."

Anders turned his gaze away from the village and found the sergeant staring at him. There was no need for words. The seriousness etched in the sergeant's face could not have been clearer, nor could the young man's confusion.

"The ultimate threat does not come from within, son. You're facing the wrong way."

Anders spun around and took his position toward the darkness beyond the fence. He surveyed the area but could see little in the dim light. As he scanned a second time, he heard the sergeant's weapon engage. Raines rushed to the fence and then abruptly stopped. Glancing left and right, he turned back toward the sentry.

"How long has the gate been open?"

Forty days had passed since the four men returned from the Outlands. Dense clouds continued to envelop the planet. The darkness still blanketed the valley, broken only by the village's artificial light. But for the men who had been to Heis Center, there was renewed hope. Change was coming. And the news was spreading like wildfire.

<u>A Brigon Daily Exclusive</u>

MERGER IN THE GLEN!!!
by Matthew Ryan

Wasting no time since the secret conference, Guy Williams of First Brigos and Otto Mettenger of Glen Community have announced the shocking merger of two power management operations. Williams made it clear this was not an acquisition, but a true merger.

"We are returning to the basics of *The Brigos Plan*," Williams explained. "Neither operation will have control over the other. Instead, we will combine the resources and experience of both to form True Branch, which will provide better management of the power system to deliver the service Brigons deserve."

Mettenger was quick to voice his agreement. "For all the good intentions over the years, we had strayed from the simple intent of the Plan. This merger will allow us to refocus, making sure we manage the system in an orderly manner while also seeking new ways to reach more areas and provide better services. Our commitment will be clear… to bring light throughout the valley."

The announcement came as a considerable surprise to the Elder Council, which had been excluded from the conference. Stanley Edwards, Chief Elder, expressed dismay at what he termed renegade tactics. "I'm not sure what the Council's response will be at this point. I have called an emergency meeting for tomorrow evening and we will thoroughly discuss this development. I can assure you of this…there will be no merger without Council approval."

Edwards declined to comment as to what actions the Council might take should First Brigos and Glen Community proceed with the merger despite Council opposition.

Equally surprising was the announcement that the top position of the new combined operation will fall to Brian Ellington. Available records indicate Mr. Ellington is seventy-six years of age and a widower. He received his engineering training at New Bedford College, finishing second in its first graduating class. For the past twenty-seven years he has held various planning and development positions with Glen Community. However, he has never held any management position, a fact deemed particularly troubling by Chief Elder Edwards.

Williams and Mettenger promised their mutual cooperation for the merger and in assisting the new Senior Manager. Neither commented as to whether New Power would be part of this effort. Rumors persist that its Senior Manager, Laura Stürn, had been dismissed from the conference. New Power will neither confirm nor deny. Stürn herself has been unavailable for comment and calls seeking information have not been returned.

Sam finished the article and placed the newspaper on the patio table. Leaning back into the cushioned chair, he looked across the well-kept backyard. Flower beds hugged the tall wooden fence that surrounded the small, green lawn. Though Ellington had often invited the Mitchells to his home, this was the first time Sam had accepted. He wished Ali and the kids could have come, too, but Ellington made no mention of the family this time.

"Here we are," Ellington cheerfully announced.

Sam turned to see his old friend with a large platter bearing a stout teapot, cream, sugar, and two cups. Ellington placed them on the table before settling into his own chair.

"I see you've read the article," he said, picking up the paper. "What do you think?"

Sam poured their tea. "The pictures of Williams and Mettenger are nice enough. Smiling, shaking hands. That alone probably created a stir. Still, I couldn't help but notice there isn't one of the new Senior Manager."

"Well, that's for the best, I'm sure." Ellington laughed. "Never have taken a good picture. Can't seem to get the hair just right." He laughed again. "Besides, I wasn't there, you know. We decided there would be enough going on with the news of the merger. My formal introduction could wait till later."

"Actually, I *didn't* know you weren't there." Sam paused and took a sip of tea. "The paper made no mention of it, and that's pretty much the only place I get the news these days."

Ellington's smile faded as he sighed.

"Ah, don't be like that, my boy. Been a rough time for me, too. It's like my whole world has turned upside down. I haven't worked this hard in a long time. There have been so many meetings, all the planning and replanning, worrying about one thing after another. I'm sorry, Sam. I certainly haven't meant to ignore you."

"That's, OK. I know you've been busy." Sam set his cup on the table. "It's just been strange not seeing you since we got back. I guess I've been feeling a little sorry for myself."

"Like you've been left out?" Ellington suggested.

Sam shrugged. "Yeah, a little."

"Consider yourself lucky, Sam. This hasn't been fun. It's like Otto told us back at Heis, there's so much pressure, so much responsibility. I honestly had no idea."

"Don't worry about it. I'm glad you called and had some time today. So…how are things going? Any light at the end of the tunnel?"

"Yes, there's been progress." Ellington nodded. "Quite a bit, actually. There was a lot of confusion at first, the two operations being so completely unalike…different territories, different directives, different personnel with considerably different training, not to mention the vastly different philosophies. When we first explained the merger to the managers, several resisted. But I have to say, Guy and Otto took control and brought everyone in line. I believe it's going to work well. There will be bumps along the way, to be sure, but all in all, I feel good about it. What's been the response back at the office?"

"Not a lot either way. The information's only been trickling down. There have been concerns about losing jobs and what the new responsibilities may involve. But there *is* one thing that should please you," Sam added, with a mischievous grin.

"What's that?"

"Roger Carrington."

"Carrington?"

"Yes. He's been very busy telling anyone who will listen about what good buddies the two of you are and how he saw greatness the first time he met you. Yes, he's been quite the little cheerleader among the supervisors."

"Oh, my." Ellington laughed. "This is the same guy who routinely admonished me for wasting my time, all the while having no idea what I was working on. That *is* amusing. Worried about his position, is he?"

"Apparently."

Sam smiled and took another sip of tea. It had been far too long since he had spent time with Ellington. He had almost forgotten how much he enjoyed it. And he also enjoyed Ellington's garden. It was not as grand as the one at Heis—no cascading waterfall and the flowers were not as bright or colorful—but there was a peace here. Sam looked at his friend and noticed he suddenly seemed distracted.

"What's on your mind?"

"Oh, I'm sorry, my boy. Sometimes it wanders. I was thinking about Davidson. Have you…" He paused. "Have you heard from him?"

Sam shook his head. "Nothing."

"No message on the sifer?"

Sam remembered the recording device Davidson had given him at Heis. Upon their return, Sam had placed the sifer in his makeshift office at home. It remained there…little used and gathering dust.

"No. I thought about reviewing the report, maybe making a few additions here and there. I haven't gotten around to it yet. But as far as receiving any communication from him, nothing so far. I did send him a message a few days ago."

"Really? What about?"

"Oh, just touching base really. I asked if there was anything He wanted me to do. The sifer seemed to work fine, so I'm pretty sure the message went out. But not a word."

"We haven't heard from him, either. I was hoping he would direct us in the merger, but like you, we haven't heard a thing. I guess Lord Mohae is busy."

It sounded odd to hear Ellington use Davidson's title. For several days at Heis, they had known him only as Davidson, their driver-turned-conference-center-manager. Then they discovered he was the one responsible for bringing power into the valley and, in many ways, for the lives of everyone in the village. Sam remembered one life in particular.

"Heard from Stürn?"

"Now that's been most curious." Ellington sighed deeply. "We have made repeated attempts to meet with her and the rest of the leadership of New Power. Not much success there, I'm afraid. We've had a few, mostly polite encounters, but nothing substantive."

"What is she going to do? Davidson made it clear she would be banished if she refused to follow the Plan."

"I honestly don't know. And I'm not certain she does either. There have been a number of secretive, closed-door meetings on their part. I believe they're confused. They don't have the means to separate from the rest of us. Their search for a new power source has not succeeded, and without it, they're pretty much stuck. Once, just once, I thought there was a glimmer of hope. She looked like she might be relenting from this crusade for independence that has so consumed her. But then it was gone."

Sam sipped his tea and stared at the flowers. The lights on the towers around the village dimmed, announcing the end of another manufactured day. Sam checked his watch.

"Ali will be waiting. I guess I'd better be going."

Ellington smiled. "I'm certainly glad you came. It was good to see you again."

"Yeah, maybe we can do this again soon."

"I hope so, Sam. And I'll try to do a better job of keeping you informed. I'm not certain what part you have in all this, but I do know you have one. And you don't need to be wondering what's going on or listening to rumors."

"Thanks. I appreciate that."

As the two men stood, Sam paused.

"Speaking of rumors, have you heard the latest going around? Seems several people are claiming to have seen a Yonder wandering about South End at night. Know anything about it?"

Sam carefully found his way to the bedroom and silently unbuttoned his shirt. His day had been a long one and he was certain Ali's had felt even longer. He loved his young kids, but they required a lot of attention and patience. Before he left Ellington, he had called home and learned they had been especially hyper this day.

"I'll be a little late," he had told her, "so don't wait up."

"Never crossed my mind," came the tired reply.

Sam undressed to his T-shirt and shorts and then eased into bed. Suddenly the lamp next to Ali switched on. She leaned up on one elbow and rubbed the sleep from her eyes.

"I'm sorry," Sam whispered. "I didn't want to wake you."

"It's all right." She yawned. "I wasn't really asleep. How did it go with Mr. E?"

"Great. It was good to talk to him again."

"Must have had a lot to talk about."

"Yeah, it did take a while." Sam's voice dropped. "I'm worried about him."

"The job? Is it too much for him?"

"I don't know. Davidson certainly thought he was capable of handling it. And I'm sure he is, it's just…"

"Just what?"

"He looks so tired. This is a huge strain. Williams and Mettenger are helping, but I can tell it's getting to him…and it hasn't been two months yet."

"Maybe that's just in the beginning. Once everything's set up, it should calm down, don't you think?"

"Yeah. You're right. I'm probably worrying for nothing." He gave her a hug. "Let's get some sleep." A faint light suddenly shone down the hall. "I'll be right back," he said, getting out of bed.

"Okay, but don't be long."

Sam followed the light up the hallway, passed the children's bedroom, and discovered it was coming from the small space he used as an office. He cautiously entered and looked about the room. Everything seemed exactly where he had left it. His briefcase by the door. A coat slung over the back of a chair. A stack of work on his desk. The sifer sitting alone on the top shelf of a bookcase. Yet something was definitely different.

Floating above the sifer was a holographic screen and in the lower right corner, a pulsing, purple dot appeared. Sam strode across the room and touched the suspended image. Immediately the purple dot steadied and a message appeared. Sam studied it carefully.

"Oh, no."

WinePressPublishing
Great Books, Defined.

To order additional copies of this book call:
1-877-421-READ (7323)
or please visit our website at
www.WinePressbooks.com

If you enjoyed this quality custom-published book,
drop by our website for more books and information.

www.winepresspublishing.com
"Your partner in custom publishing."

CPSIA information can be obtained at www.ICGtesting.com
Printed in the USA
LVOW082102200612

286910LV00002B/6/P